HERE'S WHAT REVIEWERS ARE SAYING ABOUT THE
SIX BULLS series of novels
~~~

It is easy to imagine the scenes, and to feel the adrenaline of the soldiers . . . war scenes are realistic and frightening without being gory . . . placing of the lead character on the American side at the Battle of New Orleans introduces many possibilities . . . his being from North Carolina and yet not believing in slavery is the hook that caught me.
(Create Space review)

. . . These stories bring to life the tales of American settlers who lived two centuries ago. He has journeyed throughout the world and has spent months traveling across America to search out the locations for his current novels . . . (Amazon Reviewer)

A riveting story set against a tragic time in American history . . . "The Ohioans-Six Bulls" is highly recommended. (The Midwest Book Review)

". . . 'The Ohioan' brilliantly captures the essence of America's pioneer experience in the 1830s . . . In a time of tremendous American growth, transformation, and exploration, these pioneers led the way. . . . it brings readers along for the ride along America's big rivers as a group of pioneers carve out new lives for themselves on the 1830s American prairie, revealing in the process the roots of a nation's greatness and its darkest shame . . ."
(The Seneca News Dispatch)

The American frontier in the 1830s was the land of the Six Bulls. Four families leave their farms in Ohio to raft down the big rivers of America to southwest Missouri. Along the way— adventures, wonders, love, and dangers lurk . . . as Americans expanded over the continent, Indians were forced to move to a new land simply called Indian Territory, losing their way of life. These two historical strands are woven into a wonderful story full of rich detail. Read it and I guarantee you'll enjoy it. (Star)

. . . wholly absorbing . . . the ending was so riveting that I was reading *past* midnight. The story is set against a tragic time in America's history . . . The Ohioans-Six *Bulls*" is highly recommended to community library historical fiction collections. (Michael Dunford)

Richard Puz explores the complex emotions that swirl around American and Indian relations . . . and examines the clash of cultures through Captain Vogel's struggle to reconcile Indian atrocities with the brave actions of an Indian boy who saves his life . . . (Outskirts Press)

If you are a local history buff or enjoy a good novel with lots of excitement, then you should love this book . . . The book tells of happiness and hardships, death, prejudices and misunderstandings, compassion, love and forgiveness . . . all is woven into the wonderful true adventure of these families . . . (Amazon Reviewer)

The author's attention to detail brings you face-to-face with the families and some of the fascinating true-life predicaments . . . surprises, tragedy, and emotion await you. . . . (Amazon Reviewer)

Big Jen

Other books by Richard Puz

FICTION
SIX BULLS SERIES

SIX BULLS-The Ohioans
The Carolinian
*Missouri Vengeance**

NON-FICTION
(Written/compiled by the author)

Noah Gallemore Family
Sparlin Family
Elizabeth Spurgeon Family
Sparlin & Spurgeon Vignettes

* *Coming Soon* (tentative title)

Visit the Richard Puz website at www.richardpuz.com

The Carolinian

Richard Puz

EAST 74th STREET PRESS*WASHINGTON

The Carolinian is a work of fiction. Names, characters, places, and incidents are either the product of the author's imagination or are used fictitiously. Any resemblance to actual events or locales or persons, living or dead, is entirely coincidental.

Cover photograph by John Livingston; edited by Julie Puz-Wilson

ISBN 13: 978-0-9799604-1-3
ISBN 10: 0-9799604-1-X

Library of Congress Control Number: 2009901294

Dedicated to the love of my life ~

*"If you don't know history,
you don't know anything."*
Edward Johnston

*"Courage is being scared to death —
but saddling up anyway."*
John Wayne

*"Too old to plant trees for my own gratification,
I shall do it for my posterity."*
Thomas Jefferson

Acknowledgments

Many have contributed to this series of books. Without the support of my wife and family, they would not exist. My editors are invaluable to me, especially Bill and Linda. Without Wauneta, I would be writing mysteries. My special thanks to the family on the poor farm.

SOUTH OF NEW ORLEANS

Saturday January 7, 1815

*"A hero is no braver than an ordinary man,
but he is braver five minutes longer."*

Ralph Waldo Emerson

Chapter One

"**C**ANNON FIRE!" yelled a soldier down the line.

Abraham jumped into the rifle pit again and flattened himself into the soft dirt as the knot in his stomach tightened and his knees quaked. A sob escaped him as the shot sailed overhead. *God, help me,* he silently pleaded. *I don't want to die. GOD—HELP ME!*

The British shelling had begun half an hour earlier, and at first, the Carolinian had felt a light-headed sense of invulnerability knowing when the big cannon fired by seeing the distant reddish-orange and yellow glow lighting up the mist. He imagined that he could hear the shot coming and then was awed at the sound of it passing overhead, screaming through the air like a giant fast-moving scythe. He had reasoned—*how can it hurt me if'n I can see it?*

After the second shelling, his breathing came faster at the distant sight of the bright foggy glow, and by the fifth barrage, he was sweating and stood on rubbery legs. Now he waited for the twelfth . . . or was it the fifteenth . . ., his hands shook and his pulse raced. The knot in his chest made it hard to breathe and swallowing was difficult because of his bone-dry throat. His light-headedness had vanished completely, replaced by the unshakable conviction that the enemy was trying to kill him—only him. None of the other four-thousand American troops mattered: he was the target.

"GRAPESHOT!" someone shouted.

He was lying face down in the hole and didn't see the man who jumped into the pit on top of him, but he felt him and, pushed deeper, tasted dirt. *Someone else trying to stay alive,* he guessed, as links of chain and lead chunks whipped through the air, clipping leaves and limbs before thudding solidly into the trees behind his position.

"Tarnation," the man on top said as he untangled himself and stood up. "Tank ya fer sharing yar hole, pardn'r. A body just can't make any headway along this har barricade with thet dadgum cannon blasting away at us."

Abraham spat out the dirt and looked up at the stranger in the twilight. The man was older with a graying beard and his blue eyes seemed to twinkle. He was dressed as a frontiersman in buckskins complete with a coonskin cap.

The stranger reached down to help him up.

Shaking badly, Abraham grabbed the man's hand.

The stranger gave him a hard look and didn't let go. "How old be ya, son?"

"Nineteen, sir."

"Ever been in battle before?"

The Carolinian shook his head.

"Thet cannon be purdy loud and scary, ain't it?" Not waiting for an answer, the older man continued, "Well, settle down, young man, and calm yarself. As soon as ya git this har baptism of fire behind ya, ah think ya'll be jess fine. Ah be Edmund Jennings, but most folks call me Big Jen."

"And I'm Abraham Rallemore," he answered, his voice strained and his brown hair askew.

"Good ta meet ya young Abra'm." Jerking his thumb in the direction of the camp headquarters, he continued. "I be scouting fer Ol' Hickory back yonder." Apparently seeing the baffled look on the young soldier's face, he went on. "Ya know, our leader, General Andy Jackson."

"Ahh," Abraham said brushing the dirt from his uniform. He watched Big Jen stride off among the rifle pits.

"Ya men har," the frontiersman commanded, getting the attention of everyone nearby. "Start digging yar holes deeper between tha cannon firings. When the British be changing from chain and lead to exploding cannon balls, ya'll wish yar pits were deeper than a well's bottom. Now ya men git ta digging and ya surely need ta be quick about it."

Abraham worked on his hole and watched as Big Jen surveyed the other rifle pits. No one had put the frontiersman in charge. No one had even introduced him. It just seemed natural for this man to take charge. He felt himself calming down.

"We need to survive tha night 'cause come morning, we'll be laying down a field of mooskat fire when tha English charge be acoming," Big Jen said as the men worked.

"CANNON SHOT!"

Abraham and Big Jen dropped into the hole as the metal missiles whirled overhead cutting another wide swath. Unraveling themselves once more, the two stood up. Others poked out of their holes looking at the lanky frontiers-man. They seemed to be waiting for orders.

"Abra'm, ya and me and these three fellas," Big Jen said, pointing. "We're jess going ta go find thet cannon tonight and ask them British folks ta stop shooting thet big monster at us."

Abraham felt his pulse quicken once more. *We're going to ask them sol-diers—please, sir, stop shooting at us—and they're going to do it? What kind of gall darn yarn is this?*

It didn't help that the frontiersman spoke in a muddled form of English layered over a drawler's accent that made it hard to follow his words.

Abraham tentatively asked, "What . . . what you aiming for us to do?"

Big Jen cocked his head before answering. "Why, ah expects we'll just turn thet cannon inta a pile of iron."

Instinctively, the Carolinian asked, "You mean we're going through the whole British army—all ten thousand of them—that be experienced from fighting Napoleon?"

Leaning on his musket, Big Jen asked, "Do ya always ask so many ques-suns?"

"And with only five men?"

"Yep, sumtin like thet."

"How you fixing to do that?" asked another man.

"Oh, it'll come ta me."

Abraham stared at Big Jen, who appeared to be as calm as pond water.

"Now ya fellas git some rest if'n ya can," the lanky frontiersman said to the men around him. "Ah'll be acoming ta git ya as soon as tha moon be setting, 'bout midnight ah expect. Then we'll skedaddle down tha barricade slope and cross tha canal."

A man called Smith asked anxiously, "We know that gun be raking us regularly, but why don't we just hunker down instead of risking our necks trying to put that damn thing out of action? That big gun can't get us if'n we stay low."

Big Jen stared at the man for long moments with his steel-blue eyes be-fore pushing back his coonskin hat and answering. "Tarnation, man. Tha redcoats be moving thet ol' shooter every so often and dragging it t'ward our flank. Won't be no time at all befer they're able ta fire thet big gun right down our line of men, pinning us down in tha muck when their big attack be acoming in tha morning. Yep, tha general be as right as rain, thet big thirty-two pounder got ta git, as enny fool can plainly see."

Abraham settled deeper in his hole and Big Jen joined him as another volley flew overhead.

"Cuss it all, I'm sure glad we're hunkered down behind this har barricade, ain't ya? Did ya help build it?"

"No, sir."

"Well, ah did and it were a big job. Took only two weeks, but we hauled in so many bits and pieces thet it now be nigh onto twenty feet tall sitting on top of trees, cotton bales, and casks full of swamp mud with a slope down ta tha wide ditch in front of us."

Abraham nodded again.

Gesturing, the frontiersman went on. "Yessiree, we began at tha Mississip Riva ova thet away and this har wall extends along thet canal until it reaches the swamp way down thet away." Chuckling, the frontiersman continued, "Yep, ah reckon it be near a mile long or my name ain't Big Jen."

Abraham had marched the five miles from New Orleans and had passed the eight well-protected American cannons on his way to this position behind the breastwork. Shielded by this front line, he figured that all of General Jackson's troops were nearly invisible to the redcoats, except for their big cannons.

"Where be yar home?" asked Big Jen.

"Up North Carolina way, mostly Rowan County," answered Abraham. "How about yourself?"

"Tenasee, but ah spent tha last twenty 'ears with tha Osage Injuns in Missouri. Thet be in tha land of tha Six Bulls."

No wonder I'm having so much trouble following his words, thought Abraham, *given his drawl, odd pronunciation, and unusual speaking gait. Having spent so many years talking Injun, he's plumb forgotten how to speak proper American. I'd better be learning his words fast before that patrol tonight.* Turning over the older man's last words in his head, he asked, "Why do they call it Six Bulls?"

"On accounta thar be so many bulls."

Abraham was puzzled and it must have showed.

Repeating himself, the frontiersman said, "Ya know, bulls, like flowing water . . . bulls."

The Carolinian arched his brow, still confused.

"Surely ya be seeing water springs thet be acoming out of tha ground and caves in yar young life. Don't ya know water bulls?"

"Ahh, you mean water springs, like water boils?"

"Thet be right, jess like ah be saying, bulls."

Abraham suppressed a grin. *Yes, understanding Big Jen is going to be challenging.*

"Thet Six Bulls lan be purdy with prairie grass as tall as my horse's eye and sweet running water. And tha plains be full of game. Ah reckon thet country be a bit of sweet heaven in this U S of A."

"Be that right?" Abraham asked, unable to hide the doubt in his voice.

"Looki har, ah be telling ya tha way it be. Go see tha frontier fer yarself and ya'll see what ah'm saying be as true as the heavy-headed grass that be agrowin' in Six Bulls country."

"I'd like to see more of the frontier some day, but my pa's plantation takes a lot of work. Most owners use slaves, but my pa doesn't see it that way."

"Good fer him. Ah never did cotton ta men being owned by other men. Ah think it goes against tha grain of nature. The Lord doesn't know tha color of yar skin and he don't care. Ya know what ah mean, son?"

The younger man nodded.

"CANNON FIRE!"

Hunkering down, Abraham closed his eyes tight. This time, the ground shook and part of the pit slid down as an exploding cannon ball landed close by. Almost immediately, Abraham heard a scream and a man cried out, "My leg! What's happen to my leg? Someone help me stop the bleeding!"

He looked over the top of his hole as others rushed to help the injured man. Soon they were pulling him out of his pit, blood flowing from the stub-end of his leg.

"Where be my leg?" the man screamed. "My leg be missing! Someone—help me find my leg!"

Scurrying quickly out of the rifle pit, Abraham managed to reach the edge of the breastworks on rubbery legs before heaving. Looking back, he saw five men carrying the wounded man toward the medical tent—only the man was no longer moving. He felt a hand on his shoulder.

"It be hard seeing a man die," said Big Jen, leading him back to the rifle pit. "But, yar not hurt and right now thet be counting more than anything else."

Abraham closed his eyes, again seeing the man with the stump and the gushing blood.

After long moments, the lanky frontiersman softly asked, "How be it thet ya come this far ta fight in this battle?"

Opening his eyes, Abraham spoke, at first haltingly. "A British naval squadron ... it has blockaded all of the eastern ports . . . we use to ship our tobacco . . . and this has been going on for the past two years . . . so, my pa and I volunteered for the militia. He got assigned to a supply post in Charlotte and I was sent here." Again, he felt himself calming as his trembling diminished.

"Tarnation, yar sure having yarself an adventure, ain't ya?" the older man said, chuckling.

Nodding, Abraham continued. "When my ship arrived in New Orleans, I was surprised to see General Jackson's army. I mean, the men have so many different uniforms and many wear everyday clothes. A soldier down the line told me that there are militia units here from many states as well as Baratarian pirates, Choctow Injuns, and free blacks."

"Thet be about right."

"Don't you think it be an unusual and ragtag-looking group of men? You know, kind of unprofessional and not like a real army?"

Big Jen's eyed him in the gloom of the evening mist. The man's coonskin cap was off and a beaded leather band held his graying light-colored hair in place.

"Abra'm, ya got ta be learning tha difference between a man's looks and how fine he be shooting. They've never been one and tha same. Ya git my drift?"

"Yes, sir. Still, don't you find it strange to see so many Injuns and black folks here with guns? Most of the ones back home are slaves and none are permitted to have guns."

"As ah be telling ya, son, ya git nowhere looking at tha clothes nor tha color of tha skin ta judge a man. It won't tell ya nothing about whet be inside. That's where a man's mettle be, and that's what counts."

The younger man nodded.

"Well, bess ya git some rest. Yar gonna ta be needin' it tanight."

Abraham nestled into his corner and closed his eyes. Repeated cannon firings in between the sound of shrapnel flying overhead made sleeping more like catnaps. He noticed that this didn't bother Big Jen, who was snoring on the other side of the pit. Abraham smiled to himself.

His thoughts turned to his home in Rowan County and young Mary Glass, the girl he loved. He remembered her soft brown hair and her dazzling smile that could light a fire in him. As he had departed, they had kissed. Never would he forget that moment.

When this mess is over, I'm going home and marry her, if'n I can get the old Colonel's permission, he thought to himself, nodding off until another cannon blast whizzed overhead.

Chapter Two

With his musket strapped on his back, Abraham crouched low as he made his way in the dark. The five men had slipped down the breastwork glacis and waded across the canal.

Before they left, Big Jen had warned them, "Don't ya fellas be making any noise or moving sudden-like. We don't want ta be showing ourselves and letting tha redcoats know we be acoming."

Show ourselves, thought Abraham. *That's a laugh. I can't even see my hand in front of my face on this foggy night and I've no idea how Big Jen is going to find the way.* Abraham and the other three men simply followed the best they could. Unseen branches ripped at his face as he stumbled over bushes and fallen tree limbs while the swamp-like mud sucked at his boots.

They had traveled some distance when Abraham bumped into the man in front of him. Ahead, he saw a misty glow cast by a camphene lantern shimmering in the foggy night. Big Jen must have given a signal, for suddenly they were moving again, swinging around the outpost.

Abraham knew they were closing in on the cannon, as the periodic blasts were much louder and the ground now shook beneath his feet. Every firing brightly illuminated the otherwise black misty night.

It seemed like an eternity as Abraham kept following the man ahead. Then, once again, the group stopped. A bright fog-shrouded area was ahead and he figured that they must have arrived at the big gun's location. Both fearful and excited, his hands were clammy from the tension as he swung the musket off his back. No prior experience had prepared him for such a grim situation.

The bright glow must be from many lit torches, he figured. Then Big Jen gave hand signals for them to stay put as he left to scout the big gun's position. Abraham and the rest hunkered down even lower, afraid of detection. One shout and hundreds of enemy soldiers would be upon them.

Big Jen returned and again they followed him for a short distance.

Gathering the men up close, he spoke in a hushed voice. "Thet monster be sitting on a big two-wheel carriage in a clearing and horses be staked in tha woods. They be having nine, mebbe ten, men tending thet big shooter. Most be working ta load and aim thet pile of iron. There be one officer, thet ah could see. They have mooskats, but they be stacked ta one side, nice and purdy. Tha gun position be a short distance from a company of soldiers and they jest be lollygagging about. They be waiting, ah expects, fer orders and be purdy confident 'cause they ain't even posted a picket."

Another blast went over their heads, making Abraham's ears pop from the ferocious swooshing violence of the shot. He was still staring up at the night sky when Big Jen commanded his attention with a sharp finger-poke to his chest.

Softly, the frontiersman continued. "They already be moving tha horses and one team be hitched ta a powder wagon. Probably limbering up, preparing ta move soon, so we got ta work fast. Har be tha plan. Ya two," he said, pushing a finger into the chests of two men, "be making yar way around ta them horses. When ya har my gunshot, ya take out tha guards and spook them critters right inta tha men working thet monster cannon. Them horses really got ta be moving slick-like as ah expect them ta scatter tha shooters thet away. Ya git thet?"

No one spoke.

"Young Abra'm, ya ever used a mallet and pegs?"

"Yes, sir."

"Right—ya git tha job of spiking tha cannon. Know how?"

"No sir," the Carolinian whispered and then froze as another shot thundered overhead. The powder glow briefly lit up their faces and he could better see the shadowy frontiersman squatted down, leaning on his musket.

"Tha fuse hole be on top of tha cannon barrel near tha back end. After they be loading the cannon, they fills tha hole with powder, then lights it ta fire tha monster. Ya spike tha gun by driving an iron pin down tha fuse hole till it be flush with tha outside of tha barrel. If'n they have no way ta light tha fuse, there'll be no mo'e shooting. If'n they can't be gitting tha spike out, tha gun be useless. Do ya git my meaning?"

"Yes, sir," replied Abraham. "What am I going to use for a spike and mallet?"

Abraham could just make out Big Jen fumbling in his pocket. Then the older man's hand came out with an object and he placed it in Abraham's hand. The Carolinian turned it over and ran his fingers over a six-inch iron spike that tapered to a point at one end.

"Ah had tha blacksmith make this up special jess fer tanight. Ya jam it inta tha hole and pound it in with tha stock of yar mooskat. Think ya can be doing thet, Mr. Abra'm?"

"I'll do my best," the Carolinian responded, his hand tightly clutching the spike. Even to his own ears, his reply was weak and unconvincing. He sensed the frontiersman staring at him in the dark.

I don't have a better answer, he thought as his mind quickly flitted between one notion and another. *If'n I fail, that gun will keep firing, killing our men during the big attack. But how can I do the spiking if'n I'm scared? With my shaky hands, can I even fit the rod in the fuse hole? Maybe I'll be captured. Hell, I could be dead in the next few minutes.* A cold chill swept over him. *I want to live and go home to marry my girl and—*

Suddenly, his thoughts took a new direction. *I can go home and I can be with Mary, but we have to end this war first. And that means that bloody cannon has to be plugged. I'm going to shove this damn spike right into that hole and no one is going to stop me. I'M NOT GOING TO FAIL!*

His back straightened and his hand loosened its grip on the metal spike. "Sir, I'll get it done."

"Ya do thet, son. Ah'll take out tha officer, and you, Smith, ya knock down tha stacked guns and shoot as many gunners as ya can using their mooskats. What's mo'e, ya all be making lots of noise. Surprise be on our side and we got ta make tha most of it."

"How're we going to get away," asked one of the men.

"Ya two spooking tha horses, ya follow them into tha clearing and help take out some of them gunners. Everybody watch fer Abra'm. When he makes tracks, we'll know tha job be done and we'll skedaddle back ta our side. Be careful when ya come ta our wall so ya don't git yarself shot by our own folks. Tha password tanight be 'keep America free.' Be thar any questions? Good. Ya two, git off after them horses. We'll wait five minutes and follow."

A short while later, Big Jen led the way as Abraham held his musket in his left hand and the spike in his right. They were in the dark misty shadows on the edge of the clearing outlined by torches stuck in the ground, casting a downright eerie glow in the mixture of dense fog and gun smoke. Around the gun, the British soldiers moved about in a flurry of controlled activity.

The frontiersman signaled for them to stay in the dark as he crawled crab-like behind a caisson wagon. With great stealth and quick action, he collared one soldier while decisively slashing the man's throat.

Big Jen motioned for Smith and Abraham to join him. They waited for the next blast.

"COMMENCE!" shouted the British officer, followed by a thunderous roar that shook the ground.

The three Americans charged toward the gunners shouting at the top of their lungs. "YEOOOWAAAWEE!" Big Jen's bloodcurdling yell came as he fired his musket from the hip at the closest man and then hurled his tomahawk with a sharp overhand motion, burying it in the officer's back.

Smith knocked over the stacked muskets and began firing one after another at the gunners.

Big Jen rounded on another soldier and buried his knife in the man's chest.

Seconds later, other gunshots filled the air and, from the woods, came the sound of galloping horses making for the clearing.

Abraham ran to the hot cannon barrel and jammed the spike into the fuse hole, then hammered it with his musket butt until it was tight and flush. A wavering shadow cast by the torches was his only warning that an attacker was behind him. Suddenly, he found himself on the ground. He struggled to his knees, holding a hand to the gash on his head as the world spun around before his eyes.

"C'mon! Yar down but not out," yelled Big Jen, grabbing his arm and helping him to his feet.

Unsteady, Abraham caught a glimpse of his attacker lying on the ground.

"I'm going ta blow tha gunpowder, so ya git."

Groggily, Abraham managed to move toward the trees, and tripped over Smith, who lay dead sprawled on his back. He hoped he was going toward the American line and not into the middle of the whole British army.

Out of nowhere, Big Jen came alongside again and grabbed him, hurrying him along. Moments later, a series of tremendous explosions knocked them flat as the caissons went up with a thunderous roar.

"So much fer thet monster," said Big Jen, getting to his feet and half carrying him to the American side.

Big Jen left him at the medical tent to have his head wound cleaned and wrapped. Weary, he sat down on a cot, holding a cloth to his head and waited. The Carolinian noticed the others in his group walking slowly back to their rifle pits. He thought again about Smith lying dead, his unseeing eyes open.

Across the clearing, he watched as General Jackson rode up to Big Jen on his prancing white stallion. Jackson dismounted and the two men talked for long moments. They shook hands and the frontiersman pointed his way.

Making his way to Abraham, the General said, "That was a mighty courageous thing that you boys did tonight. Your country appreciates your bravery and I want to add my personal thanks. We still have the English attack to face come first light, but we can do it now knowing that our flank is secure. God bless you and keep you safe, young man."

Abraham's head throbbed, but he also felt elated. "Thank you, sir. And God bless you, sir." He looked for Big Jen and watched him amble away.

🐾 🐾

At dawn, the redcoats attacked the fixed American positions. On the firing line, Abraham was down on one knee sighting down his long musket barrel, waiting for the order to fire. In the early morning light, the fog still covered the land and hid the English troops, but he could hear them coming through the swampland. The wait for the firing order seemed endless as he listened to the advances of the enemy accompanied by their drummers beating out a marching cadence.

His head still throbbed, but the Carolinian's heart pounded for a different reason. *This'll likely be my last morning on this good earth,* he thought. *Rumor has it that the English have already captured five American gunboats on Lake Borgne. General Jackson can't defeat this big, experienced, army with the few men he has—can he?*

The sounds of the approaching enemy soldiers grew louder as they moved through the swamp's muck and scrub brush. Still, the heavy gray mist hid them. *Surely, the order to fire will come now. They must be nearly at the edge of the canal,* he thought, as nervous expectations made his hands tremble.

Now, the Carolinian heard the beating of another snare drum coming from somewhere along the American line. He also felt a breeze touch his cheek, and then it picked up, tousling his hair. Amazingly, the freshening wind swept away the fog, and in a few moments, there, right before him, was the entire English army, topcoats red, bayonets fixed, ranks closed. Some were only yards away from the edge of the canal.

"FIRE!" the lieutenant loudly shouted, and musket balls, cannons, and arrows immediately filled the air.

Abraham was astonished at the resultant carnage. The sweep of fire mowed everything down as though God's scythe was swinging again, this time through the redcoats. His company fell back to reload the seventy caliber cartridges in their flintlocks.

"Second squad forward—FIRE!"

"Third squad to the front—FIRE!"

Then it was Abraham's turn again. He now had a few seconds to notice that the advancing soldiers carried no wooden planks to assist their crossing of the canal and no ladders to scale the American's wall. Those still standing continued to move forward in a line now broken by many fallen men, yet they attempted to close formation.

"FIRE!"

American cannons fired to his right and the swath of death was impossible to imagine as the grapeshot cut through men with impunity.

"Second unit to the line," the command sounded. "FIRE!"

The noise of battle engulfed him as he rammed the rod down the musket barrel to seat the powder cartridge and ball.

The fighting continued, although time stood still for Abraham. In his mind, the fighting became a blur.

The closed-ranked redcoats continued advancing as the concentrated fire of the Americans from behind their fortification cut down wave after wave of attackers. At one point, Abraham figured that the water in the canal must have turned red with their blood.

As the hot sun rose in the clearing morning sky, the cease-fire order was heard up and down the American line and an uncommon stillness fell on the battlefield. Abraham watched as comrades helped the wounded retreat. Then, a great shout went up from the American side and men began waving their muskets as flags and banners sprouted. The battle for New Orleans was over.

Abraham was happy to be alive and excited by the outcome. He found himself shouting and waving his hat and musket as the victory roar swept up and down the American line.

🐾 🐾

Sailing for home a month later, Abraham found himself thinking about the last time he had seen Mary. She had worried about him leaving and had smiled bravely as tears had filled her eyes. *No question about it*, he thought. *I'm going to make Mary my wife and damn the old colonel.*

Then he remembered the battle. In less than an hour, the British had suffered over two thousand casualties while the American toll was less than two dozen. The Carolinian also thought about the lanky frontiersman and knew he would never forget Big Jen. Nor would he forget his gut-wrenching fear, the open dead eyes, and the exhilaration of battle.

My pa and Big Jen are right. All men are brothers-in-arms before the Lord as God pays no mind to a man's color.

Rowan County, North Carolina ~

A Decade Later . . .

"Justice consists not in being neutral between right and wrong, but in finding out the right and upholding it, wherever found, against the wrong."
Theodore Roosevelt

Chapter Three

Abraham figured that the man was moving about as fast as anyone could, running in a semi-crouch with his head bobbing up and down among the row of chest-high tobacco plants. Leaves whipped the man's face and head.

On the hillside, Abraham and his sons, Frederick and Noah, watched as the man apparently stumbled and was lost to view. *He looks plumb tuckered out,* thought Abraham.

"Why is he running?" asked his youngest son, Noah.

"I'm not sure," replied his father as the man continued.

His other son, Frederick, pointed to the edge of the field. "Pa, look over there."

A horseback rider approached with two other white men holding the leashes of three straining dogs. As the hounds bayed, the leader on horseback rose in his stirrups, obviously searching for the man.

The runner was now coming toward Abraham as the tobacco rows followed the contours of a hillside. The rising elevation also allowed the horseman to see the man. Quickly, he and the dog handlers hurried along the edge of the field, shortening the distance to the runner.

As the stranger neared, Abraham was startled to see that he was an Indian, his black hair shining in the early morning sun. *Probably a runaway slave,* thought Abraham. At the Salisbury auction block every Friday morning, plantation owners bought and sold slaves. Mostly, these days, they were from Africa, but in the past, Indian slaves had been common. Slavers would ensnare entire Indian villages, selling everyone into slavery to work the fields.

Abraham and his sons had set out early that morning to hunt. Noah was six and too young to handle a musket, but Frederick, four years older and tall for his age, could shoot right well. He had himself a rabbit to go along with Abraham's pheasant.

The three white men were closing the gap along the edge of the field. Things had happened quickly, leaving Abraham no time to consider the situation, but in that instant, he made a decision. He reached for his knife and quickly cut off the bird's head. "Frederick, give me your musket and the rabbit. Here, take my bird."

Puzzled, the boy did as instructed, holding the bird at arm's length to avoid the flowing blood.

Slashing the rabbit, Abraham said, "Noah, hold it by the hind legs and you run up the hill. Frederick, you take the pheasant and run between the plants downhill. Each of you go for six or seven rows and smear as much blood as you can on the ground. Then drop the animal and head for the edge of the field. I'll be there and both of you boys keep quiet about the Injun. Now, get."

For the first time, the runner saw Abraham, now holding two muskets, and abruptly stopped, fear etched on his face.

Holding both muskets in the crook of one arm, Abraham gestured with the other for the Indian to go over the next rise.

The man was hesitant, then he nodded and darted over the hill, casting a fleeting glance at the horseman and Abraham.

Abraham watched him disappear and turned, walking toward the three men at the edge of the field. As he neared, he called out, "What you fellows up to on my land?"

Shouting back, the horseman replied, "I be Hooker and I'm tracking a runaway Injun slave with my men. I was him disappear into your field."

Abraham saw a pinched-face man of medium height, broad across the shoulders, wearing a wide-brimmed hat, and carrying a coiled whip. The slaver held a tight rein on his spirited horse.

"What you aiming to do?" asked Abraham.

"Why, catch him, of course, as any damn fool can see."

Abraham felt himself bristling.

"There be good reward money for capturing runaways," Hooker continued impatiently. "And we be good at tracking and catching them. Later, we'll chain him up and make a big show of parading him back to the owner as a warning to others. Haven't had one that got away from us once we're on his trail. Keep me in mind the next time you have a runaway."

What a pompous ass, thought Abraham. *To him, tracking runaways is a business, maybe even a sport. He has no regard for the broken souls he hunts.*

"There be no slaves working these fields—we only use hired hands."

Hooker gave him a curious glance and shrugged, turning his horse to enter the field.

With a loud shout, Abraham warned, "Now you hold on there, Mr. Hooker," as he quickly leaned one gun against a tobacco stalk and leveled the other. "No one is going to be riding a horse into this field tearing up my crops."

Startled, Hooker pulled up. "Ya know the law. Runaway slaves be fair game for hunting and I aim to collect the reward on this here Injun. And this one be owned by Colonel Glass himself." Gazing at Abraham hard, he jeered, "What are ya, a slave lover? Be that why ya don't have any on yar plantation? Or maybe it only be Injuns ya be partial to. Be that why ya're breaking the law?"

This man is a mean bully—no, more than that, thought Abraham. *He be brimming with sarcasm and hate as though a black cloud hangs over his head—a malignant cloud.*

Hooker spun his high-strung horse twice and then rode into the field, smashing tobacco plants until Abraham fired his gun into the air.

Enraged, the slaver stopped. "What're ya, crazy or something? Put up that gun, ya damn fool."

Reaching for the other gun, Abraham walked toward the slaver, saying in a low voice full of fury, "I'll tell you what I am, Mr. Hooker. I'm the owner of this property and you're trespassing on my land. Now hear me good—no rider is coming through my fields destroying my crop and that goes for them hounds, too!"

"Ya sure ya want to be stopping me from catching that slave?"

In a voice laced with anger, Abraham continued, "This has nothing to do with the runaway. My concern be for my crop. You can get off that horse and walk between the rows with your men as long as you like, but the dogs have to be leashed and only one for each man. As the owner, those be my laws. Is that clear enough for you?"

Hooker's face flushed and Abraham knew that the man was roundly cursing him under his breath.

Abraham continued, inching the gun muzzle higher, "And one more thing—you ain't no lawman, so don't be trying to tell me the law. That dog don't hunt."

"Gimme a dog," the tracker barked at one of his men as he dismounted. "Each of ya, take a row with yar dog. Be quick about it."

Soon, the dogs had the game scent and began baying and acting up, straining in opposite directions.

At the edge of the field, Abraham looked on, a bemused smile on his face. "You be remembering what I told you," he called out. "Don't let them dogs trample any of my plants, for then I be obliged to talk to Colonel Glass myself . . . seeing as he be family."

Angrily, Hooker cast a wicked look at Abraham and trudged off up the hill holding a baying hound while his men went in opposite directions, the dogs crazed with the scent.

Abraham met up with his sons at the edge of the field.

"Pa," the wide-eyed Frederick said. "Why did we help that slave get away?"

"You know, boys, I just figured we'd give the Injun a chance to get free and maybe let him get back to his own people. It just don't seem right to have men owning other men—never has and never will. Besides, slavers like that fella be low-lifes and they'll get no respect from me. Last of all, no one is going to be tearing up our fields while I got me two muskets and two great sons like you standing by me. Do you understand what I be saying?"

"I reckon," replied Frederick. "Didn't the man say that this slave belongs to Grandpa Glass?"

"Ahh," began Abraham, "we'll just have to let the dust settle on that score and address it another day."

🐾 🐾

"Damn this soil," muttered Abraham, continuing to hoe weeds. He was in the field with his sons and hired men. His plantation was just off Flat Swamp Creek some miles east of Salisbury, a trading town, located at the confluence of the north-south Great Philadelphia Wagon Trail and the east-running Trading Path Road to Virginia. The Rallemore plantation covered over five hundred acres of uplands and drained swamplands as it stretched toward Four Mile Creek. "This be the last season for tobacco growing in this field—this land don't have enough richness. Next year, we'll be planting grains or pasture."

"Well," Frederick responded, wiping his brow with the back of his hand, "we have that virgin land down by Buffalo Creek. How about we cut and burn it this fall and take the plow to it next year?"

"Perhaps, but I think its only value may come from logging the trees as firewood."

"Pa," said young Noah. "Where do all our rivers come from?"

"From the big mountains to the west," replied Abraham, attacking more weeds. "That also be the reason why we have so many wetlands and swamps."

"Why are the lowlands so much better for us farmers?" Frederick asked.

Abraham smiled at his son referring to himself as a farmer. *Someday, my boys will follow in my footsteps and work their own land,* he thought. Then he answered, "Over long periods of time, the swamps accumulate debris like leaves, limbs, bushes, and the like. These decay and become compost, which adds richness to the soil. After we drain the swamps, the soil is excellent for long-term farming."

"But the uplands are different, aren't they?" asked Frederick. "That's why we have to add ash, ain't that right?"

"That's right. As you know, we clear virgin land by slashing and then burning the trees, stumps, and brush to make the ash. Without it, tobacco and other crops won't grow in that poor soil." Abraham knew that in less than ten years, tobacco yields on the uplands would become minimal and he'd have to switch to planting grains or pasture until yields, again, became so low that the lands were considered worthless and were abandoned.

"Hey, boys," called out Abraham to his sons. "Don't forget to weed that corner over by the creek."

"Alright, Pa," replied Noah, as he and Frederick went to the stream for a cool drink.

Hoeing once more, Abraham's thoughts turned to his greatest challenge: the plantation's need for inexpensive workers as tobacco farming was labor intensive. Large tobacco growers relied on slave labor. Like his father, Abraham had refused, yet sticking to his anti-slavery beliefs had been difficult. Hiring itinerant workers was some help, but turnover remained high. Small-time farmers were also available, but not at harvest time. Eventually, he and Mary had greatly added to their land holdings and built up a crew of sixty men. *Pa and I probably got our views on slavery from our Puritan-leaning ancestors,* he figured.

The boys returned and everyone sat in the shade eating from the lunch basket that Mary had prepared.

Looking quizzically at his father, young Noah asked, "Pa, what be a 'century?'"

Abraham was startled. "Where in the world did you come across that word?"

"At Grandpa Glass's house."

"Well, it means a hundred years."

"He told me that he can trace his family back to the thirteenth century."

Again surprised, Abraham said, "Well, he meant that he has a list of his ancestors, probably written down in family Bibles, that goes back six hundred years."

"Where was he born?" Noah asked.

"Across the ocean in an area called the Upper Palatinate."

Frederick asked, "Was Grandma Glass born across the ocean, too?"

"Yes, but in a different area. She is from a village named Rothenfluh, which sits on the banks of the big Rhine River in a country called Switzerland. Her parents came to Pennsylvania in the early 1700s and then here to Rowan County about sixty years ago."

"How about grandpa and grandma Rallemore," Noah continued. "Did they take a boat, too?"

Abraham laughed. "Most likely. Our family has been farmers forever—at least since they came to the Carolinas over a hundred years ago. No one rightly remembers where the family originated so you boys have three choices. Some in the family say that we descend from Norsemen who settled in the Galloway region near the waterway Solway Firth that separates Scotland and Ireland. Others insist that the Rallemore clan traces back to Rory O'More, Chieftain of the Clan Rory of Ulster. And your uncle thinks we came to the Carolinas from the town of Salisbury on the plains of England, like so many others around here."

The boys looked at him, nodding. Abraham smiled and wondered how much of this the boys would remember.

"Was Grandpa Glass always a colonel?" asked Noah.

"No one is born a colonel, son," Abraham laughed. "He received his army promotion as a young man fighting at the battle of Yorktown. General George Washington himself presented your grandpa with the promotion because he fought so bravely."

Abraham had always liked the old Colonel in spite of his gruff manner, but they differed markedly on using slaves to work the fields. Like Abraham, Mary did not believe in slavery either, much to her grandfather's dismay. When Abraham had told her about the runaway Indian slave being hunted using dogs, he remembered that she had paled and asked, "Abe, how can this be God's way?"

Thinking about the Indian, he smiled to himself. *Nothing like picking a fight with the old Colonel,* he thought. *The topic is sure to be part of the discussion tomorrow.*

One of the Colonel's servants had summoned Abraham to Mary's ancestral home. *Probably wants me to pay him for the runaway,* Abraham figured. *Well, I best be getting it over with.*

Chapter Four

F lushed, Abraham watched Colonel Glass interrupt his thundering lecture as he poured more sipping whiskey into their tumblers.

"Face it, Abraham," the Colonel continued. "You can't keep going around forever like some malcontent. Tobacco farming takes lots of labor and slaves provide it. You've got a growing plantation, but you're short of help." Interrupting their conversation for a moment, the old Colonel added a finger of water to each tumbler as he and Abraham sat in the shade on the veranda. Impatiently, he went on. "What's the use of having land if you can't farm it? And when I be gone, you and Mary will inherit even more."

Abraham shifted uneasily under the tongue-lashing. He knew of the not-so-veiled whispers behind his back from neighbors and Mary's family. Some folks in town laughed at him or poked fun at his prudish concerns regarding such a commonplace practice as slavery. A few were even alarmed, thinking his views could be dangerous to the economic life built on the backs of slaves.

"Colonel, you know I've never been at ease owning other men," responded Abraham. "Hell, I'm not even comfortable with someone being a slave simply because of the color of his skin or wearing a 'For Sale' sign around his neck at the Salisbury block. Surely, there must be another way. . ."

Interrupting again, the Colonel stormed, "You're being a hard-headed fool. Why if'n it weren't for my granddaughter, I'd let you wallow in your own self-righteous poppycock." His words stung, but the smile on his face and the twinkle in his eye softened the tone.

Abraham irritably responded, "If'n you believe that, why in heaven's name did you risk your life in the Revolutionary War? Wasn't it for the equality of all men just like the Constitution says?"

"My boy, I admire a man that has principles. Hell, I fought in the war because I believed our cause was just. But you also need to be practical for your plantation to be successful. You know we get hammered by the farmers in neighboring states every time our crops be shipped."

Abraham sighed. They had covered the same ground many times in the past. Farmers in other coastal states had demanded that their politicians place duties on North Carolina tobacco shipped from their deep-water ports in order to "protect" local growers.

"I wish God had made some harbors on our North Carolina coast, or even passable rivers," continued the Colonel. "But he didn't. Those damn farmers call it 'protection.' Hell, they be nothing but a greedy pack of jackals and that includes the state politicians they bought. And to add misery to worry, we also got to be contending with our soil wearing out, poor weather, and black root rot."

Abraham picked up his tumbler and took a long sip. He knew well the rest of the Colonel's lecture.

"And you know as well as me that it forces us North Carolinians to be more quick-witted about bringing new tobacco lands into production."

Abraham knew the situation was a slippery slope and would eventually lead to his inability to compete profitably.

The Colonel paused, sipping his whiskey, and fixed Abraham with a hard look. "Just answer me this one question—just how're you going to do it? How're you going to make that plantation of yours work without slaves—be they blacks—or redskins like that one that got away last week in your fields?"

Abraham felt his face redden. Well, he hadn't expected anything different from Hooker. *Sounds as though the jackass missed his reward money,* reflected Abraham, pleased at the thought.

"And besides . . ." the Colonel went on.

The old man is sure wound up today. This kind of agitation can't be good for his health. He seems pale and drawn to me and I think he's lost some weight.

Countless times since Abraham had asked him years ago for his granddaughter's hand in marriage, the two had had similar discussions. The old man had agreed to the marriage but bluntly told him that only a fool would try to run a sizable plantation without slaves.

Maybe he's right, thought Abraham. *When I do hire more help, I can't make a profit. If'n I raise my prices to cover the higher costs, my tobacco leaves rot in my barns. If'n it has to be the way the Colonel says, then Mary and I are going someplace else where there's no need for large numbers of slaves or hired hands.*

". . . So tell me, how're you going to do it?" the Colonel concluded.

"I wish to God I knew," Abraham replied. "I keep searching for good workers that will stay with me."

The Colonel studied him for long moments until he said, "Come, and let's walk in the garden." He slowly made his way off the porch, holding onto the rail as he gingerly took the steps.

The old fella is having real difficulty walking, thought Abraham.

As they made their way in the expansive rose garden, Colonel Glass turned to him. "In England, I hear that they're developing cooperatives. Do you know anything about them?"

"Well, yes, I've read the stories in the newspaper. But they apply to owners coming together to build mutually needed facilities such as weaving mills or buying equipment they share."

"Have you thought about taking the idea and adapting it to tobacco growing here in Rowan County?"

Surprised, Abraham responded, "I'm not sure the English approach has anything to do with our growing tobacco. What I need is pure and simple—low cost labor I can depend on."

The Colonel shot back, "I wouldn't be so cocksure. If'n you're so cussed stubborn that you won't use the tried method, you'd best be finding another, and fast. Think about the English system. I have a feeling it can be adapted." Turning back toward the veranda, he said over his shoulder, "Do give my regards to Mary."

Dismissed much like a schoolboy, thought Abraham as he walked around the large two-story manor to the great front lawn where large magnolia trees bordered the entrance. He mounted his horse and was deep in thought when he heard someone riding toward him. Looking up, there was Hooker. *Dadblast it,* he fretted, *here comes the last man I want to see today.*

"Well, hot damn," Hooker cheerily called out. "What do we have coming down the lane? You've got that hangdog look, Mr. Rallemore. I'm guessing that the old Colonel tore off a strip of your hide about your slave-loving ways. I was right happy to tell him how you shot off your gun and stopped me from catching his runaway."

Abraham glared at him and rode on. *His malevolent black cloud just keeps following this ass everywhere,* he thought.

Behind him, he heard the slaver's loud taunting laugh. "I'll wager that Injun is going to cost you dearly."

Abraham gripped his horse's reins tightly but kept riding. *God, that man be a burr under my saddle and an irritation to life itself.*

"Have yarself a nice day, Mr. Rallemore," Hooker snickered, with another mocking laugh.

Turning onto the road, Abraham put the slaver out of his mind and re-called the Colonel's lecture minutes earlier. *What had the old man meant about applying the English cooperative system to working tobacco fields?*

Breaking into a canter, he recalled the letters he and Mary had received over the years from Indiana. Mary's cousins were forever writing about the rich soil and the bumper crops it produced year after year. *Besides, in Indiana, a man and his family can tend to their own farm and there be no need for slaves.*

🐾 🐾

Abraham mulled over the Colonel's suggestion for a week before he asked Mary and his sons to talk with him about their labor needs. He also invited his solicitor, Jeremiah, to come out to his Flat Swamp Creek home and add his thoughts.

In the shade of the gazebo, Abraham spent considerable time describing the English cooperative system and then said, "The Colonel thinks there's a way to adapt the cooperative approach to our labor needs. Do any of you see how we can apply it? That's the question I'd like us to chew on."

For long moments, no one spoke, until Frederick said, "These English farmers already own their land. Isn't that right?"

"Yes. That's the case most times."

"Abe, it sounds much like the plantation we own here," Mary said. "We be using special barns to cure tobacco and sorting tables to grade the leaves and wagons for transport. Ain't that similar to English folks pulling together to put up buildings and using equipment that they all be sharing?"

"It has similarities," replied Abraham.

Standing to one side, Jeremiah cleared his throat before saying, "What you need is a cooperative way to supply labor where vast tracts of land can be farmed by both owners and non-owners."

Abraham replied, "We already pay good wages. What else would be in it for them?"

"Why, I expect it would be a split of the sales money," replied Mary.

Stunned, Abraham said, "You can't go splitting sales proceeds that away. Why before we even till the dirt, we spend lots of money buying land, equipment, making repairs, land clearing, and our planting needs."

Jeremiah added, "There be truth to that."

"Well," said Noah, "maybe the sharing should be after some of those costs."

Frederick asked, "Wouldn't it be better if these folks owned some of their own land? Otherwise, they may last only one or two seasons, just like our hired hands be doing now."

Laughing, Jeremiah interjected, "Ahh, I'm not sure you're going down the right road with that idea, Frederick."

Abraham quickly followed up, saying, "You mean give them land? Free? Outright? Why, boy, we just don't have that kind of money."

"No one in his right mind would do that," observed Jeremiah.

Unfazed by the comments, Mary pursued the thought. "Why not let them buy some of our acreage, say a few acres each. We could sell it to them on credit. They could pay it off over time with some of their earnings, and at the end, they would own it free and clear. While they're buying the land and afterwards, their crops would be grown and sold along with ours."

"Now that be interesting," said Abraham.

Mary continued, "Abe, why not try out the idea with some of the good hands we already have, like Gus and Sam?"

His solicitor said, "Look, if'n you go ahead with this plan, you need to enter into a written agreement that you and the others sign, so everyone knows where they stand. You also have to anticipate that you'll get a bad apple somewhere along the line. You know, there are bound to be fellows who don't work out. The plan should provide for making needed changes."

"Thank you, Jeremiah. Those be fine suggestions." Abraham glanced from one to the other, mulling over the discussion. "I think we may have something here." Envisioning the plan working, he went on, "We would need to attract men who are good workers and interested in bettering themselves, but who don't have the money to buy their own land. So, if the man and wife had, say, four or five younguns and we had maybe thirty men—what would we call them—something like tenants—that would give us over a hundred workers plus our own efforts at harvest time. By golly, with that many dependable hands, we can do it," he finished with gusto.

Mary smiled and even Jeremiah seemed pleased with the outcome. "This has been a wonderful idea session," said Abraham. "Now, what say we get some cool buttermilk from the springhouse?"

As Abraham rode into Salisbury on the busy Friday morning, the town was full of folks resupplying their needs and it was slave-trading day at the block. After visiting his banker and getting his suggestions for the tenant plan, Abraham drove his mule and wagon home along Trading Path Road.

Ahead, there was a line of slaves walking single-file on the side of the road, headed toward Flat Swamp Creek. Chains ran between the men and women, linking their leather collars. A few also had their hands tied behind their backs. Nearing, Abraham could see guards with guns and whips at the rear and at the head of the column. Riding up and down the line on his spirited horse was Hooker, the coiled whip in his hand, urging the line along.

Abraham noticed that the slaver was having trouble with his mount as he held the reins short and heavy-handedly sawed the bit in the animal's mouth.

Approaching, Hooker sneered, "Well, looki what be coming down the road, folks. Here be that slave-lover Rallemore. Have you grown back that chunk of hide that the Colonel ripped off?" Snickering mockingly, he tightly reined in his horse and then dug his spurs harshly into the animal's sides to move away from the line of slaves. "Here be more of his new hands, fresh from the block."

Abraham noticed that the slaves watched Hooker, fear reflected on their faces. More than one had red welts on his back. Abraham started to pass.

Unexpectedly, Hooker again spurred his steed, this time blocking the wagon's path as the animal fought the tightly held reins.

Abraham had no choice but to stop. "What do you want, Hooker?"

"Oh, just seeing if'n ya want to chaw a little, kind of friendly like. After all, we both be working for the same man. The Colonel pays me and you married into his money."

Abraham stared at him hoping that the disgust showed on his face. In a hard-edged voice, he said, "Give way, Hooker!"

"In a minute," Hooker replied, trying to look assured but having great difficulty controlling his mount.

Abraham slapped the reins hard on his mule, saying, "Get the hell out of my way."

The wagon's sudden start spooked Hooker's horse, which reared on its hind legs and stepped back into the line of chained slaves.

A man went down, screaming with pain as blood gushed from his leg wound. His fall was so sudden that two other chained men in front of him were pulled to the ground while a woman behind was dragged to her knees.

"Now look what ya done," shouted Hooker, moving his horse away and dismounting.

Leaping from his wagon, Abraham kneeled over the injured man.

The man shook his head from side to side, moaning in agony and tightly holding his leg.

Abraham saw white bone jutting through the skin as he took off his belt and tied a tourniquet above the break. He noticed that red welts formed crisscross patterns on the man's shoulders and chest. "This man needs help right now. Unchain him so we can move him to my wagon, and I'll take him to the doctor."

Hooker replied, "It ain't none of your business."

"Well, maybe Colonel Glass will be interested in knowing how badly you mistreat his help," Abraham angrily responded. "Now, get the key and free this man."

"Why? So you can let another slave run away, you weak-kneed slave-lover?"

"You damn fool. How's this man going to escape on a broken leg? Set him free and do it now," Abraham demanded.

Reluctantly, Hooker nodded to one of his men.

The slave withered in agony, as he was unchained and placed in the wagon.

Hooker refastened the chains to the other slaves before turning to the plantation owner again. "Get to the back of my line, Rallemore. I want to be there when you deliver this man to the Colonel so he'll know the full . . ."

Jumping quickly up to his wagon seat and slapping the reins hard, Abraham hollered, "Not even the gates of hell are going to stop me today." Speeding away, he yelled over his shoulder, "I'll tell the Colonel the full story, Hooker. You can be sure of that."

"Why you dirty son of a . . ." Hooker's voice faded behind the clatter of the wagon wheels.

🐜 🐜

With most of his tenant plan in hand, Abraham went back to see the Colonel. Over glasses of rum and fruit juice, Abraham laid out his thinking and his plan. He had already identified a dozen men who were interested.

The Colonel listened closely.

Abraham noticed that the old man was very pale and that his hands trembled. Concerned, Abraham asked, "Are you feeling alright, Colonel?"

"Of course, I am. The heat has got me down a bit, that's all. I heard tell you had a run-in with Hooker the other day. He be a tough man and he be mean. I told him to let things be, but you watch yourself, Abraham. A man like him can be dangerous."

"He's a pompous ass with no human compassion. Why in the world do you keep a man like him working for you?"

"He doesn't work for me anymore. I fired him."

"I'm glad to hear that," responded Abraham.

"It appears to me that you may have a very workable approach for your labor needs. But I do have one question. Have you thought about management?"

"Ahh, well yes. But do you have anything specific in mind?"

"Yes, I do. Someone has to be the boss. Each of these tenants will have a small land stake in the venture, but you have the big one. Who's going to be in charge? Who makes the decision when a mule is too old or when to sell your tobacco? Who decides when you need to build a new drying shed? Who'll be the boss—you, your tenants, or some committee?"

"It be me, at least in the areas that you asked about. That be clear in the agreement we be signing. If a man can't get along, then we take a vote and the result of the vote is binding. In other areas such as equipment needs, planting and harvest times, when to ship, work scheduling, making sales, and handling the money—them all be my areas. Does that answer your question?"

"It does. Your tenant plan sounds interesting. If I were a younger man, I'd take a chance on it myself. I wish you and Mary every success."

"Well, thank you kindly for them words," said Abraham, pleased with the Colonel's favorable opinion.

"Yes sir," continued the Colonel, "you may well be introducing the new way of meeting the labor issue for all of us as the years move along."

Working outside his curing barn some weeks later, Abraham heard a horse approaching and looked up. To his astonishment, it was Hooker.

"Good day to ya, Mr. Rallemore," the slaver said, sweeping his hat off his head and smiling.

What the hell does he want, thought Abraham. Curtly, he responded, "What can I do for you, Hooker?"

Dismounting, the slaver replied, "I've heard about this tenant plan ya've cooked up. It sounds interesting. I know ya'll be searching for experienced and qualified overseers. I be between jobs at the moment and I'd like the position. I've got experience handling men and I be knowing tobacco."

Abraham was speechless at the man's brass. *No matter what my needs, I'll never hire this man with his arrogant swagger and lack of feelings for others. For all I care, Hooker can take his malevolent attitude and shove it in a well.* Trying to retain his self-control, he answered, "There be no slaves working with me in this operation. Ain't that where you have your experience?"

A bit hesitantly, the slaver responded, "Well, yes, but every worker needs urging and prodding from time to time and I'm well equipped to do just that. I can see that men don't become slackers."

Abraham again noticed the bullwhip tied to Hooker's saddle. Coolly, he answered, "My plan be a free-man operation and maybe, down the line, there'll even be some free slaves working with me. I won't need any special prodding as you call it. If'n a man can't pull his share of the work, he soon be out. I've got plenty of men who be interested and asking for one of my openings."

"Be ya saying ya don't need an overseer, or be it me that ya don't need?"

"You've got a lot of gall, Hooker, but you're not hearing me. I'm saying that I got no use for your particular experience."

Glowering, Hooker responded, "Perhaps ya don't know men as well as ya think. Ya wait and see—ya'll need someone like me one day. So, keep me in mind," he finished, as he swung up on his horse. He gave a mock-salute over his crooked grin and galloped away.

Abraham shuddered. *There be a fella who'll never hear Gabriel's horn. No sir, I don't like slavers and, in particular, I've no use for that man.*

🐾 🐾

Colonel Glass died suddenly three weeks later. After many months, Mary and Abraham's plantation increased by two hundred acres of fine bottomlands from the Colonel's estate.

As word got out about Abraham's tenant plan, men frequently asked when he would have a new opening. The Rallemore family prospered over the years and so did the fortune of his tenants.

Chapter Five

Abraham and his tenants were cutting trees along Buffalo Creek preparing for the winter firewood demand in town. Noah came along to spend a day with his father. Abraham looked at him, again seeing the resemblance between the boy and his wife. He had her hair and laughing eyes.

"You be sure you stay on the creek bank and don't be falling in, Noah," said Abraham. "You heard your ma. I don't want you to get me in trouble with her."

"Alright, pa," replied the boy, laughing.

Leaving home that morning, Mary had sternly instructed, "Noah, that creek has some deep stretches and you be sure to stay clear of the water. You hear me, young man?" Turning to Abraham, she had continued in a crisp voice, "Abe, you make sure you watch that boy. I know how you get carried away when you're working."

Abraham always knew when she had her mind set. Just like this morning, she would square her mouth and stand with her hands on her hips. Then she had thrown him one of her dazzling smiles that he loved and had said, "See you at suppertime."

Noah enjoyed his outings with his father and today was a particular treat. He had brought along his fishing pole, meaning to catch his supper. He walked along the water's edge searching for just the right spot. Frederick had told him that fish liked to hide in holes during lazy sunny days.

The young boy excitedly spotted just the place. There was a tree stump in mid-creek with water rushing around it, creating slack water on the other side. He cast his baited hook, but it fell short. Glancing over his shoulder, his father and the men were still cutting wood. Noah sat down and took his boots off, rolled up his trousers, and waded into the creek.

Again, the hook and weight went out toward the stump, but it fell short once more. Bringing in the line, he waded out farther until the water was above his knees. Casting once more, the line flew beyond the stump. Carefully pulling it in by hand, he dangled the baited hook right behind the tree stump.

Waiting, time passed slowly, but the cool water felt good on this warm day. He stared off to the distant horizon and then at the stream where the rippling waters threw off dazzling reflections. After a while, the mesmerizing glare made him drowsy as he closed his brown eyes. Warmed by the sun and lulled by the sound of rushing water, he was lost in the pleasure of the moment.

Abruptly, the line went tight and burned his hand as more line ran out. Startled, he let out a yell.

"Noah, what is it," shouted his father in alarm some distance away. "Why are you standing in such deep water?" he asked, rushing to the stream.

Noah teetered on the rocky bottom. Losing his footing, he sat down hard as water washed over him.

Wading in, Abraham picked him up and carried him to the bank. "Be you hurt? What were you doing? I told you to stay out of the water," he said, brushing Noah's wet hair away from his eyes.

Unfazed, Noah grinned and held up his fist clutching the taut line. "Pa, I got me a fish. I got me a fish on the other end of this line. Will you help me pull it in?"

He saw the surprised look on his father's face. Pulling in the line, his father brought a brown trout to the edge of the creek. "Well, I'll be . . ."

"I hooked him from that hole in front of the stump."

Abraham bent down to get the hook out of the flopping fish. Then, he held it up so they could admire it. "This be a right good one. It'll make you a fine supper this evening."

Grains on the fish's side glinted brightly in the summer sun. Noah watched his father inspect the fish, wiping some of the bright specks into his hand.

"By heavens, I think these could be flakes of gold," his father muttered, almost speaking to himself.

"What be gold?"

"Oh, just bits of shiny sand," his father replied, quickly turning and glancing toward his men cutting wood.

🐿 🐿

After supper that evening, Abraham and Mary walked in the garden.

"Mary, I looked closely at the fish Noah caught today. I'm sure those were grains of gold on the skin. Here, look at these specks," he said, opening his handkerchief.

"Gold?" she asked. "Real gold, Abe?"

"I'm pretty sure."

"What do we do now?"

"I don't know anything about gold mining or getting it out of streams. I thought I'd ride over to the mining town of Gold Hill next week. Maybe talk to some of the fellas working the streams."

Heavy with child, Mary walked uneasily. "Please be careful. Gold has a strange way of making people act crazy. Let's not take any chances. We have a good life here and we don't be needing trouble."

Riding south, Abraham stopped to watch as men searched for gold along creek banks, washing gravel and grit with large shallow pans. Others used long wooden devices that one man called sluice boxes. They shoveled dirt onto the front end and the flow of water carried the earth over the length of the box. Heavier material, like gold, caught behind ridges built into the bottom while the excess washed away.

He also met old Jamie LaPine, a wizened miner who was searching for his own gold strike. As they talked, Abraham took a liking to him. He described his find and listened to the way Jamie would work it. He decided to involve him in his hunt for the precious metal along Buffalo Creek.

Over time, Jamie built and set up several sluice boxes on inside bends of the creek where the waterways widened and changed speed. The old miner, with Abraham's part-time help, worked the creek for nearly two years, after which gold production became minimal. To be sure, this was no mother lode, yet it allowed both to split the find and each walked away happy with a deep pouch of gold dust and nuggets. Later, Abraham exchanged his share for gold coins at the newly built U.S. Mint in Charlotte.

Stopping, Abraham tied off the wagon reins outside his house just as a gang of men suddenly rode up with guns pointed at him.

"Ya be Abraham Rallemore?" asked the leader.

Somewhat hesitantly, Abraham said, "That be right."

"We be waiting for ya. Get yarself down from thet wagon. We knows ya got gold hidden here abouts and we aims to have it."

Abraham was startled. "What're you fellows talking about? There be no gold here," he blustered.

One gunman stood near the front door to assure that no one in the house would interrupt their thieving plans.

"Ya be getting down or do we have to drag ya off that wagon?"

"You fellows have the wrong man," Abraham said, climbing down.

"Oh?" said the talkative stranger. "Well, let's just say that we ran across an old coot by the name of Jamie LaPine. After a bit of persuading, he be telling us about yar strike on Buffalo Creek. We relieved him of a big pouch of that golden glitter. Be that refreshing yar memory?"

Abraham was stunned. Before he could say anything, one stranger looped a noose around his neck and another tied his hands behind his back.

"Could be ya'd like ta see how we got old Jamie to tell us straight-off where his gold be?"

With that, they marched Abraham over to a large tree. One rider threw the end of the rope over a limb and then wound it once around the pommel of his saddle.

"Now, be ya telling us where ya're hiding tha gold?"

Belligerently, Abraham stared at him.

The man continued. "I guess ya need some persuading just like ol' Jamie did. Alright boys, let's see how far this here fella can stretch himself."

"You fellows will never get away with . . ." The tightening noose choked off further words as the bandit with the rope slowly backed his horse. Abraham tried to keep his toes on the ground, then he was swinging free. An instant later, his toes touched ground again.

"Ya gonna be telling us now?"

Coughing and breathing heavily, Abraham glared at the man, sweat running down his red face. "Go to the devil!"

"Well, ya're just making it tough on yarself," said the man. At his sign, the man on horseback once more lifted Abraham until his feet dangled with toes touching dirt only enough to reduce the strangling pressure on his neck. Again, he was let down and Abraham wheezed, taking in great gulps of air.

"I'm really asking ya for the last time, Mister Abraham. Where are ya keeping that gold?"

Frederick stood inside the house with the rest of the family staring out the window. He knew his mother was frantic with worry as she clutched baby Solomon in her arms while her daughter, Suzanna, clung to her skirt. He was as tall as she was and he tried comforting her by putting his arm around her shoulders.

Turning to him, his mother pleaded, "What do they want?"

He tried to keep his voice even. "Maybe this has something to do with the Buffalo Creek gold."

His mother looked at him, tears flowing from her eyes. "No one knows about it except the family—and old Jamie."

Nodding, he thought, *I have to do something to help pa.* Staring out the window, he counted the bandits and noticed that all had dismounted except for the one with the end of the hanging rope. The leader was talking to his father while two others held his father's arms. The fifth was just outside the front door.

Frederick stepped back and silently signaled to Noah. They quietly walked into the other room and took down the three muskets hanging on the wall. Moving to the back of the house, they left through a rear door with Frederick leading the way as they ran toward a shallow ravine and around a low hill bordering the front of the house.

"Noah," whispered Frederick, "do you think you can fire this musket by yourself if'n I get it ready?"

Nine-year-old Noah answered confidently, "Sure I can. I've seen pa and you do it many times."

"Young brother, you're going to have to be careful where you aim. Don't point the gun anywhere near pa, you understand?"

"Yep," Noah answered, his voice filled with nervous excitement.

"You stay hidden near the top of the hill while I circle around to the other side. When you hear my gunshot, you stick your head up and shoot at them men. They should be looking toward me so you'll have a clear field. After the shot, you make a ruckus like there be men hiding behind this hill. Can you do that?"

Seeing the nod, he went on. "Once you shoot and run down the hill, you light out for the tobacco fields and duck down among the plants in case they come looking for you." Seeing another nod, he cocked the gun for his brother.

Moving quickly, Frederick rounded the base of the hill. When he was in position, he peered through the shrubbery at the men below. Taking aim, he had one bandit squarely in his sights. His hands began to tremble and he eased his finger off the trigger. *I can't shoot a man with no warning*, he thought.

Instead, he fired his gun in the general direction of the man doing the talking and let out a whoop. He heard Noah's gunshot and the ball apparently grazed the horse's rump of the man holding the hanging rope. The thief barely had time to let the line loose as his mount started bucking and then the horse took off for parts unknown.

Frederick heard the sound of a small rockslide coming from Noah's position. He figured the musket recoil must have sent Noah tumbling down the hill and he fired the third musket into the air.

The bandits were spooked, quickly looking from one side of the hill to the other. Even to Frederick, the rock noise coming from behind the hill sounded like it might be the clatter of horses' hooves. *Maybe they'll think it's the local sheriff's men*, he hoped. He peeked from behind the brush as the leader of the gang took a long look at the hill and then spurred his horse, galloping off with the rest of his men.

Watching until the bandits were gone, Frederick quickly ran down to his father, taking the noose off his neck. Noah was there an instant later, untying his father's hands.

Abraham grabbed both and hugged them, as tears filled his eyes. "That was quick thinking and good work, boys. But, dadgum it, you know you could have been badly hurt or even killed. You both took quite a chance."

"We didn't want to lose you," replied Fredrick, smiling.

Abraham hugged them again.

By this time, Mary and the other children were out the door, not comprehending the events, yet crying with happiness.

Flat Swamp Creek never saw the likes of those outlaws again.

THE TRAIL ~

SPRING, 1830

"You can't cross the sea merely by standing and staring at the water."
Rabindranath Tagore

Chapter Six

I t was spring and Abraham was taking a last look at the land where he had been born, feeling a twinge of nostalgia as he thought about how his father and grandfather had worked this land. He and Mary had sold over seven hundred acres along Flat Swamp Creek and Four-Mile Branch River. Early next week, they'd leave and begin the long trek to Indiana, traveling in a wagon train with other settlers.

High branches of slippery elm, green ash, white oak, and many other trees created an arched canopy over slow-moving Flat Swamp Creek. The ripples swirled as he guided his flat-bottomed skiff down the creek, poling his way through low-hanging branches. He swept aside the many draped vines hanging like nature's scarves from the trees.

Most of our family still live in Rowan County, he mused. *But our more adventuresome kin have migrated westward over the years. Some went over the big mountains to Kentucky. Others ventured even farther to Morgan County, Indiana in the old Northwest Territory. The letters from them telling about the bountiful crops and sweet water sure do sound good. The one last fall from Mary's cousins convinced us to sell and seek new lives in Indiana.*

Abraham brushed aside another low-hanging limb as he continued poling the boat. Over the past five years, his tenant plan had worked even better than he had imagined. Abraham was proud of its success and their Rallemore nest egg had continued to grow.

The Colonel was right. The English cooperative system is adaptable to farming tobacco. Yet in one way, the tenant plan worked too well. Give a group of men some say in the operation of the plantation, and the next thing you know, they want to use it. With increasing impatience, he had found himself spending more time settling petty disputes and arguments. *And the tenants are always suggesting changes—buy more mules—begin the leaf-by-leaf tobacco harvest earlier—plant later—shorten the curing time—sell grain to northern markets instead of Charlotte—build more curing sheds—*

He would never say it aloud, but he reluctantly came to the realization that there had been some kernel of truth in Hooker's words spoken many years earlier. Abraham might not have needed a prodder, but he certainly could have used someone to help manage the plantation and to field the many tenant related issues. *At times, it's been like brokering a truce between bickering mules*, he thought.

As he poled the skiff ashore, Abraham felt a wave of excitement thinking about the upcoming trip and the adventures they'd have on the trail.

All of the settlers in the train were from the Salisbury area. During their first group meeting, Abraham watched as a ruggedly handsome young man stood up dressed in buckskins. When he took off his coonskin cap, Abraham was startled to see that the man's head was bald except for a roach of long hair that began at the top of his head and continued in a line to his neck.

"Good morning," he began, smiling broadly. "I be Prairie Hawk Jennings, the captain of your train. Most folks call me Little Jen. I've got only a few words to say before I get to your questions."

That name sounded familiar to Abraham, but he couldn't place it.

"This be a big country and many folks have hankered to go west," continued Little Jen. "Over the years, hostile Injuns, bad weather, and flooded rivers have slowed down pioneers like you, but the Appalachian Mountains have been the biggest barrier to westward migration for the last two hundred years. It's no trick at all to get lost mighty fast in them confusing mountains and canyons.

"When we're on the trail, strange things can happen. We'll take care of one another like family. When anything happens to one wagon, we all fix it if'n that's what it takes." Little Jen paused, gazing at the group. "Just like a family, we have to have some rules. Every man here has signed the company articles. It be saying that you elect me as your captain for this journey. It also be saying that I make the rules. On any major issue, you'll be the jury. The punishment for killing or thievery be hanging. Break other rules too many times—like being liquored up or unruly—and you're off the train and that be my call."

He stopped, smiling at the group. "So, I'm happy you made the decision to go west and I'm pleased to be your guide. Now, who's got the first question?"

"How large be the pass through them big mountains?" asked a man from town.

"It be broad. Many years ago, the Yellow River carved a notch in the ridgeline, now called the Cumberland Gap. More than likely, bison used the pass, traveling to the rich Kentucky bluegrasses, and I know the Injuns used it."

"Be the trail well marked?" asked another man.

"Back in 1775, Daniel Boone and his axmen marked the first trail through the mountains. By the way, my pa was one of Boone's axmen when he was just a small shaver of a lad. Since that time, settlers have streamed through the pass and across the mountains." Little Jen paused, waiting for more questions.

A woman raised her hand, "You don't look old enough to be a captain. How long have you been guiding settlers over them strange mountains?"

Little Jen laughed. "I'll take that as a complement, ma'am. This be my third train with settlers. It'll also be my last, at least for a while. I've an itch to see more of the wild frontier farther west and that'll be my destination after we reach Martinsville, Indiana.

Another man asked, "What route are we taking to get to the Gap?"

"We'll be picking up the Great Philadelphia Trail in Salisbury and taking it north for about a hundred miles to the small village of Mount Airy. Then, we be turning westward for another hundred-forty miles to Sapling Grove, which some folks now call Bristol. It sits right on the border of Tennessee and Virginia.

"There, we be tracking westward along the stagecoach road for another twenty-thirty miles and then we'll take the ferry across the Holston River at Kingsport. This be a good-sized community and you'll be able to restock your provisions in town. From there, it be eighty miles of climbing the ridges and valleys to the Gap."

Samuel Hanks from Abbotts Creek asked, "It being springtime, how good will the trail be?"

"Winter and spring weather will have left deep ruts and steep drop-offs on parts of the trail," answered Little Jen. "You can expect that we'll have to rebuild it in some places so be prepared for the work. Take along your shovels, lever bars, saws, and block and tackle. We'll be using them all."

Abraham asked, "Be there any special tools we should be taking?"

"You always find low hanging branches," answered Little Jen. "With spring growth and fallen limbs, we'll have to lift them or cut them down so the bonnets of your wagons can pass freely. Before we leave, cut yourself some long poles with a fork at one end. We'll use these to raise low limbs, much like you womenfolk raise your clothesline by sticking a brace beneath."

The group chuckled at this.

"What about Injuns? Are we likely to be running into any hostiles?" a man asked at the back of the group.

That voice sounds familiar, thought Abraham. Turning around, he was unpleasantly surprised to see that it belonged to Hooker. *Where in blue-blazes did he come from? I haven't seen or heard of him in years. Don't tell me that jackass is part of our wagon train.*

"Sure, you'll be seeing Injuns," Little Jen continued. "But they long be pacified in the areas we'll be traveling. We shouldn't have any trouble from them."

As the meeting broke up, Abraham saw Hooker staring at him with a crooked smile. It was unsettling as the man tipped his hat and nodded. *That be one fella that this train don't need,* Abraham thought. *Sure as hell, he'll muck up something.*

While waiting to talk to Little Jen, Abraham overheard a man say that Hooker had signed on to drive west for a man with a crippled leg. *Too bad,* he rationalized. *Some things you can't control.*

The guide's name kept tugging at his memory. *Little Jen, Little Jen,* Abraham repeated to himself. *Where have I heard that name?*

Little Jen turned and stuck out his hand. "Howdy."

The Carolinian shook his hand, saying, "How do. My name be Abraham Rallemore and I'm glad to meet you."

"Much obliged."

Giving in to his curiosity, Abraham said, "You be a big strapping young man. How did you come by the name 'Little?' Maybe you got a bigger brother or possibly one that be even taller or broader than you?"

Laughing easily, the wagon boss replied, "I got me two sisters and they be small little things. No, I've no brothers, but my pa be a sizeable man. His name be Edmund Jennings."

That name triggered another memory, yet Abraham was still having trouble placing it. "Where do you hail from?"

"Years ago, my pa went to the frontier and lived with the Osage Injuns and married my ma. I be born out Missouri way in the land of the Six Bulls and we left after my ma died."

That finally jogged Abraham's memory. "You know, I met a frontiersman during the battle for New Orleans. He led some of us across the English lines the night before the attack. Is Big Jen your pa?"

The guide was startled and stared at him for a moment. "You mean the time General Andy's men spiked the cannon?" he inquired.

"The very same. I did the spiking and your pa was our leader. The very last time I saw him, he was talking to General Jackson."

"Well, I'll be," Little Jen said, astonished. "My pa always be talking about the monster cannon that had to be stilled. Isn't it amazing? This be such a big country, yet here we are, meeting each other after so many years have passed since New Orleans."

"That's true. Did your pa go to Tennessee after the war?"

"Yep. He settled down and got himself a new wife and my sisters."

"I don't recollect how the area in Missouri came by the Six Bulls name."

Chuckling, Little Jen said, "My pa lived with the Injuns for so long that he kind of forgot how to speak his first language." Little Jen went on to tell about the many water boils in Six Bulls that feed the streams. "When my pa says 'boils,' his words come out sounding like 'bulls,'" said Little Jen, laughing again.

"Ahh, now I recall," Abraham responded, joining in the laughter. "He and I had quite a long discussion about boils and bulls."

"I think you'll meet him again on this trip as he plans to travel with us," continued Little Jen. "He'll probably find us in Boonesborough. You wait 'till he catches up to us. Tarnation, he has so many tales and stories about Six Bulls that he'll have your ears ringing."

Smiling, Abraham said, "I'll look forward to seeing him." Left unsaid was his concern about Hooker.

🐾 🐾

The night before departure, Abraham lay on his pallet staring up at the stars. Nervous excitement kept him from falling asleep as thought after thought went through his head. His three Conestoga wagons were loaded and he figured that each wagon bed, measuring four feet by sixteen feet, carried close to a ton of supplies, equipment, and belongings.

Axes, saws, water barrels, a spare wagon tongue, and extra wheels nested on the sides below the big billowing canvas tops while tar buckets hung from the axles to grease the wheels. Gauging the width of a wagons hub to hub, he figured that they'd need trails through the mountains with at least eight to nine feet of clearance.

Here we are, the seven of us, traveling west. Ever since my soldiering days, I've wanted to see more of this great country. With our sixth youngun on the way, Mary was concerned at first, but now she's eager like me. Imagine—at the weathered age of thirty-five—I'm going west and starting over. Hallelujah, brother, it be like a dream come true.

He reached out and touched Mary as she slept on the ground beside him. There was only enough room inside the wagons for the youngest children. *I sure hope she rests tonight,* he thought as he snuggled deeper into the padded quilt sitting on top of freshly cut grass. *We had better get used to bumpy pallets as we have months of it ahead of us.*

Still, the excitement of their departure kept him awake as he again ran through his mental list of goods packed in the wagons. *I hope that collapsible iron cooking stand works well for Mary. I worry about her fixing meals outdoors and walking around an open fire with her skirts. By golly, that's a fine looking new plow we bought, but it sure takes up a heap of room in the lead wagon. I think those two flour barrels with the false bottoms and Mary's knitting basket are going to work well as hiding places for our money and gold. Each be in a different wagon in case we lose one.*

The beef jerky plus the flour, beans, coffee, dried fruit, and winter vege-tables will see us through much of the trip. Besides, we have the barrels of smoked bacon preserved in bran, our two cows for milk, and cattle in the remuda for fresh meat. Little Jen told us that we'll do some hunting on the trail and that we can buy more supplies and fresh greens in villages along the way.

Finally, sleep overtook him.

The next day, a mist lay on the land, curling up tree trunks in wisps before disappearing into overhead branches on that early morning in May. At the lead, Little Jen sat astride his stallion, as the thirty-six wagons were ready. Folks called to one another excitedly, waiting for the command that would start their journey west. The harnessed teams were also agitated as some pawed the ground or snorted, apparently as eager as the settlers to get underway.

"Wagons, ho," Little Jen loudly called out.

Excited, Abraham found his hands were clammy as he flicked the jerkline. "Get up, Lizzy," he called to his lead mule. In the usual manner, he walked on the left side of the wagon to drive the team using a single line affixed to Lizzy's bit—one quick pull for left or two for right with voice commands for start and stop.

He could ride on a fold-down board-seat affixed to the side of the wagon, but that left him with a restricted view of the trail ahead. *Yes*, he thought, *unless I'm going down a grade or the trail narrows, I'll walk when I'm driving the team.* He stumbled over a rock and thought, *by heaven, it's going to be a long walk.*

He looked over to his other wagons. A cow followed each tied on a lead just like the two horses behind his. Tall and strong at nearly sixteen, Frederick handled the second wagon, walking to one side like his father. Noah, now eleven, drove the third, seated high on the wagon's brow with Mary beside him. *Between them, they'll be able to handle their team and Frederick or I'll help them on the more difficult parts of the trail.*

As the snake-like train curled around a bend in the road, he could see some of the other wagons ahead. Some were horse drawn. *Good for speed but not the best for hauling heavy loads long distances*, he thought. *I prefer my mules I bred from male donkeys and female horses. They're stronger and less excitable.* He knew that oxen were the strongest animals in the train and pulled the slowest-moving wagons. *From birth, these fine animals learn to plow, haul, and grind wheat by trampling. I've always admired their strength and once saw a sizable brace pull a load near twice their weight-likely about four thousand pounds.*

Looking toward the rear, he just caught sight of the remuda. *I hope them young boys at the rear of the train can handle the herd of extra draft animals and cattle.*

Abraham found that the many days along the trail became interchangeable as nearly four weeks passed before they reached the ridgeline of the mountains. There were issues along the trail just as Little Jen had predicted. The train halted when there was a hard rain and, half a dozen times, they stopped and made repairs to the trail. Today, a landslide had completely blocked their way and it would take a great deal of work to clear it.

Abraham was surprised when he heard Little Jen ask Hooker to organize the work detail saying he was going ahead to check more the trail ahead.

Except for the youngest, everyone pitched in, many armed with shovels and lever bars to move stones, downed trees, and dirt.

"Rallemore, listen up," Hooker commanded in a gruff voice as he rode his horse up and down the work area like a field marshal. "We got to move that big tree that be knocked down by the slide. Ya get to digging it out and make it quick."

The bristles on the back of Abraham's neck rose, but he went over to the tree and began shoveling dirt.

"Ya four men take a whipsaw and axes to the tree," Hooker ordered. "Ya other men, start flattening out this part of the trail."

He just loves ordering folks. Next thing I know, he'll be telling Mary and the younguns what to do.

"Ya women and younguns get yarselves some buckets and begin picking up rocks. We'll use them to seat the roadbed."

Just as I guessed, the Carolinian thought.

With the help of a dozen men and harnessed mules, they were able to dislodge large sections of the tree while other men leveled the roadway.

After many hours of hard work, Abraham stopped and watched the first wagon slowly rolling over the rebuilt trail with the hillside to the left and a gully on the right. Hooker, still mounted, led the harnessed team of horses.

From behind, Abraham leaned on his shovel and wiped his brow with the back of his hand. It had been a long day and he was glad that it was nearly over. Suddenly, he straightened, staring ahead at the team and wagon slowly moving over the rebuilt roadway. Dropping his shovel, he quickly walked a few paces toward the edge of the gully. From this position, he saw that the sloop of the restored trail was still too steep. Through cupped hand, he urgently shouted, "HOOKER, STOP! THE WAGON CAN'T MAKE IT."

"MIND YAR OWN BUSINESS, YA DIM-WIT," Hooker arrogantly replied. "HELL, THIS BE A CAKEWALK FOR AN OLD HAND LIKE ME."

At that instant, the wagon started sliding sideways in the loose dirt toward the gully. For a moment, it hung suspended on its side wheels nearly pulling the four-horses to the ground from the strain until the wagon-tongue broke with a gunshot-loud snap. Then the interior load shifted and over it went, crushing the bonnet, scattering supplies as the driver jumped for his life, and dragging the horses downhill.

Little Jen rode up, sliding to a stop and asked, "What be happening here?" The closest man told him and Abraham looked around, but Hooker had disappeared.

It took all of the men the rest of the day to repair the road, haul the wagon out of the gully, and to save some of the supplies. Two horses were severely injured and put down.

The settler and his family finally had their wagon back, but men spent part of the next morning replacing the wagon tongue.

"Here," Abraham said, handing a large heavy tarp to the man. "It won't replace your wagon bonnet, but it can help keep your gear dry."

"Thank ye, Abraham. I be mighty appreciative."

Late in the morning, Little Jen call out, "Wagons, ho."

As the train resumed its climb toward the Cumberland Gap, he noticed Hooker climbing onto his wagon seat.

Chapter Seven

O n the trail, Abraham was surprised at the number of travelers headed east with cattle and wagons filled with potatoes, hay, and grains. As Little Jen rode by, he said, "I never realized that this was such a busy market trail."

"Indeed it be," replied Little Jen. "Now you know that the Gap be a trail for both west bound settlers and the east-bound market route from western farms to the coastal states."

"I see the trail be too narrow in some place for wagons to pass each other," Abraham observed. "What do we do then?"

"I'm riding ahead, blowing my cow-horn bugle to announce us. Those going east respond if'n they hear me. Then, it becomes a matter of finding wide spots along the trail."

As the caravan of wagons continued, a strange thing evolved. Abraham noticed that other wagons began joining at the end of their train. He surmised that the Cumberland Gap also served as a funnel.

The next evening, Little Jen came to their campfire with the latest news. "Me and the other train captains met earlier this evening. Our combined wagons now number just over a hundred-twenty with thirty-one joining in just the past three days."

The large number surprised Abraham. "Heavens, it'll take even longer to pass on-coming folks with this many wagons."

"Yep," replied Little Jen. "And if'n a wagon breaks down, it can easily mean that both directions are stopped until the problem be fixed."

"What happens now?" Abraham wondered aloud.

"We decided that each train will leave four hours after the earlier group departs. That should break up our long line. We be at the head of the line, so we're moving out at first light. Be ready."

"We'll be there," replied Abraham. Unable to resist, he added, "I see that Hooker is back driving his rig. Is everything alright there?"

Little Jen stared at him and shrugged. "Don't forget, first light."

🐜 🐜

A late spring was in the mountain air as the wagons finally breached the mountain gap. They were now traveling along the valley bordering the Yellow River.

Prior to the trip, Abraham had installed a simple counter mounted on his wagon, which recorded the number of times the lead wheel turned. Every day, he noted the number in his journal and reset the device. Doing the arithmetic, he could estimate the distance they had traveled. To this point, he figured they had come three hundred miles. *Well, only five hundred more to go,* he mused, as he opened his reading book on Greek mythology.

Little Jen announced that the train would be laying over for two days outside the town of Cumberland Gap, allowing time for needed repairs and rest.

The second evening, they held a family-style dinner to celebrate reaching their first milestone. Men passed around a jug and Abraham smiled, figuring it was probably good old white-lightning corn whiskey.

A man with a fiddle began playing a lively gig as others joined him, playing an assortment of "musical instruments." One kept time beating two blocks of wood together while an old-timer blew through a jews harp. Abigail Hanks, Samuel's wife, added the thump of a large wooden spoon to an upended iron kettle while Samuel blew deep bass notes on an almost empty jug. Another man raked a stick over a washboard in time with the music while still another took up his banjo. Most folks simply clapped their hands in time with the music.

Music be good for my tired soul, thought Abraham, *and this'll bolster everyone's spirits.*

A man stood on a box and began clapping his hands while calling out, "Now c'mon, get your partners, 'cause we're going to do a quadrille so be forming your squares."

Before long, men and women were sashaying left, then right, and swinging arm in arm to the music while children mimicked their parents on the edge of the dance circle.

"Allemande left . . . and do-si-do . . . now promenade back ...," the caller chanted, stomping his foot in time to the lively tune.

Abraham walked over and sat down on a log next to Little Jen as they watched the dancing.

"Bow to your partner . . . bow to your neighbor . . . now swing your neighbor's gal . . . and shuffle on back . . . ."

"What do you think of our progress so far?" asked Abraham.

"It's been slow with the pace of the oxen, maybe a couple of miles an hour at best, and some of the drivers were new to the task. The eastern-bound travelers and climbing the mountains have also been against us. I'm thinking it'll ease up once we get to the other side of the pass."

". . . now swing your partner round and round . . . and pass her on to the next man down . . ."

Abraham listened to Little Jen but noticed that Hooker was dancing with a young woman. *Really kicking up his heels*, thought Abraham. *That young gal looks like she be plumb tuckered out. I wonder which wagon is hers.*

"We have some fifteen miles along Yellow Creek," Little Jen continued. "Then we'll reach the Cumberland River and go past the Narrows, which runs through a break between two mountain peaks. There's a good river crossing there with a hard bottom for the wagons." Changing the subject, Little Jen asked, "Have you ever seen an iron-making furnace?"

"No, I haven't," replied Abraham in surprise. "Why you be asking?"

"There be one on the other side of the village. Folks found iron ore around here a dozen years ago and they built a giant wood-burning fireplace with a stone chimney that reaches maybe thirty feet high. The melted ore is hotter than blazes and runs down channels to hollows in the ground. They be calling it pig iron since it be reminding you of a sow feeding piglets. Darndest thing you ever saw."

"It sounds interesting. I'll look for it," said Abraham. Again, he noticed the girl dancing with Hooker. *He sure is holding her tight and she looks downright scared to me.*

The music stopped as folks rested between dances, talked, and aired themselves. Abraham heard hoots and hollers coming from a group of men off to one side. He knew that Mary and some of the other women in the train called them the "bachelors." They were unmarried men on their way to adventures in new lands.

Unconcerned, Little Jen kept talking, "I expect we'll raise Morgan County in the middle of July or there-abouts."

The bachelors were loudly laughing and carrying on, passing a jug around.

Suddenly, Hooker knocked another man to the ground. "That be my jug and this be my gal," he shouted as he stood over the fallen man, holding the woman by her arm.

The woman was crying as she twisted and tried to free herself from Hooker's grip. "Let me go," she wailed. With a mighty heave, she wrenched free, lifted her skirts, and ran right towards Abraham and Little Jen.

Hooker was quick to hand the jug to another bachelor and light out after her.

The young woman was running flat-out, skirts raised and flying, her hair coming undone and streaming behind her. She was clearly frightened. As she neared, she cried out, "Mister, help me! This brute keeps pawing at me."

Little Jen stood as the young woman tripped and literally fell into his arms, tumbling both to the ground.

Hooker was only a few paces behind. "Come back here, you dumb little wench," he snarled.

Before the wagon boss could react, Abraham stepped in and let loose a roundhouse right fist into the pit of Hooker's stomach.

The blow doubled the slaver over, sending him to the ground with the wind knocked out of him. For long moments, Hooker lay doubled-over, gasping for air. At length, he slowly stood. "Rallemore, you're always messing with me when I be trying to catch someone, ain't ya? Well, see how ya like this," he said, and charged low.

Both men fell to the ground as they threw punches and wrestled for an advantage.

Hooker was the stronger and Abraham knew he was on the losing side of this brawl. Suddenly, Little Jen lifted Hooker by the seat of his pants and shoved him aside.

"Make him leave me alone," the woman cried, still on the ground, her skirts awry. "He keeps pawing at me and forcing me to dance with him. I want to go to my wagon. Please make him stop, mister."

"You best be sobering up down by the river," Little Jen said, shoving Hooker toward the water. "This party be over for you."

"Let me be, ya stinking half-breed, and don't ya lay yar hands on me again," said the slaver, livid with drunken rage. "Ya got no rope over me and ya got no call to interfere. She be my woman and I aim to have her."

"Not tonight, and you'd better be calming yourself right quick. I've every-thing to say about you being in my train and you're done for tonight. Now get on down to the river and cool off. Go on, get." Turning Hooker around roughly, Little Jen gave him a hard shove.

Angry and embarrassed, Hooker stared at Little Jen and then Abraham. "Another time, Rallemore," Hooker said, as he stomped off, throwing him a dirty gesture.

Ignoring Hooker, Little Jen turned to Abraham, "I'll see that this gal gets back to her wagon." With a firm grip on the girl's arm, Little Jen walked away.

🐾 🐾

Fifty miles beyond the Gap, they were finally clear of the mountains. It was Sunday, normally a day of rest. In the morning, Abraham and Noah joined a hunting party from the train. The other Rallemores remained with the wagons parked under shade trees and some distance from the rest of the train.

Remaining with the wagons, Frederick was greasing the wheels when he glimpsed a shadow around the backside of another wagon. Rounding the rear to investigate, someone jumped on top of him from the wagon gate, knocking him to the ground. Looking up, he was surprised to see Hooker standing over him, a knife in his hand.

"Get thee up, boy," Hooker commanded.

As Frederick stood, Hooker turned him around and grabbed him around the neck from behind with his arm, the knife prodding him in the neck. "Now keep yourself quiet because ya're just in time to help me," he snarled. "I want ya to call out to yar ma and tell her to come over here. Now do it, but keep calm or else this knife will slice your throat from ear to ear."

"Why you be wanting her?" Frederick asked anxiously, the cold knife striking fear in his heart. Blustering, he added, "Anyway, she isn't here. She went off to visit a woman that be sick down the line."

"No she ain't, because I saw her just minutes ago. Now do as I say and call her," commanded the slaver, tightening his arm around Frederick's neck.

Fearing for his mother, Frederick panicked. "Leave my ma out of this," he implored, choking out the words through the stranglehold.

"Boy, do it now or die—your choice. Makes no difference to me because I'll just kill ya and then find your little brother next," replied Hooker, as his knife drew blood.

"You're not going to hurt her, are you?" Frederick hesitantly asked.

"Nope, I just want to talk to her, that's all. Call her NOW!" he whispered harshly in Frederick's ear as the knife probed deeper.

Feeling blood seeping down his neck, he called out, "Ma. Come here."

"That's a good boy," Hooker rasped in his ear.

His mother came around the corner of the wagon and stopped in surprise. "What're you doing to my son?" she angrily snapped.

"Don't be making any commotion if'n ya wants yar son to live," Hooker said, flashing his knife.

"You've hurt him."

"Nope. He's just got a little nick on his neck."

Mary was ash-faced and looked worried. "Why are you doing this? What do you want?"

"I be tired of this trip and tired of sitting on that hard wagon seat day after day staring at the butt-end of mules," replied Hooker, his mouth curling in an ugly smile. "And I be weary of yar husband and the trouble he's caused me. I wants yar money because I'm heading for new places. I've already searched this wagon, so ya must be keeping it in one of the others."

"What money are you talking about?" asked Mary.

She's scared for me, thought Frederick, as an uncontrollable tremble went down his leg.

"Don't ya be playing games with the likes of me, Mrs. Rallemore," Hooker said. "Ya sold yar land, didn't ya? That be how I know ya got money hidden in yar wagons. Get it quick or this knife is going to go through yar boy's neck and out the other side. Ya want to see that—eh? I promise ya, it won't be pretty," he continued as the knifepoint drew more blood. "Then, I'll be starting on yar other younguns. NOW MOVE IT, MA'AM!"

"Give it to him, ma," pleaded Frederick. "I don't want anything to happen to you and the others."

His mother stood tall. "Alright, Mr. Hooker, you searched this wagon so I know you overlooked my knitting basket." She raised the hem of her skirt and stretched, stepped up on the wheel hub, and reached under the seat. "This is what you're searching for," she said, holding out the basket to him. "Take it and turn my boy loose. You've got what you wanted."

"Not so quick, Mrs. Rallemore." With a nasty grin, he continued. "Come over here and open it so you can show me what be inside."

She opened the cover, turned the basket over, and dumped the contents on the ground before him. Among the needles, knitted fabric, and balls of thread, a heavy sack hit the ground with a clink.

"Pick it up and let me see what be inside," Hooker commanded excitedly.

His mother complied, untied the string tie, and shook out some golden coins into her hand. He heard Hooker's gasp next to his ear.

Laughing softly, Hooker said, "Well now, ain't that a pretty sight. Hand it to me—careful now," as he raised the blade until it was tight under Frederick's jaw.

The horror of the knife filled Frederick with dread as his leg trembled again.

Releasing his strangle hold, Hooker took the sack and again grabbed the boy by the neck, walking him backwards. "It be time for me and the boy to be leaving, ma'am."

Confused, she said, "But you told me . . ."

"Quiet down. I want your word that you'll tell no one about this until mealtime. I'm keeping the boy with me to make sure. If'n I see anyone coming after us, I'll gut him just as sure as the sunrise comes in the morning. Ya got that?"

Hesitantly, Mary answered, "Yes, I understand, Mr. Hooker." Then in a firm voice edged with tension, she went on. "Take the gold, but if'n you harm my son, my Abe and me will track you down if it takes the rest of our days. You got that Mr. Hooker?"

"Sure, sure—we understand each other perfectly, Mrs. Rallemore," he responded sarcastically. "Come on boy, we're making for them horses in the trees."

The hunting party was returning to camp when Abraham reined in as two horsemen galloped away from the train. The leader held the reins of the second horse and Abraham was astounded to see that the other rider was Frederick.

With only a brief pause, Abraham shouted, "Little Jen, look! Something is wrong." Spurring his horse hard, Abraham galloped off shouting, "Noah, you stay here."

Little Jen followed and they galloped stirrup to stirrup after the pair as the lead man glanced around.

"It's Hooker," shouted Abraham.

Seeing his pursuers, the slaver dropped the reins to Frederick's horse and the animal slowed.

Riding alongside, Abraham saw that his son's hands were tied to the pommel. Reaching over, he grabbed the bridle, pulling the horse to a stop.

"Pa! Hooker stole our gold! He threatened to kill me and harm the youn-guns, so ma had to tell him where it be hid."

Abraham untied his son's hands and watched Little Jen pull his musket from the scabbard and dismount in one smooth motion.

The wagon boss dropped his reins and stepped forward several paces before kneeling. Sighting down his gun barrel for a long second, he fired.

He can't hit Hooker at this range, thought Abraham. *It must be well over a hundred yards.*

An instant later, the horse went down, throwing his rider.

🐾 🐾

Standing to one side, Abraham watched the trial.

Presiding, Little Jen said, "You've heard the witnesses and talked among yourselves. What say the jury? Should Mr. Hooker hang?"

A man stepped forward. "He be guilty as sin. The jury says hang him."

Much to Abraham's surprise, the crowd cheered and a few even threw their hats into the air. The display made him uneasy.

"So be it," said Little Jen.

"Ya can't do that, ya rotten Injun half-breed," yelled Hooker, his broken arm in a sling, as he was marched off toward a tree with men shoving him along the way. He was sweating heavily and his eyes were wild. "Ya ain't the law and ya got no right."

Someone had already thrown a rope over a tree limb and fashioned a noose. A man held the reins of a horse while another fitted the rope around Hooker's neck and tightened it with a jerk. Several men pushed him up onto the horse's back.

A chill went down Abraham's spine. *Am I really going to let them hang this ass?* His own near hanging on Flat Swamp Creek flashed through his mind. *He be a mean man, but to carry his blood forever on my hands . . .*

"I know the law and ya can't do this," Hooker shouted, starting to rant and rave hysterically, white spittle running down his chin.

Little Jen said, "Things always be happening around you, Hooker, mostly for the bad. Now you'll hang for your thieving ways."

Suddenly, Abraham shouted, "Hold on there." Making his way through the crowd, he noticed some giving him a curious stare. Looking straight ahead, he continued parting the crowd until he was standing in front of Little Jen. "It be my family that Hooker robbed and it be my son that he held at knifepoint. You're right, Little Jen, Hooker mainly is bad news, but we don't have to burden our souls with his blood. We have our valuables back and no one was hurt bad other than scaring us to death." Abraham saw the surprise on Little Jen's face. A few men standing next to the wagon train captain actually gawked.

Little Jen studied Abraham for a long moment. "Carrying out the jury's verdict be my job."

The Carolinian continued. "Indeed it is. But my pa always told me that there be justice in mercy. I say give him a few minutes to pack his kit and to get the hell off this train so we can be rid of him for good."

"I'm not hungering for blood, not even from this scoundrel," the wagon train captain said. Staring up at Hooker, he continued, "Alright Mr. Hooker, you get to stay alive but only by the good graces and mercy of Mr. Rallemore."

Hooker's hysterics had given way to his usual mocking smile.

"But hear me, Hooker," Little Jen commanded his attention. "Come anywhere close to this train again and I'll shoot you on sight. You got that?" Turning to face his settlers, he continued, "And I'm also saying that anyone seen helping this thief will be immediately banished from the train. This man is vermin and I'll not have him or anyone helping him in my train." Looking at his settlers and waiting to let the words sink in, he finally said, "Cut him free boys."

Hooker sneered, "Ya always was soft-headed and possum-brained, Rallemore, with ya pretending to be a moneyed-gentleman thanks to yar wife's family. This Injun says I'm going to live because of yar good graces and yar mercy. But just ya wait—somewhere, some day, we'll meet again."

"That's enough, Hooker," Little Jen said harshly.

Never taking his eyes off Abraham, Hooker went on. "Ya'll just turn around one day and thar I'll be with my knife poking yar gut. I'll wait for that day when ya'll be begging me for my good graces. Only problem is, I ain't no gentleman and it'll never be in me to give ya mercy."

Abraham felt a shiver go down his back as he once more realized the depth of Hooker's hatred. *Could be he'll show up looking for me with his knife some day. He be a mean man just like the old Colonel said. His character be like that cloud that he follows him everywhere—and for him, it be black cloud.*

🐾 🐾

In Boonesborough, Big Jen joined the group. Abraham looked at him closely. The man was much older but still sporting a full beard, now snow white, and his blue eyes still seemed to twinkle. "Big Jen, I don't know if you remember me, but I be Abraham Rallemore, the fellow that spiked the British cannon with you down in New Orleans. Do you recall?"

"Lordy, do ah ever. We really had us some fun thet night, didn't we. Why ol' General Andy was just beside himself with glee and now look at him, being President of these whole United States of America. When ya stop and think bout it, ah reckon we helped Ol' Hickory get elected. Really good ta see ya, young Abra'm."

"It's good to see you, too. Where're you headed?"

"Out west a-ways. On tha trip back, ah wants ta stop and see my daughter in Wooster, Ohio. And ah guess ya all be on yar way to Indiani."

"Yes, we're traveling to find good farmland in Morgan County."

Abraham noticed that Big Jen didn't carry himself as straight as he remembered and reckoned that age was catching up to him. Everything continued to be unusual about Big Jen—the way he spoke, how he carried himself, and certainly the way he traveled.

The old frontiersman drove a stumpy wagon pulled by two mules. It may have been a Conestoga wagon at one time, but he had greatly modified it to fit his needs. It was nearly a third shorter than the usual length and had tall wheels in the rear with smaller ones in front. Overall, the wagon bed sat higher off the ground.

"Ya be curious bout my prairie schooner? Well, ya see with tha wagon shorter sitting higher off'n tha ground, ah can better ease ova and around rocks and trees thet away. And ah turns quicker with them smaller front wheels."

Abraham nodded.

"But tha inside be my real joy. I got me a place fer my food, my buck-skins, and my hunting needs. But looki here," he pointed through the rear bonnet at the wagon floor mostly filled with a thick soft down feather bed.

"I need this ta comfort tha aches thet ah picked up from 'ears of bedding down under tha stars," explained the frontiersman. "Man has ta do what works fer him and this bed of clouds be fer me."

The next night, the weary group made camp by a stream and rested around a campfire having eaten their fill of salted beef, greens, and pan-fried biscuits.

Abraham sat next to Big Jen and asked, "You ever going back to your Six Bulls country?"

"Nope, ah don't reckon so. Sleeping under the big sky with no roof ova mi head be gitting ol' fer me. Still, tha country be right purdy. Why, they've mo'e game thar than a man kin believe. It was tha bess 'ears of my life and if'n my wife had lived on, why mebbe—" He paused, staring at the ground. "Ah expects we'd still be thar. Yesum, thet be mighty purdy country, thet lan of tha Six Bulls."

Of course, Big Jen didn't stop there but told one story after another about this great land. Nearly every evening, he spun his yarns and the horse-eye–high grass was on the minds of many who sat around the campfires and listened to him. Abraham and Frederick were usually part of the group even though understanding Big Jen's words never got any easier.

I've a hankering to see even more of this great country, thought Abraham, as his mind pictured the prairie that Big Jen described. *Here we are with hundreds of miles yet to go on this journey and I'm already thinking about traveling again. Well, who knows? Maybe someday I'll see this land called Six Bulls. Kentucky has its Daniel Boone, but southwest Missouri sure is Edmund Jennings' country.*

Chapter Eight

The weather had turned hot and humid, causing Abraham to wipe the inside of his hatband again. It had taken twelve long sweaty days to travel from Boonesborough to Newport, Kentucky, which sat across the Ohio River from Cincinnati.

Here, Abraham could feel a slight breeze from the water, and he was thankful for even a little reprieve in the weather as he and his boys made camp for the night. Come morning, they'd cross the big river on a ferry.

Riding up and dismounting, Little Jen asked, "Everything alright?"

"Yep, just tired, that's all." Abraham turned to gaze at the water. "This Ohio River be so wide, it makes me nervous to think that all my wagons are going to cross on a boat. How long has this ferry been making crossings?"

"About a decade, I reckon," answered the younger man. "It should go smoothly. This outfit has several boats and each be powered by horses."

"Horses?" Abraham asked in surprise.

"That's right. At the rear, they hitch two horses to a capstan. Walking in a circle, the animals turn a center post that drives the paddle wheel. The horses have blinders on to keep them calm and a man rides one to set the pace. This form of power be very reliable."

"Well, I'll be . . ."

"Each ferry takes four wagons," continued Little Jen. Then turning dead serious, he went on. "There be only one wee problem."

Suddenly anxious again, Abraham asked, "What's that?"

"Them horses get mighty dizzy," Little Jen replied, bursting out with laughter.

🐾 🐾

In the morning, the wagon train began crossing. It took most of the day to get all the wagons, teams, people, and extra livestock across the river.

Abraham's wagon made the last crossing. The afternoon heat had rapidly cooled and, mystically, vapors rose off the water. The ferry glided smoothly with its two-horse propulsion, parting wisps of fog along the way.

Off in the distance, Abraham made out the upper decks of a steamboat coming downstream through the mist, black smoke billowing from its smokestacks and trailing behind. He tried to catch sight of Ohio across the big river and, perhaps, Cincinnati, but the far shore remained hidden by the low-lying mist.

Big Jen came to stand beside him. "This har riva and tha Mississip be some of God's wonders."

"I've never seen anything like it. I can't make out the other side through the vapors. Will we be able to see Cincinnati when we get closer to shore?"

"Not on this trip as it be five or six miles east of tha landing and round tha riva bend. Lordy, it be a sizable village wit better than fifty thousand souls living thar, kinda like ants on a sugar plum."

"Cincinnati be an unusual name," Abraham said. "Is it Injun?"

"Nope—it be called after some ancient I-talian fella and Cincinnat be its second name 'cause the first was Losantiville. This place be tha prime jumpin' off point fer westward travelers."

Nearing shore, Abraham could make out cabins and buildings on the riverbank bluff. The boat bumped into the bottom and the landing ramp came down, lowered on ropes from uprights mounted to the sides of the ferry. He drove his wagon down the off-ramp and slapped the reins hard, urging his mules to climb the steep bank. At the top, he saw that the rest of the train was camped some distance away. As he pulled up, Little Jen met him and his father's wagon stopped along side.

"Glad to see you fellas had a safe trip. Ain't that horse-powered barge something?"

"I'll say," replied Abraham.

"Thet be one slick ride," Big Jen added.

"You know," continued Abraham, "I could have used that same locomotion on my plantation when we were drilling out log centers to create piping for irrigation. I'm going to keep it in mind."

Little Jen pointed, saying, "Over yonder, me, Samuel Hanks, and some of the other men are going to the Anderson Ferry Inn after supper for a tankard of beer. Come along, why don't you."

"Beer sounds like a fine idea to me," Abraham replied.

"Ya fellas go on ahead," said Big Jen. "My cloud of feathers be calling me."

"See you after supper."

🐦 🐦

The inn was crowded as Abraham looked for his friends. Samuel stood up and waved Abraham to their table. With so many talking, there was an air of joviality.

"This be a popular place this evening," said Little Jen.

Abraham accepted a tankard of beer from a passing barmaid and took a deep drink. Smiling, he remarked, "Ahh, this tastes mighty good after all those long days on the dusty trail."

"That it be," and Samuel lifted his tankard in salute.

Little Jen leaned in so he could be heard over the din in the tavern. "We have another hundred and fifty miles until we be reaching Martinsville. There be two routes from here. If we head northwest, it be about twenty miles shorter than if we go north to the village of Richmond and then west over the National Road. But the first route takes at least the same number of days because of the many soft-bottom river crossings. I'll go either way. What do you men think?"

Abraham listened to the discussion. The shorter distance was attractive, but the soft river bottoms were a concern. Finally, they decided to take the route due north through Richmond.

A man leaned over from the next table who said, "That be a right good decision. I've walked all over this territory and going northwest from here be difficult with the many quicksand riverbeds."

Seeing Abraham and the others looking at him, the man laughed and waved his hand, saying, "Don't mean to be butting in. My name be Johnny Hill and I'm a river man and have my own barging company out of Coshocton, Ohio. You probably know that barges and flatboats only go one way—downriver. Once they reach their destination, we sell them to someone going farther downriver or they're broken up for wood. Anyway, my people and me walk a goodly ways to get home. That's how I know something about the lay of the land here-abouts."

"Aye, and he knows the rivers and barging right well," added an older balding man with Johnny. With an Irish brogue, he continued, "I be Rufus

Putman and I build the most beautiful rafts up in Loudonville on the Black Fork River." He was dressed in a cutaway coat with a yarn cap stuffed in his pocket.

The Carolinians introduced themselves and bought a round of beer for the strangers, who joined them at their table. The two brought along their jug of rye whiskey and Johnny went to the bar for more whiskey glasses.

Abraham watched as the round-bellied Rufus raised his whiskey glass in salute. "Here's to ye, slainte," he said, giving the traditional Irish toast, and downed his drink. "Saints preserve me, this sweet nectar reminds me of my dear departed mother." He refilled the shot glass and dropped it and its liquor content into his tankard of beer with a small laugh. "Ahh, this'll perk up the flavor."

Following his lead, Johnny did the same and so did Abraham and the others. The laughter and talking around the table continued.

Johnny said, "Rufus built a stout raft for a fellow who wanted to transport dried apples and grain to Cincinnati. He's wanted to ride one of his boats so he can improve his designs and decided to come to Cincinnati with me. We be starting back in the morning."

"Aye, I picked up some fine ideas to use back at me yard," said the balding man with the potbelly.

Abraham could hear the liquor slur in the old gent's voice as he talked.

Turning to Abraham, Rufus asked, "And where be ye going?"

"We're from North Carolina and we've been on the trail for weeks headed for Martinsville up in Morgan County, Indiana."

"Well, you got most of your trip behind you," Johnny relied.

"That be right."

As the evening wore on, Abraham was feeling good. Indeed, he noted all were now a jovial bunch as still another round of boilermakers was prepared, this time by Rufus who was a bit shaky in the hand. Abraham watched as the portly boat builder finished the task with the solemnity of a priest performing high mass.

"Beannachtai na Feile Padraig," he intoned, almost under his breath. Looking up from beneath his shaggy eyebrows, he saw the others watching him. "What?" he asked, with an impish grin. "I'm only wishing ye a happy St. Patrick's day in me mother's tongue." Then he turned serious with an almost crestfallen expression on his face. Looking at each of them, he said solemnly, "But ye know, the next St. Patty's day be nearly a year away."

In the next moment, Rufus's impish grin was back. With one eyebrow comically raised, he raised his tankard. "But let's not wait to celebrate." With a hurrah, they all downed his brewed mixture.

It was now late and Abraham noticed that the crowd noise had increased. With little warning, a fight started at the next table where five men were playing cards.

"Don't ya be calling me a cheat!" yelled a man standing up so fast that his chair clattered over backwards. "I'm an honorable gambler!" he stormed, emphasizing his words by crashing his fist on the table. "Ya best take back those words, mister!"

A tall man was sitting across the table from the angry card player. Judging by his dress, Abraham figured him to be a mountain man. The fellow remained seated as he leaned back staring up at the gambler. "My pappy always said that ya can't draw a straight line with a crooked stick. And ya be just like that crooked stick, dealing from the bottom."

"Back up yar words or eat them," stormed the gambler.

The inn was now silent as Abraham felt the tension building in the tavern.

The mountain man stood slowly. "That'll be the day. When I'm done, ya'll be the one swallowing your teeth, ya cheating two-tailed-possum . . ."

The gambler dove across the table and both card players went down, sending table, chairs, and other men flying. Suddenly, everyone in the barroom began brawling and the Carolinians' table was in the middle.

Abraham found himself facing a bearded farmer who gave him a good wallop to the head. He ducked low and charged as they fell to the floor.

Standing again, he glimpsed Johnny Hill and Samuel Hanks standing back to back as each swung at men coming at them. To his surprise, he glimpsed Little Jen smiling and standing near the door watching the fight with his arms folded over his chest. *He was sure fast getting to the other side of the tavern,* thought Abraham, as he ducked under an awkward swing thrown by a big tipsy man.

Ending up on the floor again and rolling under the bar overhang, Abraham found himself sprawled beside Rufus.

The older man gave him a crooked grin and asked, "Having fun, are ye?"

Abraham noticed that they had an excellent ground-level view of the fight as Rufus cuddled the whiskey jug protectively, making sure that he kept a spittoon between him and any fighter. *How did he manage to save the jug from smashing on the floor?* Seeing the big grin and rosy cheeks on Rufus' face, he decided that the old gent was really enjoying this fight.

"Hit the bugger with your fists not your head, you heathen," shouted Rufus loudly. This was followed by, "Is minic a bhris beal duine a shron."

A man on the floor near them looked quizzically at Rufus. He shouted, "Eh? What did ya say?"

"Sure ye know," Rufus shouted back, "Ye being on the floor and all, that many a time a man's mouth broke his nose."

The melee continued and Abraham now found himself squared off with the gambler and managed to punch him in the eye. He stood with his fists raised as the cardsharp staggered back and pulled a knife from the inside top of his boot.

Suddenly, a gunshot loudly reverberated throughout the room. The fighting stopped in mid-action and everyone looked toward the door.

Little Jen stood holding a smoking pistol in one hand and a knife in the other. "That's enough, mister. Drop your knife and take yourself out of here."

"You go straight to hell," said the flush-faced gambler, swinging his arm up to throw his knife.

With a swift underhanded toss, Little Jen's blade flashed through the air, burying itself in the gambler's shoulder.

"Ahh!" cried out the man, crumbling to the floor, clutching his shoulder.

Little Jen moved quickly and stood over him, one foot on the man's knife. He retrieved his own with a couple of quick jerks, causing the gambler to cry out in pain.

"Ya rotten dirty . . ."

"Shut your mouth, friend." The wagon train boss's gaze was unwavering. "I told you to depart and I mean right now. My friends and I be traveling through and leave tomorrow. Between now and then, I don't want to glimpse your face, not even once. You got that, mister. Now, git."

Cursing loudly, the man slowly stood, blood staining his brocade vest. Clutching his shoulder, the gambler glared at Little Jen but backed away and went out the door.

Suddenly, Abraham heard the tavern come back to life as everyone was talking again and the din was back. Men brushed themselves off, straightened tables and chairs, and sat down.

Little Jen said to his group, "This inn be friendly, but I think we'd best be leaving."

Johnny went to collect Rufus from under the bar. The older man in the cutaway coat was singing an Irish ditty while having trouble getting to his feet.

Abraham chuckled as Rufus pulled his floppy yarn cap out of his pocket and put it on at a cock-eyed angle. Never once did the portly boat builder release his hold on the jug. Both he and Johnny staggered out the barroom door, loudly singing—

"Oh Danny boy,
The pipes, the pipes are calling
From glen to glen, and down the mountain side
The summer's gone, and . . ."

Chapter Nine

T he animals were worn thin by the journey, and the heat took its toll on Abraham as the days passed slowly into the seventh week. Dust billowed around the wagons and stuck to mouths, food, and clothes.

He worried that Mary was having doubts about the trip and he knew that the baby was wearing on her. He watched her slowly climb down from the high wagon seat with Frederick's help. Strands of dark, matted hair framed the sweat and trail smudges on her face; her once white bonnet was the color of dust.

Still making his journal entries, Abraham sat on his wagon seat and totaled up the seventy miles they had come in the past four days. Now camped on the banks of the White River on the outskirts of Richmond, they were just west of the Ohio-Indiana border and had finally arrived at the east-west running National Road. The train would begin ferrying across the river in the morning.

Abraham felt a sense of foreboding come over him as he gazed at the river, and oddly, Hooker's threat came to his mind. A chill went down his back. *It's probably just the heat and dust,* he thought, *and I'm tired.*

Little Jen reined in his horse and asked, "Know anything about the National Road, Abraham?"

The Carolinian shook his head.

Dismounting, Little Jen explained, "It be the first roadway in the Northwest Territory built and paid for by the Federal Government, and it be pretty good in all kinds of weather because it's graveled. About seventy years ago, a young lieutenant and his men began cutting the first trail. His name be George Washington."

"Really?"

"Yep. Now it crosses Ohio and continues west to Indianapolis. I hear that next year they're going to start building a bridge over this river. The politicians seem bent on taking the road clear across Indiana and Illinois to the Mississippi River."

Gesturing toward the water, Abraham said, "This is a pretty wide river. Do steamboats use it?"

"Not hardly," replied Little Jen. "I'm told that some folks once had dreams of sailing the river and one steamer even tried it. Heard it was stuck so bad on a sandbar that it was abandoned. Still, the town be an important trading center due to the new road."

The air was very humid that evening. Abraham had watched the dark clouds gathering in the western sky all afternoon. "Looks like a big storm headed our way."

"You got that right." As Little Jen led his horse away, he warned, "You'd better figure out how to keep dry."

"Aye," replied Abraham as the Rallemore family set up camp.

Abraham and his sons stretched a big tarp to create a sloping roof using the bonnet of a wagon on one side and staked upright posts on the other. To prevent sagging when the rains came, a tall limb was wedged between the ground and the uplifted tarp to create a peak. Beneath the covering, they'd try to keep a campfire lit.

He figured the younger children would mostly stay in one of the wagons. They were always clamoring for their nightly reading and he knew Mary would oblige them. *Maybe I'll get a chance to read more from my book on Greek mythology. Those folks sure believed in a parcel of legends.*

Another wagon train pulled in making camp along the river. *We got quite a backlog waiting for the ferry*, Abraham thought. *It's going to be miserable weather tonight, but this rain will break the heat.*

Showers came hard that evening and continued for the remainder of the week. By the time it let up, Abraham's wagons were wet and soggy, and the usually mild flowing Whitewater River was a flooded roaring torrent.

Because of high water, everyone in the trains waited another three days before the ferry began moving the backlog across the White. Finally, it was the Carolinians' turn.

Abraham's wagons were in line behind the Hanks. Samuel drove the lead and his two young daughters were laughing and waving to Abraham from the rear gate.

Smiling, Abraham waved back and shouted good-naturedly, "Don't you be falling into the water, you hear." He heard Abigail call out to her mules as her wagon began to move. Her son was on the seat beside her.

The loaded ferry moved into the current. Suddenly, Abraham saw people on the opposite riverbank acting up and pointing. Looking upriver, a giant tree was coming around the far bend and heading swiftly toward the ferry.

His throat went dry and his heart began to beat wildly. He glanced back at the Hanks and then again at the fast moving hulk. *Will the ferry be clear before the monster sweeps by,* he wondered, gripping his wagon reins tighter.

Standing by his mules, Frederick anxiously asked, "Pa, how are they going to maneuver around that big tree?"

Abraham briefly turned his way and saw the worried look on his face. Silently, he turned back to watch the developing scene, transfixed.

"Pa, tell me they're going to make it! They are, ain't they?" Frederick asked again, his voice rising in panic.

"By God, I hope so," Abraham exclaimed, unable to take his eyes off the life-and-death drama. The ferry operator looked upriver for the first time and the man's eyes seemed to grow larger.

Staring upriver again, Abraham studied the monstrosity. *The branches of that ancient white ash look as wide as a barn, floating behind that massive clump of dark scraggly roots.* Incredulously, he felt a stab of terror as pictures from his mythology book flashed through his mind. *My God in heaven, that tangle of roots looks just like the evil Medusa picture with her hair of snakes.*

Abraham quickly sifted through the options. *The ferry is right in the middle of the river with ropes strung between both banks. If they start back, the tree will snag the outbound line and probably take the ferry downriver. If they speed up, it'll catch the nearest rope and the result will be the same. GOOD GOD! There's no way for them to avoid that monster.* The realization shocked him, and empathically, Abraham pulled back hard on his clenched reins and fully extended his foot on the wagon brake, as though his actions could help the Hanks.

On the ferry, the boatman froze stock-still for just an instant, but it seemed an eternity to Abraham. Suddenly, the man picked up his long-handled ax and brought it down with a powerful stroke, severing the thick outward-bound line.

Alarmingly, the raft veered downriver in the current, still linked to the Richmond side. The slewing caused the raft to heave up terribly. Then, in an almost slow-motion death roll, he watched in horror as one wagon then the next went into the turbulent water. With its load suddenly lightened, the ferry righted and swung like an out-of-control pendulum, slamming into the high embankment on the Richmond side. Almost immediately, it began breaking up.

Anxiously, he looked for the Hanks' wagons that were bobbing in the current. For an instant, he saw Samuel and one of the girls holding onto the canvas bonnet ribs with the team still harnessed. Then the marauding monster tree ran them over, sweeping everything under and out of its way.

Abraham heard Mary cry out, "God have mercy on their . . ." but the sound of the roaring river whipped away the rest of her words. The swiftly moving events staggered him and it stunned the crowd into silence.

Shocked, he began to shiver as the horrifying event hit him while a succession of thoughts flashed through his mind. *It did happen, didn't it? Or was it my imagination? Yes, I saw it with my own eyes. In an instant, five souls have gone to their maker.*

A wave of sadness overcame him. *I had a cup of coffee with Samuel this morning. Last night, our families shared biscuits. Good Lord, I just waved to the little girls minutes ago.*

Suddenly, at the ferry wreckage, the operator waved an arm. In that instant, Abraham tied off his reins and jumped down as he and the crowd came to life. Quickly, parties sped down each side of the river searching for any trace of the missing family. The ferryman had managed to hang onto a log rail and ride the ferry into the embankment. Abraham's group reached him and the wreckage. The man was in a bad way with two broken legs.

Abraham left two men and continued downriver with the others. Desperately scanning the riverbank for any sign of life, he felt that he could find and save the Hanks family if he only ran faster. His party continued for nearly a mile, but they only found pieces of the wagons and dead horses, still in harness. Abraham looked up and saw what was left of one wagon beached on the far shore. The rescue party on the other side searched, but signaled that they found no one.

That evening, women sobbed over cooking pots and more than a few children clung to their mother's skirts. There was a hush in camp as though all were trying to make sense of the tragedy.

Everyone is sad about loosing the Hanks, Abraham surmised. *We're also frightened by the turn of events that reminds us how quickly life can end.*

Little Jen wandered into the circle of their camp firelight. "Everyone doing alright here?" he asked, sitting down on a log next to Abraham.

"Aye," replied Abraham. "No use trying to figure out the ways of God." He threw a stick into the fire. Both men stared into the flames as the fire licked the embers.

Little Jen finally broke the silence. "You can't explain nature when she deals the cards. Folks can plan for most things and think they have everything under control until all hell breaks loose. It's like my pa says—there be times when you've just got to be lucky."

They sat watching the flickering fire. Abraham finally asked, "What happens now, Little Jen?"

"Me and the others have been meeting at the ferry dock with the townsfolk. In the morning, we'll form work parties to rebuild the ferry. With the help of all the men sitting in these wagons, most figure crossings will begin again in about four days."

That surprised Abraham until he figured that there must be well over a hundred men with the wagon trains and perhaps another two dozen in town. Such a large group could get a lot of work done in a hurry.

Little Jen went on, "Some will fell the trees and teams will drag the logs to the river where they'll be sized, notched, and fitted."

"Well, you can count on me and my sons."

Little Jen nodded and stood. "Night to you all," he said, leaving the firelight ring.

By the end of the fourth day, the new ferry was floating at the riverbank and fresh lines had been snaked across the water. As for the river, the great rush had passed.

The next morning, Abraham's three wagons were the first to board the ferry. This one was larger and accommodated all of his wagons on the same trip.

Abraham, gloved-hands damp with sweat, held his breath as the barge began crossing. He nervously glanced upriver, half expecting to see the snake-like root ball bearing down on him.

He breathed a sigh of relief when the ferry touched the far riverbank and it almost seemed to him that the watching crowd did the same, as they clapped and cheered. The long line of wagons began to trickle over the river.

🐞 🐞

Nine days later, they were in Martinsville, Morgan County. Farewells echoed throughout the wagon train with promises to keep in touch as the Carolinian families went their own way to seek new lands and, perhaps, family or friends.

Abraham and Mary were anxious to see their kin, James and Elizabeth Burked, who farmed several miles outside town.

First, Abraham found the Jennings to say his goodbyes. "Been a pleasure meeting and working with you, Little Jen."

The wagon boss replied, "I wish you and your family well. Pa and me will be staying in town a few days and then we're looking forward to seeing more territory." Pausing for a moment, he gave Abraham a thoughtful look before saying, "I'm thinking that you have no cause to worry yourself about Hooker showing up around here to carry out his threat."

"I agree," replied Abraham, caught off guard by the comment.

"I reckon that snake be long gone and good-riddance."

Abraham nodded, shaking off the image of Hooker.

"Who knows," continued Little Jen. "Maybe we'll meet another time."

The Carolinian had taken quite a liking to both men and he was sorry to see them leave, yet he knew that they might always have trouble settling down, at least until Big Jen's bones couldn't take it any longer. "Thank you for all you've done, Little Jen. And, Big Jen, it has been a real pleasure to be with you again, sir. I hope your back gets the warmth and comfort it deserves."

"Abra'm, it has been fun seeing ya and riding along with ya folks. I'll never forget ya and the fun we had thet night in New Orloons. Li'l Jen and ah are gonna look at some mo'e country out west aways. And one of these days, ah's hankering ta see my daughter in Woosta, Ohio. Then, it'll be Tenasee time fer me and my rocking chair sitting next ta a warm pleasurable fire. My backside jest be itching ta git thar. Ya folks stay safe, and who knows, mebbe we'll see each other agin, maybe in tha land of tha Six Bulls. Ya kin never tell."

As he spoke, there was a smile on his lips and Abraham noticed a peculiar gleam in his eye.

Chapter Ten

R eunited for the first time in a decade, the Rallemores and their cousins had a joyous celebration. James and Elizabeth Burked had come to these parts in 1822 from North Carolina and eventually put together a farm of nearly two hundred acres.

"You know," Abraham began, as the families sat on the Burked's cabin porch, "your letters were always talking about how rich the soil be here in Morgan County. And Mary and I never could get over your bountiful harvests every year."

"Well, it be as true as rain," replied James, smiling.

"Your letter last year finally convinced us that this land be for us. And we like the fact that a man can work his farm with his family without the need for a slave system or lots of hired hands."

"That be right, again," said James. "We grow no tobacco or cotton here."

He has aged, thought Abraham, *but haven't we all? Still, he seems the picture of good health and is just as good-natured as I remember. I forgot how big a man he is with his sculpted broad shoulders from long days working the plow. I reckon he be about the same age as Mary.* "Tell us more about this land."

Smiling, James responded, "I'll be happy to do that, cousin. The town of Martinsville began the same year that we arrived in Indiana and it serves as the county seat. As you know, it sits on the White River, some thirty miles south of Indianapolis. It really be growing and already has more than fifty families living in town." He stopped to fill his pipe with tobacco. Lighting it, he blew a cloud of blue-gray smoke toward the sky.

"Abe and I were surprised to see that it was so large," Mary said. "As we came through, there was an impressive town square."

James nodded. "Early on, the town fathers started a summer tradition of holding horse races every Saturday afternoon on the square. We go a few times every summer, have a picnic lunch, and mingle with the folks in town."

"How long be the White River?" asked Abraham.

"From Indianapolis, the river cuts through the middle of Morgan County from northeast to southwest and ends hundreds of miles clear across the state at the Illinois River. Along the way, we got us some gigantic trees growing on the riverbanks here abouts." Grinning widely, James continued. "Why, some of them be so tall that it's near impossible to hit a turkey with a musket ball if'n it be roosting in the crown."

"That sounds like a really tall tale," laughed Mary.

Puffing on his corncob pipe, James continued. "And many of the trees be covered with thick layers of grape vines, which wind around and climb into the overhead canopy of branches. In some areas of the woods, it be so thick that you need a lantern to find your way in the daytime," he finished, chuckling.

Abraham smiled and asked, "What about the soil? It appears to be good and your fields of corn are bursting."

"Absolutely right," replied James. "We got a saying around here about our corn—'it grows knee-high by the Fourth of July.' This here land, when it be cleared, simply excels at growing wheat, corn, and a virtual cornucopia of vegetables."

"Pretty highfalutin words you got going there," laughed Abraham.

The big man knocked the ashes out of his pipe. "What you probably don't know is that hog rearing in these parts really be big. Me and other farmers let them forage in the thick forest, but we keep them close by feeding them a small daily ration of corn. We do lose some animals that go completely wild and they become mean dangerous critters—some with six-inch tusks. Around these parts, they be called 'land sharks.'"

"Where do you suggest we start searching for our new land, James?" asked Abraham.

"There still be some government land available in the west county. But you might want to look at the Widow Henry's property first. She be trying to sell her farm. The Henrys came down from upstate Indiana a few years after we arrived. This spring, her husband was plowing in the field when a sudden storm came over the land. He died when a tornado dropped down from the sky and destroyed the crop. She told me that she never did find his body."

Mary was startled. "Oh, sweet Jesus in heaven—I pity that poor woman and her younguns. James, we know wind when we got those awful hurricane storms off the Atlantic. The rain comes down by the bucket, as you know, and the gale blows it sideways. More than once, we've lost part of our crop to those evil storms that can last for days. Are tornadoes like our North Carolina storms?"

"Mary, tornadoes are similar, but our storms tend to be shorter in length and . . ." he paused, searching for the right words. "They be more sudden. You get hard rain, thunder, and lightning, and we even get hail. Every now and then, the whirling funnel clouds called tornadoes be dipping out of the sky. When they touch the ground, they move fast and destroy everything in their path."

Mary paled slightly. Abraham knew she could take rain and even lightning, but she plain didn't like wind. Moving the conversation back to the Widow Henry's property, he asked, "What is her land like and is the homestead fully built-up?"

"She has about a hundred-twenty acres in corn, some hardwood forest, and they built themselves an ample cabin," James replied. "You can take a look for yourself and make your own decision."

The two families rode over to the Henry property the next day and James made the introductions.

"I'm anxious to get me and my younguns up north where we got kin," said Mrs. Henry, eying one of Abraham's loaded wagons. "If you can make this homestead work for you, I'll make you a good price. I hate tornadoes. They be winds straight out of Hades."

Mary stared at the woman.

"Let's walk the property," Abraham suggested. "Then we'll come back and visit with you, ma'am."

Walking outside, Abraham noticed the drying strings of apple rings hanging from the rafters of the porch and smelled the heady aroma wafting from the braids of drying onions.

At the edge of the cornfield, Mary pulled him aside from their children. "Abe, you know I don't like wind and the talk about these whirlwinds frightens me."

"I know, dear, but let's keep our heads about this. James says that they ain't had but two in this area since he and Elizabeth came here." Her look told him that was far too many.

They liked the farm and went back to talk to Mrs. Henry.

"What be your thinking?" the widow asked. "Can you make this farm work for you?"

"Well," started Abraham, "we had in mind more acreage and . . ."

"Hear me, mister. I've got to git me and my younguns moved closer to our kin. If'n you have the interest, I'll trade you the farm and livestock for that wagon and two of your mules . . ."

Her offer surprised Abraham. He knew that the government sold virgin land for a dollar and two bits an acre. Such land required hard work to remove all the trees, brush, and larger stones before leveling. Next came the first plowing to bust the hard new ground filled with roots and small rocks.

". . . and ten dollars," the widow added.

Abraham could see that the woman was sincere. "That's more than fair," he said. "Sure you want to be selling this place for that?"

"Yep. I got to git," she said as tears formed in her eyes. "Me and my husband loved this land, but those evil winds got the better of him."

"Then it's a deal."

&. &.

The next day, Abraham and his sons helped the woman pack the wagon. He and Mary stood outside their new cabin in the early morning light and saw the Widow crying as she climbed up to the wagon seat. Then, she waved farewell and slapped the reins on the backs of the mules.

Abraham couldn't help but feel sad. The Henrys had put so much of themselves into making this farm a home. Looking at Mary, he saw tears flowing down her face. "There, there, Mary dear. The Widow Henry will be alright."

"I'm real sad for her, but I also find myself being sad for our family . . . and maybe for myself," she sobbed. "There be something about this land that just don't fit in my craw."

Chapter Eleven

1832

It was August and the hot sun beat down on Abraham. There was an undercurrent of dread as he rode his horse into town. Townsfolk had built a barricade on the main street just east of the river using overturned wagons, barrels, and wooden crates. He was on his way to the best place in the county to get news—the general store.

Entering, there were eight or ten men talking and sitting around a cracker barrel. Some appeared to be anxious farmers just like him. In the air, heavy tobacco smoke hung like a tempest cloud before a storm.

As Abraham sat on a box, he noticed the bins behind the counter—usually stocked with gunpowder horns and lead musket balls—were empty.

The quick-paced non-stop discussion seemed to jump like a spark from one man to the next as one "fact" followed another. Two details, agreed by all, were that Chief Black Hawk and the Saux and Fox Indians had jumped their reservations in Iowa and had returned to Illinois to retake their old hunting grounds.

"A fella told me that ol' Black Hawk had hundreds of warriors following him when the Injuns crossed the Mississippi River," reported a man smoking a pipe. "Be that right?"

"Newspaper up in Peoria says it were at least a thousand," replied a younger fellow, using his knife to cut an apple. "And I hear tell that the chief be a living legend."

Another asked, "All ya old-timers remember Chief Black Hawk, don't ya? He be the one siding with the English back in the War of 1812. He became a legend alright—a legend of death."

"Yep, that be him, the legend of death," repeated a man with shaggy black beard.

"A friend in the saloon told me last night that the Injuns have already tangled with our militia and that they've already hightailed it back across the river," said a player bending over a checkerboard resting on a barrel.

The other player gave him a curious look. "Tarnation, you've got that backwards. Your drinking pardn'r was either too stupid to know better or too liquored up to care."

Laughing, the first player nodded. "Yar move, pardn'r."

"Heard tell that there've already been many massacres," said a well-dressed man with a handsome wax-tipped handlebar mustache standing next to the checker players.

Sitting with his chair tilted back, an older man commented, "Aye, I be hearing the same."

A man filling his pipe spoke up. "The newspaper be saying that they've killed over a hundred folks, mostly farmers and their families."

Abraham clinched his fists. *Mostly farmers and their families*, he silently repeated to himself, turning over the chilling words in his mind. *What kind of land did we come to where Injuns be killing folks, mostly like us Rallemores?*

Rolling a cigarette, another announced, "A county official told me yesterday that negotiations between the Injuns and the government have failed."

The handlebar-mustached man added, "I heard the same and spoke to a traveling drummer passing through who told me that Black Hawk's warriors have already met up with other tribes from Michigan and Wisconsin territories."

"By now, I reckon his original thousand warriors must have at least doubled," added the man eating the apple.

Still another brought his tilted chair down hard, managing to screech all four legs loudly over the pinewood floor. "You got to figure that it just be a matter of time before the Injuns be coming east."

"That be for sure and probably right our way," said a man dressed like a farmer.

The storekeeper had been listening to the back and forth comments and now came over to the group. "You know, we'll sorely miss them three dozen men who left town to join the militia up north. When the Injun attack comes, we're going to need them." He stood there looking frustrated, his apron smudged from stocking shelves.

Abraham listened, but his mind was whirling as he tried to separate reality from rumor.

Finally, a bent-over and white-haired fellow sitting next to him leaned closer and quietly said, "Keep your head about you, young man. The plain truth behind all the hot air around this cracker barrel is that no one really knows any details for sure, so rumors are spreading like wildfire in this here town. One man be telling another—and don't you know—before long the same story comes back to the first, except it be even more alarming."

I can see how that be happening, thought Abraham as he glanced at the men sitting around the cracker barrel arguing over still another "fact."

"Yep, it's just like my pappy always said," the old man went on. "'When people get scared, the dangers they know pale before their fanciful dangers of the unknown.' Heck, I've even seen people load up their wagons and head east for God knows where. Maybe clear back to the Atlantic Ocean," he finished, smacking his toothless gums and nervously laughing.

As he rode back to his farm, the Carolinian felt uneasy. He had never even heard of Chief Black Hawk until yesterday when a passing farmer had told him the latest news. He'd felt a shiver of apprehension go down his back. Being from the Carolinas, he knew about Indians and the family stories, etched in his memory, about the battles and skirmishes fought with the Cherokees. More than one family member had been lost and Indians had abducted his niece.

Upon telling Mary the news, she had voiced her own concerns. "Abe, I'm scared for the younguns. Please ride to town tomorrow so you can get more news."

Well, he thought as his horse plodded homeward, *I've ridden to town and I definitely have more rumors, but which are correct? Think I'll stop to see old Benjamin Vorshell on my way home and get his views.*

His neighbor was digging in a field when Abraham rode up. Benjamin and his wife had come to this area seven years earlier from Pennsylvania and were originally from the old country.

"How do, Benjamin."

"Ja, and a good day to thee," the farmer said with a heavy accent.

"I've been to town and heard all the stories about Injuns and war parties. What do you think? Have such Injun concerns been happening regularly here abouts?"

Benjamin pushed back his straw hat and leaned on his tall shovel. "Been a mighty long time since we be having any Injun troubles. But jumping reservation and murdering settlers be alarming and I be angry with our government. Here it be 1832 and they still be having trouble protecting settlers and us farmers. But come, get off your horse, Abraham, and take a sip of water with me in the springhouse. We talk more."

Stepping into the small cool stone building constructed over a stream, Benjamin cupped water from a bucket, handing it to Abraham. "Tell you the truth, this news has me and the wife all stirred up. My boys and me want to take down our guns and join the militia, but we've got to be thinking about the womenfolk and the farm."

The old farmer's views added to Abraham's uneasiness. Sitting on a bench, both men remained silent for long moments until Abraham spoke. "One thing we brought with us from North Carolina be our signal bell," referring to his cast-iron bell mounted on an outdoor post. "You know, with a favorable wind, I can hear it a good long ways from home. I know you got one. Let's agree to signal each other if'n we think there is danger. Then we can join forces to meet the threat.

"Ja."

"Maybe we should get some of our neighbors thinking along the same lines?"

"Ja, good idea."

"You've got the most stoutly built barn in the county with its limestone foundation. We could use it as the meeting place."

"Ja by golly, them all be good notions. I'll go see the Youngs. Maybe you can talk to your kin, James. Then, with our signaling, we could all get enough warning to protect the lives of our people. But you know some farms will be left with no protection."

"True enough." Abraham noticed the concern on the older man's face. "Think of it this way—you can rebuild a barn and replant a field, but you can't replace your family. And I've yet to meet anyone who can put his scalp back on."

Looking at the Carolinian, the old farmer nodded. "Ja, I see what you mean."

"I'll go see James now. Let's gather the men tomorrow at my cabin after supper and we'll work through a plan."

&. &.

The next day, the men from all four families met. Each reported his news. However, it was the information from James that riveted them.

"Folks be concerned about the Injuns jumping their reservation and men in surrounding states be signing up for militia duties. I was in town today. Militia supply wagons were passing through from Ohio. A Captain Vogel led the escort troop. Well, the whole town wanted to talk to him and he had quite a group listening to him as he sat a spell in the general store.

"He had seen reports of Black Hawk's eastern route. He didn't know of any major battles yet with the militia, but he was confident they'd eventually find and defeat the hostiles. Captain Vogel figures Black Hawk be trying to join up with other tribes like White Cloud's Winnebago Injuns." James paused, looking at his neighbors. "And, he told us it was likely that Black Hawk was moving toward St. Joseph County, perhaps in the South Bend area."

Abraham knew that this area was about one hundred-seventy miles north of them.

"Anyway," continued James, "this wagon train turned northward expecting to intercept the Ohio expedition force coming through Lafayette up in Tippecanoe County."

Abraham couldn't hide his shock. *That area is only a two-day ride from here. If'n the Indians are already there . . .*

Mary cried out, "Oh my God, are they that close?" Others displayed similar feelings. A hush descended over the adults and, for several moments, the silence hung heavy.

"Ma," cried out four-year old Solomon in a frightened voice, "them Injuns coming to get us?"

Abraham's youngest children were looking around at the adults for assurances. He figured that they felt the tension in the room as Mary soothed the boy. Abraham looked at Benjamin and the older man was shaking his head.

"This be a big step backwards for the whole state," the old farmer remarked. "Who'll want to settle around here when Injun massacres be happening? Men, we best be thinking about our defenses."

Everyone agreed to use Benjamin's barn as the meeting place.

"Perhaps we could bring some of our cattle and horses over to your pasture, Benjamin?" asked James. "They'd be more protected than being left on our deserted farms."

"Ja, you do that."

"We can use our signal bells to warn of danger," added Abraham. "Let's agree that three clangs mean trouble is coming and it's time for everyone to move to Benjamin's barn. Two bell strikes will be a call for a meeting that day just after supper." Again, there were nods.

The group broke up and each went their own way. As he watched them leave, the Carolinian figured all were working out the routes they'd take to Benjamin's barn if the need arose.

More than a week went by with no additional news. Abraham didn't know whether to feel better or worse. His mind conjured up all manner of circumstances—mostly bad—just as the old man in town had predicted.

On the twelfth night, the Rallemore family went to bed as usual. After midnight, Abraham quickly jumped out of bed, as one bell could be heard ringing three times and then others. He and Mary roused their sleeping children.

"Frederick, be sure you take our two extra muskets and get the extra powder and balls—and go ring our signal bell. Noah, you and the other boys saddle the horses and hitch up the wagon for ma and the younguns—and take them lamps we set out to light our way."

In minutes, they were ready.

Abraham led the way holding one of the lanterns while Frederick drove the wagon. "Aha!" his son called out, slapping the reins on the backs of the mules.

As they drove up under a half-moon, Benjamin said, "Hurry. A rider passed through earlier tonight and reported that he be seeing Injuns crossing the creek."

The women and children hustled inside. All the men took defensive positions behind the barn's thick limestone walls. Frederick and Abraham went up to the hayloft to stand watch.

Everyone waited as several hours went by with little stirring except the rustling of leaves in the trees.

Noah was tense at the thought of a possible attack. He was also aware of Letha Vorshell's presence as she sat at the edge of the haystack in the barn. She was Benjamin's second oldest daughter and he thought she was just about the prettiest girl he had ever seen with her brown hair, large brown eyes, and a smile that seemed to light up everything.

There were no lanterns in the barn except one kept behind the walls of a horse stall that provided enough light to reload the muskets. Within this dim light, the eyes of Noah and Letha occasionally met and Noah felt a spark of mutual excitement pass between them as he turned away sporting a teenage blush even though it was too dark for anyone to see him.

Probably recognizing that Noah couldn't overcome his shyness, Letha got up, brushed the straw off her nightgown, and pulled the shawl closer around her shoulders. She walked toward Noah and whispered, "Have you seen anything?"

Noah shook his head as he looked up at her. He could barely see her small smile and he caught the faint scent of the jasmine sprig pinned to her shawl. He stood and, impulsively, took her hand in his. Letha glanced around to see if anyone was watching, but no one was paying them any mind. Noah drew her around to the other side of the haystack.

He saw her dimpled cheeks in the dim light as she looked at him curiously, her long hair falling to her shoulders. "I've wanted to talk to you for a long time. Now isn't such a good time, still . . .," whispered Noah, nervously.

"What about?"

"I've wanted to tell you how much—" He paused, searching for the right words, "—how much I admire you," he finally blurted out.

"That be right?" Letha said shyly, staring at Noah in the dark. "And why be that?"

"Well . . .," Noah paused again, stalling, not knowing how far his speech would take him. *You don't always get to pick the proper time and place for talking,* he thought to himself. "Because I think you're mighty pretty," he finally managed to stammer.

"Oh, Noah, how you talk."

Noah wondered if she was blushing. He knew he felt flushed.

"You behave yourself," she admonished with a smile, and gave his hand a quick squeeze. "You're guarding everything we own and all that be in this barn. You just keep watch for them Injuns." She turned away and sat against the barn wall.

Noah was unsure about this sweet girl's reaction to his bold talk right in the middle of an Indian crisis. Nevertheless, he felt a warm inner glow and a wave of elation. *She squeezed my hand,* he marveled.

Now the moon was lower in the night sky. Still, they waited with nothing to disturb the arriving morning except the occasional sonorous call of a bullfrog seeking a mate or the pawing at the dirt by one of the animals.

Up in the loft, Abraham went over and gently nudged Frederick, who had fallen asleep against a haystack. "Son, if'n their fixing to attack, dawn be a likely time. Best you be alert."

"Ahh, sure pa. Sorry, my eyes just went and closed themselves for a few minutes."

False dawn silhouetted the hills while leaving everything else in black shadows. Once more, Abraham checked his own musket until movement on the horizon caught his eye. He froze, staring. "Frederick, what do you make of that?"

Peering at the dimly lit horizon, his son said, "It looks like smoke."

"Yes, that be what I figure . . . and now look . . . see the flames?" Turning quickly, he called down from the edge of the loft, "I see fire and smoke on the horizon, maybe a mile away across Honey Creek."

"Whose place?" someone shouted back.

Abraham shrugged. He could see some of their faces peering up at him from below. Most were pale and anxious. "I can't tell," he answered, moving back to stand beside his son.

It seemed an eternity as the families waited. Abraham gave updated reports from his vantage point, but nothing new had occurred in the last few minutes.

Time dragged on slowly. Feeling edgy, he paced in front of the open loft door, staring toward the creek for any sign of danger. Suddenly, he turned and shouted to the group below, "I hear horses crossing the creek and they be coming at high speed."

Tight with anticipation, he strained to see the approaching riders. Every second, the rhythmic thud of hoof beats in the lane grew louder and then stopped as horses, breathing hard, came to a halt near Benjamin's farm-house.

Suddenly, a nanny goat dashed out of the darkness and, with nary a de-lay, James shot it dead. At the sound, several other guns went off, as shadows became targets.

Abraham, still standing in the loft, saw no one as he anxiously scanned the darkened trees and bushes.

"Hello, Benjamin," someone shouted. "Don't shoot. It be Richard and Gail Sparlin from the farm up the river. For God's sake, can you hear me? We've come for help as the Injuns be right behind us and they've burned our barn."

"Everyone, lower your guns right now!" commanded Benjamin. Then, he shouted toward his cabin, "Come along quickly. We'll not be shooting you."

The two ran toward the barn, reins in hand, with their horses trotting behind.

They made it through the large barn door just as Abraham heard other horses coming down the lane fast. "Here come more riders!" he shouted.

"Stay here, Gail," said Benjamin as the sounds became louder. "Richard, find cover over there behind the wall."

Around the corner of Benjamin's house came three Indians, riding fast, and keeping low.

"NOW!" shouted Benjamin and nine guns fired together. The Indians fell, two as their horses were hit.

Abraham watched in amazement as most of the men and boys in the low-er level instinctively ran out of the barn, yelling loudly at the top of their voices, and brandishing spent muskets and hayforks.

The Indians were quick to regain their footing and took flight around a shed. They continued toward a pasture and into the trees beyond.

The charging "farmer regiment" followed them to mid-field where Abra-ham, running to catch up, commanded, "Hold here. No sense risking an ambush in them trees."

With that, everyone ducked down in the pasture and reloaded their muskets. The sun was just cresting above the trees, blinding them as they tried to scan the deep forest shadows.

Again, the splashing sound of horses fording the creek could be heard and Abraham panicked, figuring that there were Indians in the woods and others coming from behind. "Back to the barn and hurry!" he commanded. Soon after, the farmers again had their guns aimed from behind the barn's stout limestone walls.

Long before anyone could see the new riders, they heard calls announcing a large group of armed men from town. The leader, a man named Saunders, rode up and said, "We saw the smoke on the horizon and set out at dawn. What be happening?"

Benjamin told about the attack on the Sparlins' and pointed to the woods. The townsmen rode across the pasture and into the woods, guns held at the ready.

Abraham returned to talk with the Sparlins.

Richard said, "An Injun raiding party torched our barn before we even knew they were near and then started toward our cabin. That's when we opened fire."

"Then what happened?" asked Abraham.

"The Injuns ducked for cover and we snuck out a back window and rode off." Somewhat sheepishly, Richard continued. "We've been so nervous, what with all the stories and rumors about a possible Injun attack, that we've been keeping the horses saddled and tied to a back rail every night."

Just then, Saunders rode up with his men. "Your Injuns have run off, but let me tell you, there were big happenings last week. An army scout rode through last night and told us Black Hawk's warriors were chased into territory west of Lake Michigan. There be several battles and the Injuns have been defeated at Bad Axe River with most of them killed or captured. The danger of Injun attack be over. A few that got away must have come across you folks."

"Praise the Lord," said Mary. "He has answered my prayers for good news!"

The night had been long, but Abraham felt a heavy burden lift off his shoulders. Smiling, he watched his neighbors laughing as old Benjamin tossed his straw hat high into the air. James let out a "Hurrah" and Mary smiled at her husband as she hugged their young children.

Some distance away, Noah suddenly shouted, "Pa, come quick. Hurry!" There was no mistaking the insistence in his voice.

Abraham and others ran over to the bushes where he stood. On the ground lay a lifeless body. Abraham motioned Noah back and then turned the Indian over with the end of his musket.

It was a young boy, perhaps ten or eleven years old, with his face painted and his black hair pulled back and tied off. He wore buckskin pants, a government-issued plaid shirt, and had a sheathed knife on his belt.

"Oh my God," exclaimed Abraham. "He be just a youngun—no older than one of my boys—caught up in a man's world filled with hate—and we killed him—" He staggered back a step or two and leaned on the end of his musket.

"God help us," muttered James.

A tear slid down Abraham's face as he wrestled with the reality of the dead boy on the ground and the heart-stopping fear he had known only moments earlier.

A few riders from town rode over and stared down at the boy.

Abraham looked around, seeking answers, but he only saw the anguish on the faces of James and Benjamin. Noah turned away with tears in his eyes.

Saunders got down from his horse, saying to the farmers, "We'll take him back to town. The folks will want to see what they've feared." He kneeled and grabbed the boy by the hair, drawing his knife. Smiling crookedly, he continued, "We'll probably hang his scalp in the mercantile store window."

Without warning, Abraham's musket butt caught Saunders in the chest so hard that the townsman went over backwards, his knife flying. "You'd do such butchery on a youngun?" snapped the angry farmer, as Hooker's face came flooding back to him. "There be so much hate twisting in your guts that scalping a boy be passable to you? Well, it ain't passable to me—not on this here morning—and not at this here place—"

With grief and rage spilling over, he continued, huskily, "And I suppose next you'll be taking the scalp of that dead nanny goat over yonder. After all, she be the only thing that attacked us."

Saunders finally had enough wind to ask, "What're you saying?" Probably trying to poke fun at Abraham and cover his own embarrassment, he let out a derisive laugh. "What be ya, an Injun lover? Maybe you're a defender of savages?" Getting to his feet, he continued. "Pick him up, boys. We'll be dragging this one back to town."

There was no mistaking Abraham. The barrel of his musket slowly came up until it was level with Saunders' belly. Then Benjamin leveled his musket, then James.

Stopped, Saunders mouth was agape. "Well, I'll be damned . . ." and his words trailed off.

Abraham, never taking his eyes from him, said, "We'll take care of the youngun. You fellas best be getting back to town to ease the burden of those waiting and worrying for your news."

There was an awkward pause and then one townsman after another turned his horse away and started back.

Saunders spat in disgust and left.

🐾 🐾

Before the families departed for home, the young Indian boy was laid to rest. The rising sun was shining on the newly dug grave as Abraham said a prayer. Benjamin, standing next to the signal bell, rang it slowly—three times.

Chapter Twelve

O ver the next three years, Abraham and Mary added to their farm with the purchase of sixty-five adjoining acres from a neighbor and a land patent on another eighty virgin acres. Everyone worked to turn the new lands into productive parts of the farm. By 1835, their expanded cabin and fields were a complete farming operation and, sure enough, the tilled Indiana farmland was wonderful for growing crops.

One day, Abraham and Mary stood outside talking as Mary fed the chickens.

"This be good land, Mary."

She turned and looked at him. "Yes, it be . . . for growing crops."

"It be good for raising the family, too," he said. "After all, we'll have one more addition coming soon," referring to Mary's pregnancy and her due date early the next spring. "And there be no slaves."

"It's them winds, Abe. I keep thinking about that poor Widow Henry and her husband. I can't get those winds out of my mind, especially around this time of year."

"So, you're yearning to move again?"

"Oh, I'll be alright," she answered softly.

"I know it has been years since we seen the Jennings, but I still think about Six Bulls country. When I'm alone, my mind drifts back to the stories Big Jen told."

"Abraham, I'm carrying our seventh youngun, and you're again dreaming about another long trip?"

"Yes, I am. Strange isn't it? I still have this hankering to see more of this big country before you and me are permanently settled into our rocking chairs."

Abraham and Benjamin had become good friends. The older farmer was always talking about expanding his farm that sat in a valley below the Rallemore property. This was difficult for him to do, as one side of his land bordered Honey Creek and the other abutted Abraham's place.

When in the mood, usually after a couple of pulls on the white-lightning jug, he intimated his interest in Abraham's land. "Ja," he would say with his heavy accent, "You be good neighbors. Don't be thinking of leaving. But if'n you do, you speak to me first about the farm."

Abraham discussed his thoughts and Benjamin's words with his oldest sons. Frederick was enthusiastic about the thought of another adventure, but Noah seemed reluctant to consider leaving.

He also talked with Mary, who had mixed feelings.

"You know, we be settled now and have the farm in good shape," she reasoned. "We have family and friends here. Town be close for the things we need and we can socialize and watch the horse races on summer afternoons in the town square." Then, she trembled.

Abraham could tell that she was recalling the winds called tornadoes, and the thought was sending shivers down her back.

Their back and forth discussion went on as the hot steamy summer dragged into late July. Their crops were doing nicely and their youngsters were doing well.

Everything changed on Tuesday, the eleventh day of August.

It started out like most with the bright morning sun coming up over the fields, indicating another hot day. The humidity seemed heavier than usual, and virtually any activity brought sheens of sweat. By late afternoon, the sky had darkened with big black thunderclouds quickly rolling in from the southwest. The deep rumbling sound of thunder rolled across the heavens and, in the distance, flashes of lightning lit the dark clouds.

Abraham and Frederick were working in the fields and they stopped to watch the sky and the unbelievable show God was putting on for them and everyone else in Morgan County.

"This one's going to be a gully-washer," said Frederick, as the wind picked up strength and blew off his hat.

"Aye," replied Abraham, as he recalled the Widow Henry and her husband. "Let's be getting back to the barn. No sense standing tall in this field with all that lightning coming our way."

They unhitched the mules and made for the barn as heavy rain started to come down, soaking them. The wind was blowing harder now.

Mary was waiting by the door with quilts as they came in. "I'm glad the two of you had enough sense to come in out of the nasty weather," she lightheartedly said.

She's poking fun at us to keep her spirits up, Abraham guessed, looking closely at her. She had already closed the shutters on the cabin's two windows and had lit the oil lamps.

Abraham listened as the force of the wind intensified, now squirreling around outside. Gusts came down the chimney, agitating the ashes in the fireplace. Seated and holding the youngest against her breast, Mary gathered the younger children close to her.

Noah was standing at the window looking at the darkening sky through a crack in the shutter. "Pa, come see this."

Lightning illuminated the black clouds of the advancing storm with several flashes every second or two. A bright bolt jaggedly arched from the sky down to the ground.

Abraham began to silently and slowly count, "One, two, three, four . . ." and the cabin shook as a ferocious thunderclap boomed and echoed about them. "It still be a ways off. Maybe the wind will take it north of us."

Instead, the storm continued straight toward them.

Abraham looked at his wife. Her face was ashen as her fingers wound into and around the corner of her shawl. "Mary, would you feel more at ease if we went out to the root cellar?"

Mary didn't reply. She simply stared at him, pleading with her eyes.

Abraham figured that nothing would comfort her until the winds stopped. "Right—Frederick, you get the tarp from the loft. We'll use it to shed the rain."

The family ran to the cellar some ninety feet away. Unusually, the hole in the hill had double doors at the entrance. The two older boys managed to open one despite the wind and all hurried into the darkened shelter. From the stash of flint, wool, and kindling stored in the cellar, Frederick lit an oil lamp. Dropping the crossbar, Noah sealed the doors from the inside.

The battering sound of the wind-driven rain changed. At first, it came as light tapping. Soon, it increased to a crescendo as hail bombarded the hefty doors.

Looking through chinks and knotholes, Abraham exclaimed, "The ground be covered with balls of hail." Focusing more closely, he continued, "Heavens, they're not balls—they be gnarly pieces of ice!"

Mary came and stood beside him in her hooded cloak and looked through another opening. "It can't hail in the summer, can it Abe?"

"It sure seems that way." He looked up at the sky and suddenly his throat tightened and his heart began pounding. There, a small dark cloud shaped like an upside-down pyramid was beginning to form. At first, the pointy shape dipped toward the ground and then retreated. It repeated this several times over long seconds and each time the pointed funnel dipped lower.

Then, it was down. In a furious scene, trees, grass, bushes, crops, and fences disintegrated in its path. At its current course, it was coming directly toward them.

Abraham felt Mary trembling beside him and he drew her close as his other hand tightly gripped the crossbar.

"God have mercy on our souls," Mary exclaimed.

Then for no reason that can be understood, the funnel rose and retreated toward the main body of clouds like a truant child caught playing in a neighbor's haystack. It didn't disappear right away but hung below an immense black cloud before being absorbed. In the stormy gloom, Abraham looked at the tornado's path and was amazed to see the damage.

Suddenly, Mary's grip on his arm became vice-like as she looked down the valley. A new and larger funnel descended amid a deafening roar, headed straight for the Vorshell's barn. Moving at an incredible speed, it struck, engulfed, and disintegrated the barn. Rather than dropping the mangled pieces, the scraps of the former barn took on new life, suctioned up into the whirlwind cloud. Unstoppable, the funnel continued around the next hill and was lost from sight.

"Oh, Abe, pray that the Vorshells are safe and well shielded in their root cellar."

"Yes, we can only hope."

Noah was nearly sick with fear for the Vorshells and Letha. *Have they survived? Is Letha's hurt?* These questions kept racing around in his head as his mouth went dry and his pulse beat rapidly.

Despite a continuing drizzle, Abraham and his sons saddled their horses and rode to Benjamin's farm. The wind was still blowing hard and lightning illuminated the sky off in the distance as the main body of the storm had moved away quickly.

Despite his anxiety and the knot in his stomach, Noah couldn't help but marvel at the quick pace of the lightning-lit sky with multiple strikes every second. No Fourth of July fireworks could match what he saw as the distant billowing black storm clouds were continuously silhouetted in the sky.

As the three Carolinians neared the site of the Vorshell barn, Noah's breathing came faster, dreading what they'd find. There was little remaining to indicate where their former refuge against Indian attack had once stood. Even most of the thick limestone walls were down. The three rode past and headed for the cellar.

"Hello, Benjamin," called out his father. "Benjamin, are you and the family in the root cellar?" Hearing no response other than the wind, he called again, "Benjamin, it be Abraham. I'm here with my sons. Are you all right? Do you need help?"

Slowly the stout wooden door opened. Benjamin carefully peered out and then a smile lit his face as he opened the door. "Ja by Jove and by all the saints, I thought at first you might be the grim reaper calling us. Ja, we be shaken but not hurt, thank the Holy Mother," he said, making the sign of the cross.

Noah's eyes searched anxiously beyond the open door into the darkened cellar until he found Letha returning his gaze. He smiled and felt a warm wave of relief. He saw that her hair was wet and he couldn't help but notice how the rain-soaked clothing hugged her body, showing womanly curves. She managed a thin smile at him and he grinned wider.

They had seen each other a number of times since that night in Benjamin's barn, but they never had a chance to exchange private words. He often thought about her and simply hoped that she remembered him, too, and that night when she had squeezed his hand.

It was after this that Mary was steadfastly in favor of leaving Indiana once the baby arrived. She was shaken and clearly distrustful of this part of the country. Forcefully, she let Abraham know her feelings the next day when they were alone in the barn.

"Abe, you told me that the seven hundred miles we traveled on our last trip from the Carolinas would help keep us young. I have to tell you that whirlwind last evening took ten years off my life. I'll never be able to feel safe again in this country. I know we have family here and we dearly love being with them, but it's this place, these winds, that I can't take. I'm pleading with you—let's make our lives somewhere else. I can't live with the thought that I, too, could end up like the Widow Henry."

"Mary, you know I be ready to make a move, and we've talked all summer about Six Bulls country. All the same, let's keep our wits about us as every-place has something poor about it. Back home, we had those hurricanes that lasted days. Other folks on our trip contended with many things like sickness, the flooded river, and our train losing the Hanks family. Maybe we just have to take some things in stride, wherever we are."

Mary had been standing with her back to him. Turning, she stiffened and stared at him, tears glistening in her eyes. "If you're staying here, Abraham Michael Rallemore, you're staying by yourself," she sobbed. Slowly, she sank to her knees, covering her weeping face with her apron.

"Hold on, old girl, times will get better," said Abraham soothingly, raising her to her feet. "Things do work out. You know, I've never been able to get Six Bulls out of my head. I best be getting on with it and talking to old Ben about selling our land. Then, we best be getting on down Missouri way. James has similar thoughts. He says he'd up and move in an instant if someone could verify the farming qualities of the land in Six Bulls. My guess is he also had a long talk with Big Jen before the old man departed."

Mary looked up at him and smiled. "Thank you, Abe." She laid her head against his shoulder, her tears still flowing.

The strength of Mary's convictions surprised Abraham. He tried his best to comfort her, but he knew they'd have to leave. In the barn the next day, Abraham again broached the idea of Six Bulls country with Frederick and Noah.

Noah asked, "Ahh, pa, what does Six Bulls have that we don't have right here? We've good land and good water. And the soil be fertile year after year, not like our land back in Rowan County."

"The winds have made your ma distrustful of these lands. Besides, Missouri has fewer people and the land is cheaper. I'm told that the soil is good with first-rate water, and the game be abundant," recited Abraham from the tales he knew by heart. "And one more thing, son, I still have this hankering to see more of our country. I don't know if you can understand what I'm saying, but I feel right strong about it."

Noah rolled his eyes and gazed up at the barn's beams.

Abraham knew that Noah wanted to stay right here and some day farm his own land. *Maybe,* Abraham thought, *Noah's thoughts of staying include Letha Vorshell.*

Frederick had been listening. "Pa, perhaps we could sell the additional land we bought last year to Mr. Vorshell. He wants more farmland and we got it pretty well cleared. We could keep the rest for now."

Following his brother's train of thought, Noah added, "That way, we'd be going to Six Bulls and if'n it wasn't what we expected, we'd come back. And maybe Mr. Vorshell would accept the deal if he had the possibility of buying the rest of the farm someday."

Abraham looked at his two boys. Both suggestions were good and he again was amazed at how fast his sons had grown up. "You know, that sounds like a workable plan you boys just spit out." Impressed with their ideas, he reckoned both boys would be making their mark in this world, and soon. *Boys?* . . . he mused. *You are fooling yourself old man. Frederick already be twenty and Noah be nearing sixteen.* Looking from one to the other, he continued, "You make sense, but your mother can't travel with the baby coming and all."

Frederick suggested, "Why don't me and Noah go on ahead and scout the area? Then we can come back and tell you and ma what we found."

"You two can handle yourselves well, but your mother would be frightfully worried."

"What if Tommy Burked came along with us?" asked Frederick, "He be nineteen, and he knows farming as well as we do. Why not talk to Mr. Burked and see if his interest in Six Bulls be strong enough to let Tommy come along? Our cousin could help provide the information his pa has talked about."

"Boys, your minds are working at high speed now. That's another good suggestion. I'll talk it over with your mother and, if she agrees, I'll talk to James tomorrow."

That evening after dinner, Abraham took Mary outdoors and, as they walked, he voiced the boys' suggestions to her. Mary was in her fourth month and already feeling heavy. The weather had again turned hot and the humidity was high. Abraham knew that she was very uncomfortable.

Walking stiffly with one hand on her waist, she said, "Abe, I'm just not fit for travel at this time. You know I would follow you anywhere, but this isn't the time for me to be thinking about leaving here, even though I distrust this land. My keenness for such a long trip will come after the baby arrives."

"Well, that's just the point," replied Abraham. "We should see to the birthing here where you have Elizabeth's help, but we could let the boys inspect the land now. If their reports be favorable, we can follow when you're feeling more like yourself."

"You mean send Noah and Frederick ahead to the wild frontier?"

"That's exactly what I mean, but with Tommy Burked along, too. James wants someone to view the farming qualities of Six Bulls land. Our Frederick and Noah have good heads on their shoulders and they know good land and water when they see it. Tommy has been working his father's farm since he was a youngun. Between the three, they have sound farming judgment. Heck, they could even mark the new land if'n it looks good. What do you think?"

Mary nodded and looked at her husband, then smiled and asked, "Could it be Mr. Abe, that you've contracted a sickness called 'Six Bulls fever'? Alright—I won't be comfortable, but I can cope with your plan."

"James, me and Mary have been talking about Six Bulls country again," said Abraham. "You reckon you might have an interest in moving there one day?"

James had a quizzical look on his face. "You know, Elizabeth and I were just talking about that the other day. We met those Jennings fellows in town and they talked our ears off. Yes, if'n I could be sure that everything that old Big Jen told us was true, Elizabeth and I would have an interest. Cheap good farmland always interests me and there's great demand for existing farms here from all the new settlers that be arriving. Why do you ask?"

"That tornado scared us right bad, particularly with us watching the Vorshell's barn being destroyed. It's affecting Mary's nerves. I've promised her that we would seek another area to live after the baby arrives—one where there is no slavery, like the Missouri frontier. No offense meant to you and Elizabeth, James, but it's just these dadgum storms. Frankly, she just won't sit still with the thought of living in this area any longer than we have to."

James stared at him, but remained silent.

"I've talked with Noah and Frederick about Six Bulls," continued Abraham. "They've suggested going ahead now to explore the area. If it seems like a good choice, we would leave next year in late spring. Both Mary and I have a concern about sending them alone, but we would be mighty comforted if you'd allow Tommy to go along. That way, you could get a first-hand report from him."

"Well, that's a lot of news you've laid on me, my good friend," said James. "I'm going to have to think on it. When would the boys be leaving?"

"It's not decided, but probably in the next week to make sure that they can return before the winter snows come."

"Let me talk it over with Elizabeth and I'll let you know."

The Burkeds agreed with the plan and their son, Tommy, was thrilled at the prospect of the adventure.

Noah did manage to find a few minutes alone with Letha before he left.

"You'll be back, won't you?" she asked shyly in a small voice, her brown eyes lustrous.

"Of course. We're just going to scout some frontier land—you know, take a little look-see, and report our findings. Just the same, I expect you'll be out fancying someone else with me being gone and all."

"Oh, Noah, how you do go on. I wish thee a safe trip. Come back soon. Then, we can talk some more." She gave his arm a squeeze and turned away, but not before he saw tears in her beautiful brown eyes.

The three young men left on the following Saturday.

Chapter Thirteen

F rederick had two items to help guide them. One was a traced map from the army supply depot in Martinsville and the other was his father's compass. Leaving their farms in central Indiana, it took the boys six days to make the first one hundred twenty miles. They followed the White River until it emptied into the much larger Illinois and camped outside the village of Vincennes. In the morning, they would cross on the ferry. Inquiring at the tavern, Frederick learned more about the area.

"Yep, this here village be the oldest town in this part of Indiana and it be important in American history, it be," said the tavern owner. "Right here, there be two major battles fought during the Revolutionary War."

Frederick nodded, eager to find out more about the trail but less interested in the small village's history. He resigned himself to listen.

"In 1778," the owner continued, "King George sent his men on a surprise attack and captured this here village. Then, the next year, frontiersman George Rogers Clark captured Fort Sackville and liberated the town. And that was the end of the English in these parts."

"That surely be a lot of history for you folks," acknowledged Frederick. "But let me ask you, what be the trail like from here over to the Mississippi River?"

"Well," began the talkative tavern owner, "most folks traveling west use the old Cahokia Trace and it be taking ya right to St. Louie. When you get to the Mississippi, the big city be on the other side."

"Be the trail well marked?" asked Frederick.

"It be well used and called after them Injuns, mysterious ones they were, by the same name—'Cahokia.' No one rightly knows anything about them and no one can even recall seeing one. Those Injuns just up and disappeared maybe a hundred or more years ago, but everyone knows that they were here because of the big dirt mounds they left behind. Some reckon it must have taken them two maybe three hundred years to build 'em. Yessiree, keep on the trail due west and you'll see their work and you'll be at the Mississippi in about a week's ride. St Louie be your destination?"

"No," Frederick replied. "We be on our way to southwest Missouri."

"You'll want to take Boone's Lick Trail west of St. Louie to Booneville on the Missouri River. There, you can be inquiring about the last part of your journey."

Frederick was puzzled. "Ain't Boonville and that trail you mentioned in Kentucky?"

"Nope, you be thinking of the father. This trail be named after Nathan and Daniel, his younguns. Yep, that old salt spring provides most of the salt for folks west of St. Louie. Anyway, you'll also be following in the same footsteps that the Lewis and Clark expedition took when they set out to survey the Louisiana Purchase territory for President Jefferson, traveling up the Missouri River."

"Thank you for all the information," replied Frederick. "It's mighty help-ful." He was awed at the thought of following the same trails taken by so many legendary frontiersmen. Again, he felt the thrill of adventure as he briefly lost himself in the tavern owner's accounts.

The older man brought him back to reality when he said, "But you take care, young man. Keep a sharp lookout for thieving scoundrels. On the trails, some prey on travelers like you. Any of them scallywaging thieves caught twice in these parts have their ears cut off. The judge figures that they don't need them as they sure ain't listening to the law."

🐾 🐾

The next morning, Frederick and his companions continued their journey. "According to the tavern keeper, we'll just keep going due west following the trail. He believes we can ford the Embarras River on our horses at the small village of Charlottesville near a Shaker mill."

Noah looked at his brother. "I wake up every morning and still can't be-lieve that we're really on our way to the frontier. I wonder if'n our family is ever going to settle down for good."

"Oh, you're just pining over that Vogel gal, that's all," Frederick replied, with a laugh.

"I can't believe you Rallemores are actually thinking about moving again," said Tommy. "But I'm mighty glad you asked me along. This trip is probably going to be the biggest adventure of our lives. Ain't you excited to be taking this trip, Frederick?"

"Sure I am. I must have more of my pa in me than Noah has," Frederick said, laughing. "I like seeing new country and this journey reminds me of our travels from North Carolina." He quickly turned away as he suddenly recalled Hooker and his fear as the naked blade had slid up his throat. Looking toward the horizon, he thought, *well those days be long behind me. Best leave it buried in the past.*

Along the trail, they passed a number of the huge mysterious Indian mounds just as the tavern owner had said. By the end of the week, they were on the banks of the Mississippi and ferried to the other side on a bright sunny afternoon.

"Did you ever see so many boats?" asked Noah excitedly, standing on the ferry's bow. "And this river sure be wider than the Ohio. Why it must be two or three miles across—maybe more."

"And look over there along the far shore," said Tommy in amazement. "Be them steamboats? Why there must be near a hundred tied up along the riverbank. Those tall black smokestacks look like a forest. Have you ever seen such a sight in your life?"

Boats of every shape and size were busying themselves on the river— flatboats, keelboats, log rafts, steamboats, and small skiffs. Their ferry docked at the foot of the bustling city.

Everywhere Frederick looked, there was more to see. He watched as muleskinners took wagon after wagon up and down the high riverbank over roads cut through the limestone rock formations underlying the bluff.

Walking their horses up the hill and through the narrow streets, Frederick was amazed to see that the streets were paved with cut stones. In the center of town, they passed a large public square where teams of workers were constructing new brick buildings. "Never have I seen the likes of the comings and goings as this city offers."

A passing stranger told them that many travelers camped on the western outskirts of town. They came over a rise and the next sight stopped them in their tracks.

Tommy exclaimed, "Good God, almighty."

"Heavens," echoed Noah.

There stood the largest building the young men had ever seen. Four huge columns framed the stone entry porch, fronting two lofty spires. Behind, there was a huge dome with a cross high on its peak.

"Good Lord, I've never seen anything this big," Tommy exclaimed.

"Be it a house of worship?" Frederick asked incredulously. As he rode closer, the immensity was awesome. Old scaffolding on one side of the building held a large sign that proclaimed—

Dedication

Cathedral of St. Louis

October 26, 1834

"I simply can't believe my eyes," Noah said. "How can people build places this large?"

Slowly they rode away, glancing over their shoulders at the structure. At the edge of town, they made camp. Between the treetops, they could see the cathedral's bell tower peeking through.

"Let's go back and take a better look at the city," suggested Noah.

"I don't think we should leave the horses alone," said Frederick. There were some campfires in the distance, but no one was close.

"Ahh, it'll be alright," replied Noah. "We'll only be gone an hour."

"You two go on ahead. I'll stay."

🐿 🐿

Wherever Noah looked, new sights delighted him—tall buildings, horse-drawn carriages, and people busying themselves in a bustling city.

As he and Tommy crossed the main square, his cousin said, "I've never seen anything like this. Say, Noah, let's buy us a drink in that saloon over there."

"Ahh, I don't think that's a good idea."

"And why not? We been on the trail for weeks and a beer would really quench my thirst."

"Since when have you started drinking beer?"

"Oh, come on. What's the harm? Then we'll get back to camp."

Pushing through the door, Noah was amazed. On one side of the room, a long bar ran the full length of the saloon and behind were a series of mirrored shelves filled with bottles and glasses. Half a dozen bartenders were working the customers as the sounds of men talking and laughing filled the air while heavy tobacco smoke created a haze.

At the bar, Tommy asked, "What'll it be, Noah?"

"I think I'll have a glass of milk."

"Barkeep, one milk and a beer, if you please."

Frederick gathered wood and started a fire. The saddles packs were on one side of the camp with his horse and the packhorse hobbled in the trees.

Frederick rested on his horse blanket with his head against the saddle. A coffee pot sat near the fire and soon there was a pleasing aroma of brewing coffee mingled with smoke from the campfire. Closing his eyes, Frederick dozed in the late afternoon.

With a start, he awoke. The end of a gun barrel poked him in the nose and a rough looking bald-headed man with a shaggy beard was standing over him. Frederick was equally startled to see that the man had ugly scars on his head in place of his ears.

"Ya appear like ya've been traveling some," the older man commented, eyeing him for long moments.

"Who are you?" demanded Frederick, spying a second man standing a few feet away. "Why've you got that gun pointed at me?"

"Say, don't I know ya?" replied the bald man. "I be seeing ya somewhere before."

Wide-awake, Frederick asked, "What do you want?"

"Hot damn, now I recall. Ya be one of them Rallemore brats, ain't ya? Don't ya be recognizing yar old pardn'r? Take another look and pay no mind that I be missing me ears and hair," the man grinned evilly.

Frederick stared hard. There was something familiar about the man but without the ears and hair . . . Suddenly, Frederick knew and cried out, "Hooker?"

"That it be. How be yar pigeon-headed self-righteous pa? Be he still looking out for Injuns and wayward slaves?"

The other bandit let out a gruff laugh, mindlessly repeating, "Pigeon-headed, pigeon-headed."

The second man was huge with broad shoulders and ham-sized arms who stared at Frederick with a lopsided snaggletooth grin while holding a pistol in his hand.

Looking back at Hooker, Frederick asked, "Where did you come from?"

"Now ya listen ta me," commanded Hooker. "I be the one asking the questions. Stand up. Ya have some dusty horses over there. I think we'll be relieving ya of them. They should fetch us forty or fifty dollars. Perhaps ya got some money, too. Be that so? Maybe some of them shiny gold coins like ya had the last time. Are they still in that leather purse?"

Frederick was unsure what to do, remembering the last time Hooker had asked him the same question. His stomach was doing flip-flops and his hands were clammy. One of his legs began to tremble as he clearly recalled the steely pressure of the naked knife against his throat years ago. Hooker's gun muzzle rose as he stood.

"You didn't get away with stealing the last time and—"

"Don't be stupid and don't be putting me off," Hooker said as he poked Frederick hard in the ribs with the barrel of the gun. "Ya couldn't do it before and it won't work now. Can't ya tell by my missing ears? Thieving be my business these days and I'm good at it. Now let me see yar money. And I mean right now."

"See yar money, right now," the big man parroted.

"It be in one of those saddle packs over there," stammered Frederick, nodding toward the other side of the camp.

Hooker prodded him again with the gun. "Well, don't just stand there, go get it and stop yar meandering."

"Go get it, go get it," Hooker's partner childishly repeated.

Frederick thought the second man looked oafish with his loose grin. The red-rimmed eyes were bright, yet somehow vacant.

With Hooker following, Frederick began hunting through the packs. As he moved them, he saw his lariat. Grabbing it in one hand and a saddle pack in the other, he swung around quickly, tossing the pack in a high arc to Hooker.

As the earless man stretched and reached up, the gun muzzle dropped.

The young man brought the coiled lariat around fast, whipping it across Hooker's face and eyes, momentarily blinding him, and quickly followed with a fist to the slaver's jaw, knocking him to the ground.

The big oaf quickly stepped in-between, slowly flourishing his pistol back and forth under Frederick's nose, and shaking his head. Still wearing the lopsided grin, he said in an odd voice, "Ya no hurt my pardn'r or me git mad."

The slaver was bleeding from a cut lip that framed his yellow teeth. Getting up, he snarled, "Ahh, ya young devil. Ya always were one to try and play games, weren't ya?"

Frederick glared at him, unsure what would happen next.

With an ugly laugh, the earless bandit said, "But where be my manners. I guess I failed to introduce ya to my pardn'r here." Snickering, he continued, "I call him 'Brick' because his wits are as dim as one and, when he hits a fella, it feels like one."

Frederick looked at the big man with the pistol and involuntarily shuddered. The man's vacant eyes were unnerving.

"Well, looki thar, Brick, young Rallemore looks scared, don' he? Just the way ya like it."

Frederick looked around wildly, but no one else was near. *I don't want to mess with this brute*, he thought, *yet I can't outrun a bullet*. Clenching his fists, he said defiantly, "Go to hell, Hooker."

"Such crude words coming from the son of a gentleman." Motioning toward his partner, he explained, "Brick be a strange one. Like some animals, he regularly needs his red meat and he gets his by beating fellas to a pulp. And looki who comes along to oblige—my favorite Rallemore brat. Ya and yar pa are downright lucky to have an old penny like me keep turning up to make yar lives so interesting."

Frederick took a step backwards, feeling a rush of emotions. Brick moved forward and the man's eyes no longer seemed empty.

"We'll search his kit after yar done with him," Hooker continued. "Give me yar pistol, ya oaf. We don't want this lad to claim that it wasn't a fair fight—a just fight," he laughed mockingly. With a strange gleam in his eyes, he hissed, "Get him!"

The big man's crooked smile never changed as he advanced—now intimidatingly pounding one fist rhythmically into the palm of the other.

Frederick retreated, blindly stumbling through the edge of the fire and scattering embers, as he took a fighter's stance. *He'll crush the life out of me with those strong arms and big hands,* he thought. *Well, if'n I'm going to die, I'm going to die fighting.*

Quickly reaching down, Frederick picked up a stout limb from the firewood stack. "C'mon you big lout, let's see what you've got," he shouted, dodging the lumbering man's awkward punch and swinging the firewood with all his might. The blow hit the man squarely across the head and face, cutting his lip and knocking out the snaggletooth.

Brick slumped to one knee, but then he arose and seemingly shook off the blow, much to Frederick's dismay.

"So, ya wants ta play rough, do ya," Brick bellowed, in a voice now deepened with rage. "I likes it when there be fight in a man cause it's more fun that away." He rushed at Frederick like a rampaging bull, smashing a shoulder into Frederick's chest as his momentum took him to the other side of the campfire.

Down went Frederick, barely avoiding the blaze.

Hooker shouted, "Finish him, ya big fool."

Brick came at him again, this time low.

Still on the ground, Frederick scurried out of the way, picked up the coffee pot, and flung it and the hot coffee into the man's face.

"Ahhhhhh!" Brick screamed, dropping to his knees and burying his face in his hands. For long moments, he moaned in agony. Softly at first, then loudly, he repeatedly chanted, "Ya hurt Brick—YA HURT BRICK."

Now standing, Frederick again raised his club, watching the big man's every move. Glancing briefly at Hooker, he moved back a step.

With a shake of his giant head, Brick wiped his face with the back of his sleeve and stared at Frederick; his face was red and full of hate. "After I kills ya, I'm going to smash ya to death."

As the adrenalin pumped through Frederick's body, the big man's chilling words sounded like the omen of doom.

"But first I'm going to rip ya apart starting with yar arms." Brick's voice was now deep and raspy as he finally stood. "Then, I'm going to twist yar head clear away from yar body."

Brandishing the wood, Frederick nervously stood his ground.

An instant later, Brick charged.

Once more sidestepping the big man, Frederick retreated awkwardly and tripped over the woodpile. Flat on his back, he saw Brick coming toward him fast with hands outstretched that looked as big as anvils. Frederick grabbed the limb and raised the end at the last moment, sticking it in the soft part of the man's stomach.

Atop the club-like lever, Brick's forward motion carried him up and over Frederick.

Swiftly, Frederick stood, wielding the limb again, and prepared for the next attack.

Brick lay on the ground motionless. His large head rested at an odd angle to his body.

Frederick poked him with his wood, but still there was no reaction. Brick's unseeing eyes were open, but his neck seemed to move separately from his body. The giant had come down headfirst on a good size rock and broken his neck.

"Eh?" stormed Hooker. "What be this? Get up, ya big ox." Kicking him in the shin, there was no response.

Frederick stood there and realized that he was staring down at a dead man as he dropped the firewood.

"Damn ya, Rallemore, ya killed my pardn'r," Hooker growled, a look of incredulity on his face.

"You saw the fight—" Frederick stammered, "—he was trying to kill me."

Quickly recovering, Hooker pulled a knife. "Shut yar mouth and don't whine like yar natural-cull pa. So, let's see how good ya be dealing with me, yar old pardn'r. Come meet my other friend—the sharp pointy one. Ya remember him."

Frederick froze, his terror returning.

"He'll stick ya now just like he did before," Hooker continued. "Still, ya know that I'm a merciful man and maybe, by my good graces, ya'll live. Then again, maybe ya won't," he said, coldly.

Frederick slowly backed away.

Suddenly, the loud, deeply reverberating sound of big bells came from the cathedral. Hooker was startled and glanced over his shoulder.

Seconds later, Frederick heard horses approaching.

Infuriated, Hooker turned to Frederick. "Company's acoming and I best be going. Ya Rallemores keep dodging me, probably thinking ya can do it forever. Sure, ya can—as sure as crows die when the sun goes down. Be seeing ya again, young Rallemore." Backing quickly, he rounded the trees and was gone.

Frederick heard the beat of his departing horse and, moments later, his companions returned. He turned and stared down at the lifeless Brick as shock set in. His face paled and he began to shake uncontrollably. Dropping his head into his hands, he silently asked, *Lord, what happens now?*

Frederick and his companions stared at the big man for long moments.

"After all this time, I can't believe that Hooker came after you and brought along this giant," said Noah.

"I don't believe he was looking for me," answered Frederick. "I think we just stumbled on each other and I was his next victim."

Tommy finally said, "God, this be one big ugly fella." Pausing to collect his thoughts, he continued. "A man in the bar be saying that Boone's Lick Trail follows the Missouri River out of town. Let's break camp now, load the robber on our packhorse, and find the river. We can cover him with our tarp during the trip."

"And?" questioned Noah.

"We'll set this fella floating downriver on his last voyage," replied Tommy. "No need shedding tears over the likes of him."

Hesitantly, Frederick asked, "Don't you think we should give him a proper burial?"

Tommy responded, "With what, a Christian prayer said over the man who tried to rob and kill you? Come on, let's get going before we lose all the daylight."

"I agree," Noah said, peering at the area around them. "And besides, it's not likely that Hooker would come back this evening with three of us here, but . . ."

Frederick nodded. He sensed the uneasiness in his brother's voice.

Silently, they sat around the campfire on the riverbank. Finally, Frederick broke the quiet. "I really had no choice. First, there was Hooker with his gun on me and then that creature came at me saying he was going to tear me limb from limb. But I never meant to kill him. Heavens, I didn't even know the big lout other than Hooker called him Brick."

"We understand," said Noah.

"You were defending yourself, pure and simple," Tommy added. "You've got to accept that because it be true. If'n I wasn't in that saloon having my beer, I'd have been there to help you, and they probably wouldn't have tried to jump the three of us."

"One minute, we be fighting, then the next, he be dead," continued Frederick.

"Well, we did the right thing hauling him to the river," said Tommy. "He'll just float downstream until he be caught on some snag or buried in the bottom muck."

"I don't know how I'm going to tell pa," Frederick said, hanging his head.

"You'll know when you see him," replied Noah.

The three young men continued west, keeping the river to the south. Two days out of St. Louis, Frederick spotted a brown haze on the horizon. As they neared, hundreds of Indians were slowly walking with most carrying packs on their backs that seemed to contain all their worldly positions. A body of cavalry escorted them as two privates brought up the rear. One dropped back as the three Indiana boys approached.

"Howdy," Frederick called out. "We just be riding through and were attracted by the dust cloud in the sky. I be Frederick Rallemore and these fellas be my brother and cousin. What's going on here?"

The trooper gave them a hard look and then seemed satisfied as he relaxed in his saddle. "We be taking these Injuns to their new lands by order of President Jackson under the Government's Injun removal program. We've been having a heck of a time doing it, too."

"Why be that?"

"They've been walking since late in the spring when we left Columbus, Ohio. We marched down to the Ohio River and tried to load them on a big old steamboat except about half wouldn't get on the dang thing despite the prodding from my captain. They said anything that big, floating on water, and spouting black smoke just had to be bad medicine. They just plain weren't getting on."

Noah asked, "So, what happened?"

"We split up our detail and half of our troopers went with the Injuns on the boat. And we be the ones taking to the trail, picking up more supplies along the way, and are now crossing Missouri to Injun Territory."

"Thank you kindly," said Frederick, "we'll be on our way. Good luck on the rest of your journey."

As he turned his horse away, an Indian woman holding a young boy at the rear of the column quickly dropped back. She dodged to the side before the second trooper could contain her with his mount and held the child up, as though offering him to Frederick.

Startled, Frederick asked, "What she doing that for?"

Grimly, the first trooper replied, "This has been a hard march for these Injuns. Half the time, we don't have enough food and the shelters won't ward off the colder nights. Over three dozen have died so far on this trek and I expect there'll be more."

"I'm still puzzled. Why is she holding up the boy? Surely, she isn't asking us to take him with us?"

"That probably be exactly what she be hoping for, thinking her son has a better chance of surviving with you fellas than with her and her people."

🐾 🐾

Following the trail along the Missouri River, Frederick led the way. Beyond a bend, he saw large white clouds rapidly rising above the treetops. Unsure, he reined in.

"Be that smoke?" asked Noah.

"It doesn't quite look like it to me," Tommy observed.

Rounding the bend, a sign informed them that they had arrived at "Boone's Salt Lick." The young men were amazed at the sight of the bustling activity before them.

Along the riverbank, men were busy shoveling salt from wagons into the hulls of keelboats for transport downriver. In a large cleared area, gangs of men stoked blazing stone furnaces with wood. Nearly obscured by steam, fifty or sixty large iron kettles sat atop containing boiling water.

"So that's where the clouds are coming from," exclaimed Noah.

Frederick was fascinated as he watched two men "dancing" on platforms above the kettles, manning a flume that brought brine water to the boiling pots from nearby springs. Pointing them out to his companions, he observed, "That job looks mighty dangerous."

"Indeed, it does," agreed Tommy.

After all the water had boiled off in one heavy pot, a log gantry swung it onto a mule-drawn cart, which carried it up a dirt incline where it was dumped on top of a white "salt mountain." In the distance, Frederick heard the distinct sound of many axmen felling trees and cutting wood to feed the hungry furnaces.

"Can't think of a better place to fill our salt pouch," noted Frederick.

As the young men continued toward town, Frederick rode up to an old-timer sitting outside the trading post and asked, "Is this Booneville?"

"Nope, but yar close. Booneville be a mile up river. This be *New* Franklin."

The way the man said the town's name sparked Frederick's interest. "What happen to 'old' Franklin?"

Chuckling, the man answered, "The river swallowed it about two years ago and, I reckon, spit it out down near St. Louie."

"Well, my kin and I are on our way to southwest Missouri and the lands called Six Bulls. Do you know someone who can direct us toward the trail?"

The man smiled, asking, "Ya say Six Bulls? Ah've been in them parts and can direct ya. The easiest way be to travel with the next caravan hauling salt that be headed for the pueblo of Santa Fe down Mexico way, like the one pulling out in the morning. Ya'll follow along for maybe a hundred miles and then, just shy of the Platt River, you'll turn due south. Another several days and ya'll be riding in the land of the Six Bulls."

"Much obliged. We saw the salt works as we rode into town and found it mighty interesting. How long has it been working?"

"Maybe twenty-five or thirty years, I reckon. Started by ol' Boone's sons. The men boil maybe three hundred gallons of water and, don't ya know, out of it they be getting a bushel of salt. Yep, most of the folks on the frontier, and even down New Orleans way, depend on salt that comes from the springs here abouts for everything from preserving meats to tanning leather, besides eatin'. Take some advice from this ol' buffalo hunter and carry an extra sack with ya. Comes in mighty handy when yar trading with the Injuns." Sizing up the three men, he asked, "How be it that you boys are headed for Six Bulls country?"

"Old gent named Big Jen told my folks and me about the area," said Frederick.

The man's smile broadened. "How be the ol' rascal?"

Frederick was surprised. "You know Big Jen, the frontiersman?"

"Sure do. Him and me traveled them prairie lands years ago. It sure be mighty pretty country."

The next morning, the caravan of pack mules ferried across the wide Missouri River and then headed southwest as the Indiana men brought up the kite-tail end. Near the Platt, they turned their horses south.

Overall, they had been on the trail for nearly six weeks and had covered, by their figuring, over six hundred miles. Many things stuck in Frederick's mind as he thought about the sights that they'd be describing to their folks. Two images, however, seemed to be constant: Hooker's bald earless head and Brick floating down the river.

On a late afternoon, the three breasted a knoll and the sight stopped them in their tracks. The prairie stretched across the horizon as far as the eye could see, dotted with stands of tall trees, and the grasses were as high as a horse's eye. In the distance across the lush valley, a farmer was plowing furrows in the virgin soil with his two-horse team.

"Boys," said Frederick. "I think this be Six Bulls country."

Chapter Fourteen

Andres pushed back his hat as he detected three riders on the distant hilltop. He was standing in a furrow with the reins over his shoulders and his hands on the plow handles, but his eyes strayed over to the wagon where his musket sat in the boot. He tied off the reins and walked slowly, his eyes on the approaching riders.

Occasionally, a drifter or neighbor called, and Indians frequently stopped at his trading post, yet three white men, well mounted on horses, was a different matter. He recalled the bushwhackers that had tried to rob him last year.

Standing by the side of the wagon, he waited and watched, his musket now resting in the crook of his arm. One rider appeared to be in his middle teens and the other two were grown men, yet they, too, were young. The barrel of his gun lowered.

Closing on him, one of the young men shouted, "Howdy. Is this Six Bulls country?"

The question surprised him. These three had obviously traveled a long way. They were dusty and their horses needed a good grain feed and rub-down. By their looks, they had probably been on the trail for weeks.

"Ja, that it be," he replied in his German tinged voice. "We call this area Lost Creek Valley. Who be thee?"

"I'm Frederick Rallemore and this here be my brother, Noah. Over there is our cousin, Tommy Burked. We be from up north in Morgan County, Indiana."

"Well, pleased to meet you all. I be Andres Sommer and this here be my farm. What're you doing here? Where be your kinfolk?"

"We come ahead to scout Six Bulls country for our families. They're back in Indiana."

Well, this was the day for surprises. Andres looked at the boys and they seemed genuine enough, although sending three lads on such a long journey to scout new territory seemed far-fetched.

"Well, get thee down and come have a sip of water from my bucket. You just arrive in this country? You got a place to bed down yet? Why don't you stay and have supper with us tonight?"

Frederick and his companions were heavy with trail odor. Getting directions, they rode over the hill to wash body and clothes in the clear sweet running water of a small river. "Lost Creek," the farmer had called it. Frederick managed to find a washed shirt in his saddlebags and finger combed his wet hair.

At supper, Andres introduced his five children and his wife, Elsie.

Andres be in his thirties, Frederick guessed, seeing a handsome man with light colored hair and blue eyes. He noticed Andres fingering his blond beard as he spoke. *His wife, Elsie, be about the same age and they have four boys and one girl. The oldest boy, Curtis, looks to be about ten or eleven.* The Sommer children stared at him, wide-eyed with wonder. *I reckon they don't get many strangers like us coming through.*

Andres told them they were from Holmes County, Ohio. "Us and three other families put all of our belongings and animals on flatboats and drifted down the rivers to the town of Marietta on the Ohio River. There, we caught a tow with one of them steamboats." He went on to tell them about some of their adventures.

Frederick was fascinated. "How big was the steamboat?"

Andres started to reply, but Tommy interrupted him. "How fast did it go?

"Where did you sleep?" interjected Noah.

Andres smiled as he answered all their questions.

Frederick liked this man and looked around the cabin. It was well fashioned with two rooms downstairs and a full loft above.

Elsie brought a steaming pot of coffee and set it on an upended wood-round.

Shifting himself on the seat created with rawhide webbing, Frederick leaned over to Curtis and asked, "What be that thing that my brother be sitting on?"

"We call it a chiller and we use it to store our churned butter. There be a crock inside and the barrel is watertight. Between the two, we fill it with water and that keeps the inside cool."

"Amazing," replied Frederick as he heard his companion continue with their questions.

"Did your livestock survive the trip?"

"How long did the journey take?"

"Now, you boys hold on a minute," said Andres, chuckling. "We told you something about ourselves and our journey, but you have yet to tell us why you be riding this far just to have a look at this here pretty country."

Frederick began, "Well, Mr. Sommer, Noah and I be originally from North Carolina. We set out with a wagon train in 1830 bound for Morgan County. Our guide was a fella named Little Jen. His father was . . ."

"Big Jen," interrupted Curtis.

"That be right," said Frederick, surprised.

"You know Big Jen or maybe his son, Little Jen?" inquired Noah.

"Ja, we met the Jennings first in Ohio. Big Jen was visiting his daughter in Wooster. Big Jen, he went back to his home in Tennessee and he died there a year later."

"Big Jen died?" asked the surprised Frederick.

"Ja, he passed away sitting on his porch in his rocking chair," replied Andres. "And Little Jen, he died on our trip here to Missouri. The steamboat was carrying cotton and a four-hundred-pound bale fell on him. The boat captain figured that the ties holding the cotton had broken during a fearsome storm we survived at the mouth of the Arkansas River several days earlier. With all of the boat's maneuvering, it shifted and tumbled down. Little Jen was standing on the deck below."

There was a long silence until Frederick spoke. "It sure don't seem right for them fellas to have helped so many folks find Six Bulls only to die elsewhere."

There was another pause, and then Andres was again asking more questions of the three young men. "How long did your trip take and which route did you follow?"

Frederick replied, "Our folks be farmers and the Jennings told us about the horse-eye-high grass and sweet running water in the land of the Six Bulls. We've been on the trail for almost six weeks." He told about their trip, the mule caravan, and traveling south from the Missouri River until they came upon Andres plowing the field.

Andres continued asking questions as the hours slipped into the night: Why are their families thinking of moving to Missouri? What's it like in Morgan County? Is the farming good there? How about the water, is it good?

As the evening got late, Andres stood up. "I guess you boys best be getting to bed. You're welcome to stay in the barn during your visit to Lost Creek Valley. What do ya say?"

Frederick rose, nudged Noah awake, and shook Andres' hand. "We're much obliged. We'll be happy to do some hunting and work around the farm to repay ya."

"I imagine you'll want to look over the valley and find you some good land," Andres commented as he headed to the door with the three boys.

Frederick nodded. "Yes, sir, that be our goal."

"Well, then, you get some sleep and the folks around here will be happy to answer all your questions. I'll take you down to Lost Creek tomorrow and point out the adjoining land that is similar to mine. Tell you the advantages and disadvantages. How's that sound?"

"That sounds fine."

As Frederick left the house, he turned to his companions and said, "I like these people. I think our folks will fit in right well."

The Indiana men spent the next several days exploring the rivers, streams, and valleys of Lost Creek. One day, Noah asked Curtis, "You have a favorite fishing hole in that river?"

"Sure do," replied Curtis. "If'n you like, I'll show it to you boys seeing as my chores for the day be mostly done."

"Sounds great," answered Tommy.

As they sat on the riverbank with their lines in the water, Curtis told them the story about shooting a big black bear that tried to eat them for supper when they first came to Lost Creek Valley.

Noah finally asked the question that had been busying the boys' minds: "Where did the name Lost Creek come from?"

Curtis broke out laughing. "Since we had lost Little Jen on our trip, pa, me, and my cousin, Seneca, came ahead to scout Six Bulls and left the rest of our party at Fort Smith down in Arkansas Territory. We ran across some Osage Injuns that had known Big Jen. After we had a meal of fish and bear steaks—and I mean to tell you those steaks were mighty good—we set out the next day to lay out our new land. After we completed marking it, we wondered how we could identify our claim. My pa came up with the idea of burying his iron teapot beneath a tree."

"But where did the name come from," asked Tommy impatiently.

"Land's sake, hold your britches on, I'm coming to that part," Curtis replied, chuckling. "After we returned to Fort Smith, everyone in our party traveled to Six Bulls. When we got here, the stream seemed smaller than the one that we remembered and we couldn't find the teapot. The next day, we found that the smaller river branched off from the main one and my pa named them Lost Creek and Little Lost Creek. And yes, we dug up the old teapot."

Frederick and his companions slicked up on Sunday as Andres had told them that guests would be coming for their monthly prayer meeting and meal. *I like the way these folks are so friendly,* he thought. "Is there anything we can do to help?" he asked Andres.

"No," replied the farmer. "Just bring your appetites. We're having chicken, roasted opossum, collard greens, sweet potatoes, and Ilse's oven jewels, her sourdough biscuits with honey. Our friends will be surprised that you're here and they'll want to ask you questions about your trip and your farms in Indiana."

"And it'll be a chance for us to get their views," replied Frederick.

"Ja, these be the same folks that traveled with us from Ohio to Lost Creek Valley.

Frederick turned as a wagon arrived pulled by a brace of sleek looking horses.

Andres made the introductions. "Fellas, I want you to meet Sarah and John Leach and these be their children. Let me help you down, Sarah. These three young fellas be from Indiana and are staying with us. They've been on the trail for weeks and have just arrived."

"Welcome to Lost Creek Valley," said John, shaking the boys' hands.

"Them be mighty fine looking horses you got," Frederick observed.

"Thank you," replied John. "I breed them from a pair I bought in Fort Smith. I figure this frontier will be filling up with folks and I'll have me a good business someday selling horses. Stop by my place and I'll show them to you."

"Thank you. I'd like that."

Another wagon drove up, interrupting them.

"Boys," Andres said, "this be Amos and Nancy Running Bird Hanks. They have a farm and lead mine about three miles northeast of here. The lead balls you see in my trading post come from his mine."

What a beautiful name this woman has, thought Frederick, admiring the Indian woman with her long raven-colored hair.

"Glad you're here," Amos told the boys. "This be my son, Seneca. Are you fellas staying long?"

Seneca was a striking looking boy and Frederick figured he was about Curtis' age. Wearing a headband, his black hair fell to his shoulders in a braid. He wore moccasins and a soft deerskin leather vest. On his waist, was a hunting knife stuck into a scabbard decorated with a fine Indian design. When they shook hands, his smile was bright.

"And here," interrupted Andres once more. "Here comes Captain Renke Vogel and his family. Boys, let me tell you about the Captain. He be the strongest, bravest man I know. I had five bushwhackers come around last year trying to rob me and the Captain took care of them by himself." Andres smiled as he spoke and the Captain looked embarrassed.

The man Frederick met was tall, brawny, and looked every inch like a man who might be able to handle five bandits all by himself. Turning to speak to Tommy, Frederick had to catch himself from bursting out in laughter.

Tommy was staring at the Captain's pretty daughter, whose name was Samantha. His cousin was blushing bright red looking down at his boot, which was tracing small patterns in the dirt.

No question, he be struck by this gal, Frederick thought. *In fact, he looks downright smitten.* He noticed that the strawberry-blond girl returned Tommy's look and curtsied.

"Nice to meet you all," she said in a small voice.

The group moved to the outdoor tables. Andres conducted their prayers and gave thanks for the new arrivals from Indiana. Then, they all dug into the food with gusto and appetites born from long, hard days of work.

After the meal, the younger children wandered off to dig tunnels in the haystack near the barn. Noah left for Lost Creek with Curtis and Seneca to see who could catch the most fish.

Frederick walked over to the Captain to ask about his war experiences. He noticed that Tommy and Samantha took a different path towards the river with her younger brothers following and teasing both with fiendish delight.

🐾 🐾

A thrill ran through Tommy as he walked with Samantha down the hillside toward the river. Although the teasing of her brothers embarrassed him, he couldn't help but enjoy the presence of this lovely girl and the fact that she even noticed him.

When Samantha's brothers finally got tired of teasing, they wandered off.

She sashayed along the path and asked, "So, Thomas, what's it like in Indiana?"

The use of his formal name unnerved him, yet he also liked it. It made him feel manlier. "Well, I . . . I . . ." For the life of him, he couldn't seem to get a string of words out of his mouth.

"Do you like it here, Thomas?" she went on.

"Sure do," he replied without hesitation.

"What do you like best?" she asked demurely.

Tommy paused, determined to speak one or two sentences that didn't make him seem foolish. "You are mighty friendly folks and I like that." *Good, I got one out, so let's try another.* "I mean, you got good water with the two rivers, although they be smaller than the one we got back home. There be plenty of game and I've never seen prairie grass that grows as tall as what you have here.

"I like the lay of the land, which looks and feels like good dirt for farming. We got fine soil in Morgan County, but the land be filling up and a man gets to feeling closed in, if'n you know what I mean?" he said, borrowing thoughts he had heard his father say.

Tommy could see a gleam in the pretty girl's eyes as though she might be as fascinated with him as he was with her.

"I heard the talk during our meal that you and your folks be thinking of settling here. Have you decided what you'll be a telling them, Thomas?" Samantha paused, then went on. "I mean, are you going to recommend that they pack up, and make this land their home?" Now, it was her turn to blush a bright pink.

Tommy looked at her and he knew the answer. "I think this land would be perfect for us, and I think I'd like to spend the rest of my days right here," he answered, and caught himself just in time as he was about to say, "with you."

🐾 🐾

Meanwhile, Noah was casting his line into the water when Curtis asked him almost the same question. "What you thinking of saying to your folks about Six Bulls country?"

"Well, the land be good here and so be the water. We got both back home, you know, yet I reckon my pa is itching to make the move and I know my ma is. I expect it'll probably happen next spring after she gives birth to the new baby."

"As I hear you, it wasn't many years ago that you made the move from North Carolina," said Curtis. "You say the ground be producing well in Indiana and you have good water. Why is your family looking to move?"

"My pa be hankering to see more of the frontier and my ma be just plain scared of tornadoes. We had two come through this past summer."

"I've heard of them storms. What're they like?" asked Curtis.

"I'm no expert, but it started out as a rainstorm. Then, the thundering began and the lightning was nearly continuous. The hail came next. We sat in our root cellar and watched through the chinks of the cellar door as a funnel dropped out of the clouds and moved down the valley next to our farm. Our neighbor had a big stout old barn with limestone walls for a foundation— thick walls they were and maybe seven or eight feet tall. Well, that black funnel headed right for the barn and smashed it to pieces. Scariest thing I've ever seen."

The Lost Creek Valley boy looked at him in amazement, peppering him with questions. Curtis finally commented, "No wonder your ma and pa want to live someplace else." Then he asked, "You and the others going to lay out some land claims while you be here?"

"Yep. We're going to be making some marks tomorrow starting with that hill over yonder that borders your farm. I think Tommy be doing the same."

Curtis shared with him the marks he and his father had used in laying out the Sommer farm. "You might try using them. When are you heading back to Indiana?"

"We've been discussing it," replied Noah. "We want to get back before the snows start. I think we'll leave in about three days. That'll be plenty of time to make our marks on the land and to fill your larder with some game as a way of thanking you for your kindness."

That evening, Noah talked to Andres about laying out property lines and marking the land.

"That be a good idea," said Andres. "Take Curtis with you so we know what you have in mind. We'll be keeping an eye on it for you, have no worries about that."

Noah turned away, then stammered, "Say . . . say Mr. Sommer, do you know of any old teakettles we can bury to show them marks be our claim?" he asked, turning to face Andres with a wide grin on his face.

At first, Andres seemed puzzled and then he caught on and began to laugh. "You know, I got me an old iron teapot that I could let you use. It being experienced and all in such things, it'd make you a fine claim marker."

They laughed together.

The Indiana boys stayed busy hunting during the following days. Tommy managed to talk Curtis into going over to the Vogel farm one evening to see Samantha for the last time. He said his goodbyes to her as they walked down the veranda steps under a brightly lit moon. He could see a wistfulness come over her.

"Don't worry. I'll be back before you know it, and next time I'll stay. I done marked the land I think my pa will want and . . ." He paused, looking directly into her big, shinning eyes, "I also marked another parcel I aim to farm."

Impulsively, Samantha put her hand on his arm. "Come back, Thomas. Here, take my hair ribbon so it'll remind you of Lost Creek . . . and me," she added, blushing mightily under the moonlit sky.

The night before departure, they finished their evening meal and the three from Indiana were sitting outside around a log fire with Curtis and Andres.

Andres said, "Well, boys, I hope you'll be coming back with your folks next year." He really liked these boys.

"I think we will," Tommy replied.

Frederick smiled. "You've got some mighty fine lands here in Six Bulls. I expect you'll be seeing more of us and our folks. We bought an extra sack of salt up at Boon's Salt Lick. Please accept it with our thanks for your hospitality."

"Thank you very much. Salt be precious here on the frontier."

As the conversation paused, Andres stared at the flames licking the wood, lost in his thoughts. *The frontier be for people who can work hard and carve out a life for themselves. Judging by these young men, their folks will be a welcome addition.*

A burned log collapsed in the blaze, sending a shower of embers skyward and bringing him back to the moment. Looking at the visitors, he saw Noah watching him. "You look like you've a thought festering on your mind, Noah. Be that right?"

"I have, Mr. Sommer. I don't be meaning to bother you, but there was a strange thing that occurred on our trip. And I just can't get it out of my mind. Can I tell you about it?"

Fingering his beard, Andres looked at the boy in the firelight. "Ja, you go right ahead."

"Thank you. A few days west of St. Louis, there was a haze in the distant sky. At first, we didn't know what caused it, so we approached with care."

Andres looked at the boys and sensed their uneasiness.

"It turned out to be dust raised by maybe two hundred Injuns," Noah continued. "They were walking across Missouri and carrying everything they owned on their backs. A body of cavalry was escorting them to make sure they arrived at their new home in Injun Territory. A trooper told us that it was part of the Government's Injun removal effort.

"We thanked the trooper and were turning away when a woman dropped back from the column and held up her youngun, offering him to us. The trooper told us over thirty Injuns had died during the forced march, worn out by the trip and the lack of food and shelter. He figured the mother thought her youngun had a better chance of staying alive with us."

Noah paused with his story. "Mr. Sommer, how come the army be removing the Injuns and why are they forcing them on such long marches?"

Andres remembered seeing much the same thing on his trip down the Muskingum River when his family had traveled to Missouri.

Noah went on, "Are we hurting them so bad? Be that why the woman be offering her youngun to us?"

Andres stared at the boys, unsure how to answer. He could have told them about Captain Renke's idea of keeping white and red folks apart to stop the killing. He could have talked about the bad blood on both sides. After a long pause, he chose a different way to answer the question for the boys and for himself.

"My relatives, they come to this country from Europe across the ocean, seeking a better life. My grandpapa wanted to escape always being in danger because of the way he worshiped God. In the old country, cruel men used harsh ways with many killings and farm burnings.

"So, all of us came to America and carved out a new life on the frontier to suit our ways and we built a country in the process. It be different when it comes to them Injuns who were already here, whose hunting grounds and villages we be plowing. We act toward them in a way like those that forced my grandpa to cross the ocean."

"Are you saying that the army be doing the same things to the Injuns that forced your kin to leave the old country?" asked Frederick.

"Well . . . in a way. You see, the idea is that your parents, me, and others, we all be part of the problem. I reckon it don't make any difference whether we be talking about the Carolinas, Indiana, Ohio, or right here in Missouri. All of us settlers want cheap good farmland for setting our plows. We be seeking to build better lives for our families. We carve our farms from the frontier, sell them, and then we be doing it all over again. We be the ones displacing the Injuns and, in truth, the army is just doing what we want.

"I don't exactly understand why the Government is going about it in the way they are. I do know your fathers and me like the result—good land and good water and being safe from hostiles. So, the government must be doing things right. But be God as my witness, it is a god-awful tragedy for the Injuns."

Frederick lay awake that night thinking about Andres' words and recalled the runaway Indian slave long ago in Rowan County. America had been Indian lands forever and the whites had forced them off. He understood that he and his family were doing their part to undo the Indian's way of life and they must share the blame. *Why is progress for us whites so wrong for Injuns,* he wondered. *Why can't we all just get along together?* He didn't know the answer, but he hoped God would be forgiving.

The young men left the next morning. Andres was working in the same field as he had when they had first appeared on the distant hill. They waved from the distant hill and he waved back. Andres hoped someday soon to welcome them as neighbors.

Chapter Fifteen

When the young men arrived home, Abraham and Mary invited friends and neighbors for a picnic to celebrate. Their trip and stories about Six Bulls country fascinated everyone. The three boys obliged by describing it in detail and sharing their many memories.

James and Elizabeth arrived and their oldest daughter, Annie Rose, was with them. She had just turned sixteen and Frederick seemed to notice her for the first time. The shy awkward girl he remembered had grown up in more than one way with soft curves topped by her long brown hair and a dimpled smile.

He managed to find a way to sit next to her during the picnic. "What do you think of our going to Missouri and the land of the Six Bulls?" he asked.

Shyly, she looked at him and replied, "It sounds exciting, and the trip would be a true adventure. If'n we go, I'll really be looking forward to seeing some of the marvelous things you described. Did you run into any trouble during the trip?"

Thinking about Hooker and Brick, he replied, "Ahh, not too much. There be rivers to ford and ferries to ride. Just you wait until you see the size of them big rivers and you'll be amazed when you see them steamboats. Those floating palaces be as big as hills excepting they be moving on water."

While he spoke, Annie Rose watched him.

He hoped that she was as interested in him as she was in his tales about the trip. "And that isn't all. The prairie grass be as high as a horse's eye and there be large stands of trees dotting the land. I figure Six Bulls be where I want to do my farming."

"I hope my folks decide to go. I'm just dying to see more of this big country."

"Sure they'll go. My folks are keen to leave next spring. Tommy says your folks have the itch, too. Along the trail, I'll show you many amazing things. Have you ever seen a working salt lick?"

The Vorshells attended the celebration and Noah waited until he had a chance to talk to Letha alone. As they walked toward the creek, she asked, "Do you really like Six Bulls?"

"It be fine prairie country," he replied, happy to be walking beside the pretty girl with the long hair. "But I still like this area and, if'n it was left to me, I'd stay right here." He watched her face brighten with his last words.

"Is there no chance you'll be staying in Morgan County . . . I mean your family and you?" asked Letha, her cheeks now burning.

Looking at her, a heavy weight gripped his heart. "I reckon we'll be leaving in the spring. Your father is already thinking about buying some of our land and renting and working the rest."

Her eyes filling with tears, she managed to say, "Will you write to me and let me know how you're doing?"

"Sure I will," Noah replied as the lump in his throat made talking difficult. Taking her hand, they walked along Honey Creek.

Several days later, Abraham walked to the barn with Frederick.

"Pa, I need to talk to you about something that happened on the trail."

"Sure, son. Let's go into the barn for a spell." Sitting on kegs, Abraham saw the worried frown on his son's face. "What is it?"

Straightening, the young man took a deep breath and blurted out, "I had a run-in with Hooker and . . . I killed a man."

Alarmed, Abraham asked, "Hooker? You killed a man?" He looked closely at Frederick and his obvious agony. In a softer voice, he continued, "Tell me about it, son."

Frederick told him the whole story. Then, hanging his head, he continued, "After Hooker rode off, we sent the dead man's body floating down the Missouri River. I've been waiting for a chance to talk to you. I've never had such a miserable burden on my soul and . . . I just needed to tell you."

"Thank God you and the others weren't harmed." Abraham felt both shock and relief. Seeing the mournful expression on his son's face, he said, "There be all kinds of men in this world, and you came across some of the worst ones."

"I didn't mean to kill anyone. I was just defending myself and then . . ." Frederick stared at the barn floor.

Abraham rose and put his arm around his son's shoulders. "In one way, I'm glad that you feel so much hurt at the death of another man. It shows that you have kindness in your heart and a respect for life. That's the way God intends for us to live."

Gazing up at his father, Frederick remained silent.

Abraham continued, "But now you know that there are times when a man has to protect himself. Hooker is a cruel man who lives his life walking under a cloud—a malignant cloud. He has no sympathy for other people or their souls. And the big man you fought was cut from the same cloth."

"I'll never forget seeing his open, dead eyes," murmured Frederick.

"It be true that killing be bad. But, defending yourself be part of living just like I helped protect the country down in New Orleans. There are times when a man does what he has to do. That's part of being a man."

Frederick stood, his face more at ease as the two men clasped each other at arm's length.

"Thanks, Pa, I'm glad we talked."

Afterward, the two walked toward the cabin. Abraham's eyes suddenly clouded and a wave of nausea hit him. Turning quickly to hide his tears, he said over his shoulder, "You go on, son. I left my coat in the barn."

As the tears rolled down his face, he thought, *I'm just a stupid old fool. I knew Hooker was bad right from the start. Still, I pleaded mercy for him and it nearly cost me my son.*

Walking farther, he stopped, looked heavenward, and silently asked, *Lord, what happened to my boy—that was the justice of mercy—wasn't it Lord?*

Chapter Sixteen

1836

T raveling in late spring, Abraham thought the journey to Six Bulls country was marvelous as the Indiana families took the same route that the boys had traveled. Mary seemed much like her old self, as she tended baby Mary who suckled at her breast.

They stayed several days in bustling St. Louis as Mary and Elizabeth shopped and were thrilled at the selection of goods. On Sunday, everyone went to mass at the St. Louis Cathedral, marveling at its size and taken with the gold lettering over the portico.

Inside, Abraham was astounded at the height of the soaring columns supporting the high ceiling and moved by the beauty of the marble altar sanctuary fronting the magnificent painting of Christ. Along the nave, shimmering light filtered through stained glass windows colored with saintly images and frolicking cherubs.

Besides all the new sights, Abraham figured that there was another difference on this trip. Frederick and Annie Rose spent hours riding together and Abraham could see that his son took great delight in pointing out the many new sights to her.

Arriving in Six Bulls country, Abraham and James established their encampment near Lost Creek. Their livestock was in the Sommer's corrals with their equipment and household goods stored in the adjacent barn.

Without exception, Abraham and James accepted the lands marked by their sons the prior year. Abraham admired the way Andres had laid out his land years earlier in a checkerboard fashion. The Carolinian adopted a similar approach beginning with the land just west of his new neighbor. The property lines had stepped saw-tooth corners, running west and north up the hill from Lost Creek to the meadow on the upper prairie. Similarly, other zigzagging lines ran down the other side. Abraham figured that if a flying mockingbird could see the outline, it would resemble a series of squares on a checkerboard running from one corner to another.

He and Mary figured that this layout would readily permit them to section off parcels of land in the future to their children as each started a family of their own.

The Rallemores and Burkeds also laid out the locations for their new cabins, barns, and springhouses.

Abraham bowed his head, listening to Andres' prayer welcoming the families from Indiana to his Fourth of July picnic. His new neighbor had invited them and the former Ohio families to the celebration.

Abraham still couldn't believe that he was in Big Jen's land of the Six Bulls. Smiling, he watched as folks sat at tables under the trees bordering Lost Creek. They were in an area of Andres' farm that everyone referred to as Wela Park.

The women congregated and helped Elsie with the food. Abraham had taken an immediate liking to her and Sarah Leach and all the women seemed to get on fine. Nancy Running Bird was more retiring, which was probably her way, he thought.

Abraham could hear the waters of Lost Creek rushing downstream below the deck that Andres had built overhanging the riverbank. "This is a marvelous setting, Andres."

"Ja, I feel at peace here. I've never been inside a cathedral, but I saw a picture once. I think of Wela Park as God's cathedral with the tall arching trees providing a canopied ceiling the same as in the picture."

"That it be," replied Abraham, thinking back to the St. Louis Cathedral.

"And the river," continued Andres. "It's God's choir. It always be singing to me."

Abraham smiled at the poetry in Andres' thoughts. Yes, he thought, I like this territory and these people. It's good to be in the land of free men.

Tommy strolled across the deck to where Samantha Vogel was standing with her father. "Good to see you again, sir."

"Tommy-me-boy, welcome back," Captain Vogel answered.

Tommy turned and the big red blush was back on his face. "I'm happy to see you, too, Samantha."

The Captain continued, "And I be glad that your family made the trip to Six Bulls." Probably noticing the two blushing young people, the Captain went on, "Will you excuse me, Tommy? I want to meet your papa."

After her father left, Samantha raised her eyes to his. "I knew you'd come back, Thomas."

Tommy blushed even brighter as she brushed away a small tear of happiness.

🐾 🐾

Andres passed around wooden mugs filled with cider. He thought Abraham and James fit right in as though everyone had known each other for years. "You both knew the Jennings fellas, ain't that right?"

"Well, I can only recollect meeting them once when Abraham and Mary first arrived in Morgan County from North Carolina," replied James. "That Big Jen talked so much about Six Bulls that he just naturally planted the seed of this frontier land in our heads."

"I knew them quite well," spoke up Abraham. "Little Jen, he be the leader of our wagon train from North Carolina, and Big Jen, he joined us on the trail. It turns out that Big Jen and I go back to the War of 1812. I met him there at the battle of New Orleans. He was a scout for General Jackson and I was a rifleman. He and I set out one night to spike a big British cannon that kept shooting at us. Afterward, Big Jen held the view that our work that night probably helped Old Hickory Jackson get elected President."

This piqued Captain Vogel's curiosity. "You mean you and Big Jen spiked a cannon in the middle of the whole British army? Why, I heard they had at least ten thousand men at that battle."

"That be about right," Abraham replied. "I was sitting in a rifle pit in the middle of a swamp when I first met Big Jen and heard him talking about horse-eye–high prairie grass, plains full of game, and sweet running water. He darn near talked my ear off he was so full of stories."

"You surely got Big Jen described right," laughed the Captain in his big booming voice.

Andres judged that Abraham and the Captain were about the same age. The Carolinian was slender compared to his Cousin James's broad shoulders, yet even James paled before the size and brawn of the Captain.

"Why if'n it hadn't been for the Jennings fellas," continued Abraham, "I reckon neither James nor I would be in Six Bulls. They filled our heads with all them tales that prompted James and me to send our boys here that you all so kindly received. Thank you for your generous hospitality to them. We be mighty appreciative."

"It be our pleasure," answered Andres. "They be fine young men."

"Say, Amos, your name be Hanks, ain't that right?" asked James.

"Yep."

"My wife and I were born in North Carolina, the same as Abraham and Mary. Many years back, I knew of a family by that name. You got any kin there?"

"My pa used to talk about some relations who be somewhere in them parts," answered Amos.

"This Hanks fellow, his name was William and all this happened before I be born," James continued. "The tales about him were legendary in Rowan County where we hail from. He was some kind of high county official, a justice of the peace, I believe. They even named a river and a village after him.

"Come the War of Independence, he sided with the English and they made him a colonel in their home guard. After the fighting, the state convicted him of being a traitor and confiscated all his land holdings, and let me tell you, he had a parcel. As a result, he up and skedaddled to Canada, abandoning his wife, children, and property to save his neck. His wife tried to fight the state by telling everyone about her aid to Nathaniel Greene, the American general, and her son scouting for him, but she lost everything."

Andres could tell that Amos was listening with a growing measure of discomfort. There was a moment when no one spoke.

Then, Amos said, "My pa, he be a patriot. He volunteered to fight in the War of 1812. They took him up to Cleveland and, of all things, made him a sailor on one of them warships on the big lakes. He was in several battles and the redcoats captured him and took him to some Godforsaken prison called Deadman's Island. He came back to us and lived another fifteen years, but ma always thought he was never the same."

"By golly, Amos, I meant no disrespect . . ." began James.

Interrupting, Amos continued, "Pa sometimes talked about our kin and this William you mentioned. Mostly, it was after he had one or two pulls from the jug he kept at home to ward off the fever. William was his great-uncle and pa had heard that he'd gone off to Canada. To my recollection, we ain't heard from them folks for maybe thirty years."

"Let me tell you," spoke up Abraham, "I heard the same stories as James. This William, he had some younguns, including one also named William. That man worked for thirty years and built himself up one fine plantation. He did so well, he bought back every single acre the state had confiscated. One of his sons and his family were in our wagon train from North Carolina. We were only a week away from Morgan County when we had to stop and wait for the White River to subside after days of heavy rain. Well, the rains ended and the ferry began operating.

"The Hanks' two wagons were next to cross the river and got about half-way when a huge ash tree came around the bend of the river heading right for them. The ferry operator tried to avoid it, but the tree ran them plumb over. We searched for a long time but only found pieces of the wagons."

Andres looked at Abraham, then at Amos. The sad story had dampened all their spirits.

After long moments, Amos broke out in a big smile, saying, "Why, you folks being from the same area as my kin, you're practically family your-selves." With that, everyone laughed, clapped each other on the back, and shook hands all over again. They were now all speaking at once, the joviality having returned to their voices.

Captain Renke spoke up. "Abraham, I was in Morgan County a few years ago. What part be your home? Maybe I know it."

"We farmed outside of Martinsville."

Looking at the Captain, James said, "Say, I remember a captain who was with the militia and came through our town during the Black Hawk War. Be that you?"

"Yep, I was leading a wagon train with supplies for the Ohio volunteers chasing Black Hawk and his war party."

"Well, I'll be," said James. "You know, you gave all of us the proper warn-ing at the right time. We did have an attack on one of the farms a few weeks later. Abraham and my family, as well as others, we all took up our defenses together one night in a neighbor's stoutly-built barn."

"And that's not all," piped up Abraham, beginning a deep hearty laugh. "We did get attacked that night as we sat in the barn with our muskets primed and pointed down the road. But the attacker was an old nanny goat that came out of the dark shadows running straight at us." Laughing harder now and having difficulty getting his words out, he went on, "And you . . . and you . . . James, my old friend, you up and shot that old vicious nanny goat deader than a graveyard slab with your quick trigger finger."

Both men broke up with laughter. The others smiled, a bit unsure where the tale was going. James and Abraham managed to stop laughing long enough to explain the details of the incident to the others whereupon they were all laughing.

Abraham walked to the table and poured himself another cup of cider. Unspoken was the shooting of the Indian boy and our praying over his grave. *Maybe we'll talk about it another time with our new neighbors.* He stood smiling as he watched the other men laughing and talking.

Lost in his own thoughts, he mused, *America is a big country just like Little Jen said. Here we are, thousands of miles from our old farms, building our lives in Missouri, yet our kin or we've been crossing paths over the years. This be more like a gathering of friends, not strangers. The wonder of life and the many turns be truly amazing. Yes, we're all God's younguns,* he thought as another round of laughter broke out. *We be carving out new lives on the frontier as free men.*

Chapter Seventeen

L ate the following winter, Noah approached his father as they were mending harnesses in the newly built barn. Removing his hat, he ran his fingers through his hair. "Pa, I've been doing a lot of thinking and I'd like to talk to you."

"Sure, boy," replied Abraham. *He now be nearing eighteen, a savvy young farmer, and no longer a boy.* He looked up at his lanky son, who was now taller than Frederick. *I think I know what's coming.*

"We still have the farm in Indiana," began his son. "Mr. Vorshell bought part of our acreage and he and his boys be renting the rest and splitting the income with you."

"Yes, son, I be recalling all those facts. You're kind of beating around the bush, aren't you? What be on your mind?"

Noah hesitated, then, squaring himself, he looked at Abraham. "I want to go back to Morgan County. I've always felt a kinship there and that's where I want to do my farming and live my life."

Abraham was not surprised, as Noah had harbored these feelings since leaving Indiana. He also knew that his son had received a letter from Letha the week before that traveled with the latest Burked relatives to arrive from Morgan County. "Well, your mother and I would be real sad to see you go. Have you made up your mind?"

"Yes. The soil is so rich and always producing bumper harvests and the water be good, and . . ."

Smiling, Abraham interrupted, "I know all those facts, son. I suspect a certain young lady be another reason. Ain't that so?"

"Ahh, yes, Letha be there. I got a letter last week and she says she misses me and asks if I'm ever going to return. Pa, I want to go back to Indiana, and, if she'll have me, I'm going to marry her."

This also didn't surprise Abraham. *Well,* he thought, *Letha is a fine young woman.* "Your mother and I have been talking about the Indiana property for quite a while. How about we deed the farm to you? Consider it a wedding gift. You'll need money to fix up the old house and buy seed, livestock, and the rest. We'll lend it to you and you can pay us back as your crops come in."

"Pa, your offer be very generous, but it's too much. Why couldn't I just buy the farm and also pay for it like you said when my crops come in?"

"Noah, your mother and I have acquired Missouri land with the thought of splitting off parcels as our younguns grow up and get married. Frederick received the first, as you know, and has filed a patent for more land. Your mother and me are never going back to live in Morgan County because of her fears. The land there is going to be yours . . . or sold. I got a letter last week, too. It was from Benjamin asking me again if I wouldn't sell the rest of the farm to him." Abraham could tell that this news got his son's attention. "You can't walk on just one leg, son—what's it to be?"

"I'm really thankful for your generous offer and I accept."

"When you figuring to leave?"

"I'd like to help with spring planting, and leave right after that."

"That be good," Abraham said with a smile. "It'll allow the rivers to subside and be a time when you can count on the weather. Son, your ma and I'll miss you and it'll break our hearts to see you leave, but we know you will be in God's hands—and Letha's."

TOWARD THE NEW HORIZONS ~

Many years later . . .

"It is curious that physical courage
should be so common in the world
and moral courage so rare."
Mark Twain

Chapter Eighteen

B right sunshine filled the sky. From the hillside, Abraham gazed down on Lost Creek Valley and the growing village, now called Seneca, as he sat under a tree with Frederick having lunch. "We got a letter from Noah. I can't believe how fast time has flown since your brother returned to our old Indiana farm."

"How are they?" inquired Frederick.

"He and Letha are expecting their sixth youngun this winter. His letter says the farm be producing fine wheat and that the soil be so rich on the last parcel we bought that everyone calls it 'Rallemore Soil.' Noah even sells some of it to other farmers."

"Imagine that, selling dirt," laughed his son. "I'm glad to hear that they're doing well. Maybe one of these days, Annie Rose and I'll go north and pay them a visit. Of course, it'll have to wait until our younguns be grown."

"I brought the letter for you to read."

"Thanks, Pa. We'll read it with interest." Scanning the meadow, he continued, "I appreciate your helping me clear this land. Next year, it'll be fine pasture for cattle."

"I'm happy to lend a hand. Those wagon trains coming through from the southeast on their way to Oregon Territory and the California gold fields sure have added to the demand for our farm goods. Both Andres's and John Leach's trading posts are doing well and we're doing the same selling to them."

"That be true. That's why I'm adding more grazing land for my cattle. Annie Rose and I figure that we can sell more beef next year to the travelers passing through."

Abraham again looked at the valley spread out before him. "I just can't get over how many folks are settling in Six Bulls. The new sawmill and blacksmith shop are mighty busy these days as more prairie ground is plowed and new stores go up in town."

Frederick nodded. "You know, I was working on the new church building last week and it appears that it'll be completed this fall. I never thought we'd get it done in such a hurry."

"Well, once Andres put his mind to it, everything got organized. People want a place where they can worship together with their neighbors. I hear tell that some folks are even talking about adding stained glass to the front windows, similar, I suppose, to the ones we saw in St. Louis."

"Can you believe that?" laughed Frederick. "What in the world would Big Jen say if'n he knew that folks were figuring on stained glass windows in his Six Bulls country?"

"I reckon he'd roll over in his grave and say something like, 'Tarnation!'" Abraham joined in the laughter. "Did you hear that Andres donated some acres down by Lost Creek for a cemetery?"

"Yes, I did. Has he named it yet?"

"Oh, I suppose it'll be called 'The Sommer Cemetery.'"

Shimmering in the morning sunlight, Abraham could make out Lost Creek in the valley below and, off in the distance, Little Lost Creek. The view from the hillside was one of his favorites. Turning to his son, he asked, "How be Annie Rose these days?"

"The morning sickness seems to be behind her as she figures she be in her third month. Early next year, you and ma are going to have two more grandbabies from your sons. How does that make you feel?"

"Tired and old," replied Abraham, smiling. *Frederick and Annie Rose are a good fit even if they be distant cousins,* he figured. *Hell, it's not unusual for cousins to marry here on the frontier where folks are scarce.* "But babies are for you young folks. Nine younguns are all your ma and me could handle. These days, I find that it's much easier for me to play with my grandbabies at your cabin." Chuckling, he continued, "That way, I can go home and have peace and quiet."

"Are you going to the monthly prayers and supper at the Sommer farm on Sunday?"

"Most likely. The group has changed, hasn't it? We don't see much of the Hanks family any more since the death of Seneca. Andrew says that Amos keeps busy with his lead mine."

"That John Leach sure be an enterprising fella," Frederick said.

"That he is. I really admire him. Without his enthusiasm, I'm not sure when our town would have been laid out. I think you, me, and the others will get all of our money back that we invested in the town lots plus a little extra. And I like his idea of building a bridge over Lost Creek. It be just what the town needs. What's more, I also admire Sarah. She really be a strong force in that family."

"That she be," laughed Frederick. "When she puts her mind to a matter, our friend John really jumps."

"Well, that's the way some people are, son."

"I expect that Tommy and Samantha will be attending the gathering on Sunday and I hear they're expecting another youngun."

Chuckling, Abraham noted, "He sure got over his bashfulness in a hurry, didn't he?"

"You got that right. What do you hear about Captain Vogel's boys these days?"

"They be hard working, but they seem to keep to themselves."

"I've got the same view. I saw George down at the new mercantile store last week and he seemed to avoid me."

"I think it began all those years ago when their pa rode out of the boys' lives on the day we were celebrating the founding of our new town. God, what terrible memories that day brings back."

"I'll never forget that Saturday when Seneca was murdered and Captain Vogel took on those dozen ruffians."

"Amen," agreed Abraham. "There was quite a bond between that young man and the Captain. I guess it goes back to the days when the Ohio folks were traveling to Six Bulls and Seneca risked his life to save the Captain's."

"And you recall that Seneca had just won the horserace? He was so happy. And I remember his new bride, Flower On The Water, being excited for him."

Lost in his memories, Abraham went on, "Then all hell broke loose."

"That beer-soused rowdy started it by insulting Flower On The Water and lashing Seneca with his bullwhip."

Abraham was staring at the valley again. "It's still hard for me to believe that they killed Seneca right in front of his family and the whole crowd. Some men be plain mean like those rowdies. It was a sad day for all of us and it was a day of reckoning for them rough men—men cut from the same cloth as Hooker."

"Even I felt intimidated watching the Captain that day."

Abraham gazed at his son for long moments. "I share the feeling, son, yet the Captain was a kind-hearted man and big and strong like a horse. I don't expect we'll ever see him again in this valley. He was right when he said that we should name the new town in honor of Seneca and I'm glad that we did. Wish I'd had the chance to know the Captain longer. He reminded me of the men I fought with in New Orleans— proud, straight forward, and, having made up their minds, set on their purpose."

"Speaking of purposes, about time we got back to ours," said his son, with a laugh.

Chapter Nineteen

Most creeks ran dry and water boils stopped flowing in the summer of 1854. Less than usual rain had been the pattern for the past two years, but this year had been nearly bone-dry. Abraham wondered how long it would last.

One September morning, Abraham rode his horse over a northern hill bordering his property where there was a vast view of the prairie beyond. He had no particular destination as he was simply trying to gauge the effect of the drought on the land and vegetation. Some cattle were off to the right, trailing a lead cow almost single file, and he watched them disappear over the hill. *Going off to drink from Lost Creek,* I reckon.

Breasting another hill, he reined in. To the northeast, there was a large dark smudge in the sky. He decided to ride in that direction and, crossing a valley, traveled about two miles to the top of the next ridge.

Astonished, he saw a distant fire line that seemed to extend for miles to the left and right. Billowing smoke blocked the horizon. He felt a strong sense of apprehension as many thoughts raced through his mind. *Prairies are one of nature's wonders that are seeded, watered, and tended by God, but wildfires are a terrifying scourge. Depending on the wind, one can travel faster than a galloping horse, and the smoke is as deadly as the blaze.*

Gauging the wind, this wildfire was coming toward him and he realized that his farm was directly in its path. *Such fires can last for weeks until they burn themselves out or rain quenches their insatiable thirst .We might be able to divert it, but stopping it totally is in God's hands.*

Aloud, he said, "This looks like a fire straight out of hell."

Spurring his horse, he galloped toward home. Stopping at the Sommer cabin first, he shouted to Elsie, "Wildfire coming our way from the northeast!"

Briefly startled, she recovered and said, "Thanks for the warning. Andres be down by the barn."

Abraham whirled his mount toward the barn where Andres was fixing a wagon. Skidding to a stop, he shouted, "Andres, wildfire heading right for us!"

Andres appeared startled and dropped his tools. "How bad be it?"

"There was a black smudge on the horizon and I rode northeast until I could get a better view. I saw smoke everywhere I looked, and the fire line extended across the horizon. I figure it must be several miles from us. With the direction of the wind, it be coming toward our farms."

Turning, Andres shouted loudly, "Curtis!" As the young man came out of the barn, Andres said, "There's a wildfire coming from the northeast. Take the black stallion and ride up to the top of that hill over there! Take your gun and two flour sacks from the barn with you. Raise one when you can clearly see the fire. Raise two when it be close and coming right at us. Fire the gun to get our attention."

Curtis quickly mounted the horse bareback and left.

"I'm going to my place," said Abraham, "and I'm going to start moving as much of my stock and feed grain toward the river as I can. The best place to fight this monster is at the base of these hills."

Andres was normally a decisive man, but at this instant, he seemed at a loss.

"Andres, we need to do something and do it fast. You be remembering what I told you about the slash and burn method we used in North Carolina to clear new land? We sometimes lit a backfire to control the main blaze by burning a break in the ground cover so the main fire couldn't jump over it.

"I think we should plow a break at the bottom of these hills. It should cause a draft of wind from the river that'll feed the backfire so it burns up the hill toward the main blaze. If the plan works, it can save our cabins and barns. Let's try it."

Andres thought for a moment and then said, "Those be good ideas. Let's harness up our two plows. We can both plow the grasses to make a break at the foot of the hill."

"Right," said Abraham, as he wheeled his horse. Over his shoulder he shouted, "I'll get started just as soon as I can organize the moving of my animals."

Riding up to his cabin, Abraham shouted, "Mary, come quick!"

"What's all the commotion about, Abe?" she asked, running out of the cabin.

"Wildfire coming! Get food and clothes for the family and get the youn-guns organized to take these down to the river. If'n you need to, dampen everything with river water. Send Henry to warn Frederick and Annie Rose. Then, you and the younguns get all of the stock to the river that you can. Andres and I are going to plow a firebreak and set a backfire."

Mary paled, but she turned without a word.

Quickly harnessing his mule team, Abraham began cutting a furrow and saw Andres coming toward him, plowing in a different line. Andres shouted without stopping, "I sent one of my boys to warn the folks in town and to ask for help."

They both stopped as they heard a shot fired. It came from Curtis who was waving a flour sack in the air.

"It be coming," said Abraham as he continued plowing.

Soon, the four Vogel boys arrived in their wagon. Two dropped off near Abraham, and began cutting brush uphill from the plowed rows using a sickle and long-handled axes to drop the smaller trees.

Abraham shouted to one of his boys, "Solomon, you run to the barn and get the hay rake. Then gather the cut grass uphill from the plowed area. We'll burn it in our firebreak."

Spurred by the fear of the approaching fire, all worked feverishly. Sud-denly, they all stopped at the sound of another gunshot.

Curtis was waving both sacks and riding down the hill fast. "It be coming right at us," he shouted as he dismounted. Quickly, the young man began stacking the cut grass and limbs.

Abraham continued plowing as he now came back with another furrow. Andres had disappeared over a small rise leading to his farm. The first folks from town arrived in wagons and on horseback. Some set about helping Mary move grain and stock toward the river. Others went to assist at the Sommer farm.

Sweating heavily, Abraham once again turned, beginning another furrow. Some of the men from town attacked the grass with hoes and shovels to turn over the prairie sod. More townsfolk arrived and began cutting down some of the larger trees on the hillside.

As Abraham and his mule cut still another furrow and neared the cabin, he shouted, "Sampson, you get the bucket and fill it with hot coals from the fireplace. Then bring it out here. Clay, I want you to bring out the two oil lamps from the cabin. Step quickly now."

One of the men from town galloped down the hill. "Abraham, it be only a quarter of a mile from the crest of the hill and the wind be coming directly this way."

"Solomon, take the plow and mules to the river," shouted Abraham.

Men and women from town formed a long bucket brigade bringing water from Lost Creek and were wetting down Abraham's cabin and barn.

Abraham swung onto a nearby horse and quickly rode off to Andres' farm. The Sommer family was making similar preparations. "Andres, a man just reported that the fire be a quarter of a mile away from the hilltop and the wind be blowing it at us. I think it's time to light the backfire." Andres nodded and turned to rush over to a small barrel of lamp oil.

Without waiting, Abraham rode back to his farm and jumped off the horse. He grabbed the oil lamps and shouted to the assembled group, "BACKFIRE! Watch out for the backfire and stand on the river side of the plowed area."

With that, he and Sampson started broadcasting the oil. "We need more oil. Solomon, get the oil barrel from the barn and hurry."

After spreading the oil along the edge of the furrows, men began lighting it. The fire quickly spread along the line in the dry vegetation.

As the fire burned uphill, Abraham felt a new breeze coming from the direction of Lost Creek. The flames spread as smoke filled the air. "Get down!" he shouted. "Everyone stay down and lay on the ground!" Covering his face with his handkerchief, he saw that his boys and most of the town folks followed his directions.

The wait seemed an eternity to Abraham and then he felt the breeze freshen, as the small blaze expanded and raced up the hill. Beyond the crest, he now heard a shockingly loud noise like the roaring sound of a huge waterfall as the big prairie fire moved up the other side of the hill. Peering through the smoky haze beyond his fire line, animals of every type ran for the river, fleeing from the inferno.

Abraham kept trying to see up the hill through the smoke. It took about fifteen minutes before he could make out the crest of the blackened hill. The backfire had made it to the top and soon big wisps of brown and black and white smoke were visible.

Suddenly, there was a loud cheer as the voices of everyone rang out in victory.

🐿️ 🐿️

Hours later, Abraham found Mary crying outside the cabin as she surveyed the destruction.

"I can't believe all the soot and ash," she sobbed, her once clean apron blackened. "It's covering everything," There were dark smudges on her face as she stood looking at the scars of the fire.

"The charring looks worse than it really is, Mary," he soothed. "You know our land clearing in North Carolina produced the same as we see here. The ash will add richness to the soil and things will be greening up before we know it."

"I know," she responded, running a hand through her graying mussed hair. "But I just can't help but feel low seeing all the burned area. Thanks be to our holy mother that no one was injured or killed in this wicked thing, but I'm so sad that Annie Rose and Frederick lost their cabin."

🐿️ 🐿️

In the fall, Mary planned a picnic party for Abraham's sixtieth birthday. Andres offered his Wela Park deck above Lost Creek for the celebration and all of their neighbors and family attended.

"Hey, old timer," called out Andres. "It be your birthday and you being so ancient and wise . . ." He paused as many chuckled over his good-natured ribbing. "I figure you must have some keen insights to share with all your friends. Give us a few words."

"C'mon, everyone," John Leach shouted to the group. "Let's give him some encouragement," he said, clapping his hands.

Abraham was embarrassed, but he stood to address the gathering. "Well, my hair has turned nearly as white as snow, but I don't know that my advancing years give me any special wisdom."

Raising his cup of strawberry wine, he toasted the group. "Here's to my family and friends, and particularly to you, Mary, as you are my life." He saw her beaming, her silvery hair shining in the sun. "And thanks to all of you for being such good neighbors and helping us beat the wildfire last summer. We can thank God for the new life that already be sprouting out of the ashes."

"Amen" echoed among the group.

"All of you know that Mary and I be from North Carolina and that we tried farming in Indiana before we came to Six Bulls. We left North Carolina because the soil was wearing out too fast and farming there depended on using slaves. I'm glad that we settled where slavery isn't a way of life."

Several people gave him a surprised look.

"Slavery be an evil thing and Mary and I know because that was the way it was in the Carolinas. I've thought my whole life that it be against God's wishes. A wise friend once told me that what be inside a man is his true mettle and that God be blind to color. During my life, I've learned that he was right.

"One reason I love this valley is because we have men and women who are willing to work. They be self-reliant and are people who value family and God. I love the smell of free air and I love the fact that our valley be free of slavery. Good health to each and every one of you, and thank you for celebrating with me," he concluded, lifting his cup again as more clapping broke out.

There were shouts of, "Here, here!" from some, including the Vogel boys, but he also noticed doubtful stares from others. The thought crossed Abraham's mind that some were disagreeing with his slavery remarks. There were a few slaves in this corner of Missouri, but he knew that that was the extent of it. Much to his surprise, his friend and neighbor, Andres, was one of those giving him a curious look.

Chapter Twenty

There was an unusual chill in the air during the spring of 1855. Rainy days gave way to frosty nights, and glimpses of the sun lacked warmth. It was then that it began.

Abraham heard in town that some folks on an outlying farm first came down with the ague, then it spread. No one knew how or why it came. Headaches, high fevers, and shivering fits of chills were the signs. Some got better—some died.

One dark cold morning, Mary said, "Abe, I've got both the chills running up and down my body and I'm hot with a fever. I'd like to lie down again and try to sleep some more."

Alarmed, he answered, "You probably just caught a draft of that north wind."

"Just the same, why don't you take the younguns to Frederick's so they can stay there for a few days?"

On his way home, Abraham thought about the remedies people were using to ward off the sickness. Some put sliced potatoes on their foreheads covered with a damp cloth, saying that a headache would be gone when the potatoes turned dark. Others concocted and drank a thick syrupy potion made with noxious weeds, bitter roots, and onions, then sweetened with honey. A few wore garlic in a cloth bag around their necks to ward off the illness. He'd try some of these with Mary.

Once he had the potatoes and damp rag on Mary's forehead, he turned to a remedy that his mother had taught him. He set a pot over the fireplace to boil beef kidneys. He wrapped the heated organs to the soles of her feet with a cloth, which caused Mary to break out in a sweat.

After a spell, Mary whispered, "I feel a might better, Abe." As she turned away to cough, the white streaks in her hair caught the weak sunlight.

Abraham stayed at her side feeding her chicken broth and wiping her face and arms with a damp cloth. In the following days, Mary grew pale and her eyes became red as coughing spells wracked her.

The town of Seneca now had a doctor and he visited Mary, but there was little that he could do. Outside the cabin, the doctor gave his opinion. "Best to let her rest and keep her wiped down with a damp cloth. You can try the kidneys again, but I've little faith in such remedies. I'm sorry, but there's nothing more that I can do."

After the visit Mary murmured, "Abe, my strength be failing and I think my time be near."

"No, don't talk that way!" said Abraham, his voice cracking with concern. "You'll get better, you'll see. Can you take more hot broth?"

When Mary slept, Abraham prayed. *God, she's been my best friend and wife for over forty years. Please, let her get well. The younguns need her . . . I need her.*

The next morning, she seemed worse.

As he wiped her forehead, she hoarsely whispered, "My husband, thank you for marrying me. I've loved you all my life and I love our children. Please write to Noah. Tell them all how much I love them. And you, I want you to watch over them. Promise me you'll do that."

"You'll get better, just you wait and see. It just takes time to get your strength back."

"Abe, promise me," she repeated.

"Of course, my dear, and you'll be right here helping me."

Mary looked at him, tears clouding her eyes. After a long pause, she whispered, "Please hold my hand . . . ."

Mary died the next day.

🐿 🐿

"My friend," said Andres. "It would be an honor if'n you'd let me help you dig Mary's grave in the cemetery."

His mind adrift, understanding came slowly to Abraham. Focusing on Andres, he answered, "I appreciate your offer, but my Mary, she has to be sheltered from the wind in her last resting place. There be a hollow on Frederick's farm. I'll rest her there."

"I know she'd like that," added Elsie. "She needs wrapping and I have a fine old quilt for her."

Abraham mumbled his thanks, having trouble separating his muddled thoughts. *My beautiful Mary, she be gone. I'll never again see her bright smile, feel her long hair between my fingers, or see her standing with her hands on her hips giving me that look. God, I'm going to be lost without her.*

Straightening, he lectured himself. *Buck up. The younguns will need a strong shoulder. No carrying on now—there be plenty of time for that later.*

The new preacher, Minister Hood, led the prayer as family and friends stood at the gravesite, heads bowed, tears flowing.

The youngus will miss her, thought Abraham, *but no one will miss her more than me.*

🐾 🐾

Two weeks later, Ilse Sommer died from the same illness. It seemed to fly up Lost Creek Valley and then down again.

Abraham helped to dig her grave. Tears filled his eyes as his friend, Andres, stood stoically at the site, head down, hat in hand, gathering his youngest children close. Ilse was forty-eight, and attending the funeral were her ten children and ten grandchildren.

Curtis was standing next to Andres. The young man closed his eyes as men lowered his mother to her final rest.

The year of death be upon us, Abraham thought as Minister Hood again solemnly presided over a fresh grave.

🐾 🐾

When James died, it happened suddenly and it shocked everyone who knew the big good-natured man.

Nearly beside herself with fear, Elizabeth sent for Abraham. She told him that James had been chopping wood when the ax slipped, causing a deep gash in his leg. At first, she said that James had dismissed it as simply another one of his small accidents and had stopped the bleeding by wrapping an old cloth around the cut.

Abraham examined the wound and he, too, became concerned.

James joked about it and the fuss they were making over him.

Abraham cleaned the wound and packed the spider webs gathered by Elizabeth into the cut before tightly wrapping the leg with a clean cloth.

The following day James began having headaches and muscle spasms in his jaw. In the days that followed, a high fever set in and he had increasing difficulty moving his arms and legs. He died the next week, his body wracked by pain.

Tears came to Abraham's eyes as he, Frederick, and Tommy dug the new grave. He had sat with James in those final hours and reckoned that his friend had died of lockjaw. He wondered how Elizabeth would fair, and the memory of Widow Henry came flooding back to him. With the help of her grown children, he thought Elizabeth would manage.

Abraham felt like his world had turned upside-down as the loss of Mary struck him hard. He found himself moving about the cabin, picking up items she would have touched every day. In quick succession, so many others had died that there seemed to be no end. His mind replayed the many burials he had attended presided over by Minister Hood.

On the last day of the year, Abraham pulled his quilt closer around his shoulders to ward off the night's cold as the winter wind lashed the snow outside his cabin. He stooped over from his rocking chair and prodded the fireplace embers trying to stir up more heat.

Sitting alone, he thought back on the year of death in Lost Creek Valley. *I'll go to bed for the rest of my days missing my Mary and all the friends I've lost. Things around here can only get better as it surely can't get any worse.*

There was no way for him to know how wrong he was.

Chapter Twenty-one

S tiffly, Abraham dismounted his horse near Lost Creek. Many years earlier, he and Andres had jointly constructed a waterwheel that provided irrigation to both their cornfields. Today, they were going to repair it.

A chill had come into their friendship. Their recent discussions about slavery and states' rights had become angry arguments, with neither man backing down, like the last time a few months ago.

"I don't understand how you can be defending slavery," Abraham had said, irritably.

"And I don't understand how you can be so hard-headed that you don't see the obvious. The Washington bureaucrats are taking away our rights to decide things for ourselves. The election of 1860 will be all about the rights of states to set their own laws," Andres had retorted.

The Carolinian knew the increased distance between them was more than their political disagreement. As he rode to the river that morning, he recalled how it had soured when Andres had taken another wife about a year after Ilse's death. Marrying again wasn't unusual on the frontier. After all, Andres was a successful man, having passed his fiftieth birthday, and he had youngsters to think about and a large farm to run.

The age of Andres' bride had troubled him. Ella Mae, a girl from a neighboring farm, had just past her fifteenth birthday, nearly the same age as his youngest daughter. Abraham had found this unsettling and, not knowing what else to do, he responded by avoiding his long-time friend.

That's not to take anything away from Ella Mae, thought Abraham. Even from a distance, he had learned over the years to admire her gumption and grit.

Shaking his mane of white hair, Abraham thought about those early days in the young gal's new life. *I can't even imagine what that family went through and what that slip of a gal confronted. Why, seven of Andres' younguns were older than she was, and rumor had it that at least one of Andres' boys had been sweet on her earlier on. Sure, Andres had asked them* to call her "auntie" instead of "ma," but that didn't solve anything. *That big family had its own routine only to have this young gal show up with the children's grief still fresh over losing their mother.*

There was bound to be trouble and there was, recalled Abraham. *Andres' older children hadn't cottoned to taking orders from a new mother figure. The natural function of discipline and respect between parent and youngsters had been broken and the stress showed. Two of Andres's boys, Marion and Jonah, had run off, apparently joining a wagon train bound for the west. To the best of Abraham's knowledge, there was never any word about their whereabouts, although he knew Andres had sent Curtis as far as Independence, Missouri, to search for them.*

For a young gal thrown into that family stew, she came through it well. She has a lot of get-up and backbone, mused Abraham. *As for Andres, he thinks he's a stud, looking to sire most of the new younguns in the county all by himself. He already has three younguns with the new wife to go with his previous ten, and Ella Mae be pregnant again. That be a parcel of younguns.*

His back stiffening, he walked slowly along the riverbank, waiting for Andres.

🐞 🐞

The man riding toward them seemed familiar to Abraham. Trail dust covered the horse and the man's head hung down, hiding his face beneath the wide-brimmed hat.

"That fella looks plumb tuckered out," Abraham observed.

Coming closer, the horseman waded through Lost Creek, his tired mount just managing to climb the bank.

"If'n I didn't know better, I'd swear that it's . . .," said Andres, as his words trailed off. Shaking his head, he continued, "Can't be."

As the stranger stopped and lifted his head, Abraham heard Andres say, "Ja, by Jove!" Striding toward the man, Andres called out, "Captain, be that you?"

The stranger nodded. Covered with trail dust, he was dressed in a dark suit from his black hat to his black boots. His shirt must have been white once, but now it was a dirty gray. The man's silvery hair hung down to his shoulders.

"Hello, Andres."

In that moment, Abraham recognized the voice. It was Captain Renke Vogel.

"Renke, my friend," Andres greeted him. "Where've you been?"

"Around."

"Come, get off your horse," said Andres. "You look dead tired."

The Captain dismounted with difficulty and Abraham noticed that his face looked drawn.

In the next moment, Andres was hugging him and smiling broadly. "My God, it's good to see you again. You remember Abraham Rallemore, don't you? He and his family came to Six Bulls from Indiana?"

"How do, Abraham. It's been a long time."

Abraham shook his hand and said, "Glad to see that you're back. Are you staying for awhile?"

The Captain looked at him and a thin smile came to his haggard face. "Forever," he answered.

The three men walked to Abraham's springhouse for a cool drink of cider.

"Tell us what you've been doing," said Andres. "Where did you come from?"

"Out west in the California gold fields," replied the Captain.

"My God, man," said Abraham. "You mean to say that you rode all that way on horseback?"

The Captain nodded.

"You look much thinner and . . . tired," said Andres, concern reflected in his voice.

"I am."

Studying the Captain, Abraham noticed the dark shadows beneath his eyes. The suit hung on him as though purchased for someone even larger. The man had really changed.

In a low matter-of-fact voice, Renke said, "I've been to the old homestead and talked with my boys. They be about as cold as a high mountain lake, saying that they've been living with the shame I brought on the family ever since the day we celebrated the new town. And I guess I did. All my life, I've always been one to let out my passions."

"Nonsense," replied Andres. "Those rowdies were drunken rabble just looking for trouble. Only they never expected to meet up with someone like you."

"Perhaps," said Renke, in a tired voice. "But that be water down the stream."

"Where are you staying?" asked Abraham.

"With no welcome from my boys, I guess I don't know."

"I've got a spare bedroom and you're welcome to stay with me," replied Abraham. "My Mary died some years ago and my younguns be grown and married."

The Captain gave him a long look. "Thank you. That be a generous offer and I'll take you up on it. I'll not stay long."

The way he said the words sent a shiver down Abraham's back as though a chill wind was blowing. He noticed Andres staring at his friend.

"Renke, what is it?" Andres asked.

"I've got a cancer," the Captain replied. "I came home to be buried in Six Bulls."

🐦 🐦

After a welcome home supper at Andres' cabin, the three men sat outside in the warm evening. Night was coming and already crickets and the loud saw-like buzzing of the cicadas serenaded the evening as Ella Mae joined them.

Abraham noticed that the Captain gave the young woman an appraising look before he turned to Andres.

"I've got a message for you, Andres, from your boy, Jonah," the Captain said.

"What did you say?" asked the startled Andres. "You've seen my boys? Are they alright? Where are they? Are they coming home?" he asked in quick succession.

"They be fine," the Captain replied. "They be in the gold fields the last time I saw them. Jonah says he'll see you some day after he travels the Oregon Territory."

Andres seemed to be having difficulty catching up with the notion that his boys were in far away California. Interestingly, Abraham also noticed that Ella Mae was now leaning forward, her eyes fixed on the Captain.

The Captain fumbled in his vest pocket. "And Jonah asked me to give you this," handing a small rock to Andres. It glinted strangely in the flickering firelight. "It be a gold nugget from his prospecting."

"And what about Marion?" Andres asked. "Did you see him? Did he send a message, too?"

The Captain didn't speak for long moments, staring at the fire. "He goes by the name of Frank these days. All he would say was that he has no home."

Andres paled and looked away. To Abraham's surprise, Ella Mae quickly rose and left, saying she had chores to do, but not before he saw tears in her eyes.

🐿 🐿

Over the next days, Andres visited his friend often at Abraham's cabin. The once proud and strong Renke was weakening fast.

"I took Renke with me this morning when I visited Mary," Abraham told his neighbor.

"It be restful in that hollow," the Captain added.

Intuitively, Abraham knew that Renke was thinking about his final resting place, perhaps in the Sommer Cemetery. With the acrimonious relationship with his sons, it was unlikely that it would be on the land the Captain had originally settled.

"How be your pain?" Andres asked, his voice reflecting worry and concern.

"I've got something that helps," Renke replied.

These fellas are too sorrowful thought Abraham. *Best we be talking about something else.* Turning to Andres, he asked, "Who're you going to vote for in the presidential election this year?"

Without hesitation, his friend replied, "Well, it won't be for that Lincoln fella. If'n that man be elected, he'll split this country apart."

"Why be that?" asked Renke.

"That man be bent on destroying our republic form of government and denying the rights of states to set their own laws," Andres replied.

The Captain gave his old friend a long look. "If war comes and Americans end up fighting each other—what then?"

"If'n that's what it takes to have the rights my pa fought for in 1776, so be it," retorted Andres.

"Ahh, Andres, I wish you hadn't said that," the Captain replied in a low whispered voice.

🐾 🐾

The next day, Abraham returned from his daily visit to Mary. The Captain was gone, but a small nugget weighed down a note on the table—

> *"Abraham,*
>> *It be my time. I ask for one last favor. I would be much obliged if you would allow me a final resting place in the hollow. Thank you for your kindness.*
>> *Renke"*

Sad and weary, Abraham set out for Andres' cabin.

Chapter Twenty-two

N earing his sixty-sixth birthday, Abraham found that the days were long and life was empty without Mary. Over the passing years, his heartache had eased, but he missed her presence, hearing her talk about everyday life, and sharing things that only occur between two people who are nearly one. Many days, he sat beside her grave.

Rain had fallen steadily during the past week as Abraham sat at a table near the fireplace, a quilt wrapped around his shoulders. Stiff and aching with the pain of age, he was writing a letter to Mary, as was his way when the weather prevented him from visiting her. He'd leave it in the hollow log behind the cross with the others.

> *"Dearest Mary,*
>
> *Again the weather keeps me from visiting you these many days, yet I long to be sitting beside you and talking to you.*
>
> *I am worried, Mary dear. There be an angry smell in the political winds these days and changes are coming. If you were here, I know how worried you would be.*
>
> *Some politicians said that the 1860 presidential election was about states' rights, but there is little doubt in my mind that the question of slavery has brought the whole country to a breaking point.*
>
> *I am not politically active, as you know, but I was surprised to find out the other day that only 10 men in the county joined me in voting for Lincoln.*
>
> *We got us a weekly newspaper in town now called the Seneca News-Dispatch and it carried the stories about the secession of states led by South Carolina. Missouri is the largest northern state and it is highly prized by both sides*

as St. Louis straddles three major rivers. How lucky can we be?

I miss you and comfort myself knowing that we'll soon be together, but I need to watch over our family now more than ever during these dangerous times.

All my love,

Abe"

🐾 🐾

As other states withdrew from the Union, some of the strangest things Abraham could imagine began to happen. The administration in Washington, D.C. had demanded that Missouri provide four regiments of troops. Claiborne Jackson, the newly elected state governor, had refused, leading the Union Army to seize the St. Louis arsenal. Then Washington had issued an edict replacing all the state office holders followed by Missourians holding a state convention to reaffirm the previously elected state officials, including the governor. In a short span of time, Missouri had two sitting governors.

Hearing that a rump session of the "duly elected legislators" was going to meet in Neosho, Abraham decided to attend, trying to make sense out of the bewildering events. Sitting in a crowded gallery, he was astonished to hear the representatives of the people vote for secession and elect legislators to the Confederate Congress as most onlookers cheered.

🐾 🐾

Abraham shifted uncomfortably in his saddle. *My rheumatism really be acting up today*, he thought, as he rode home from Neosho.

He was deeply confused and troubled. The colonies had stood together to fight for their independence from England, the most powerful nation in the world. Again, the two countries had fought in the War of 1812. He recalled his days in New Orleans and the many men from all walks of life and races that had fought together and won against overwhelming odds.

If it came to war, he guessed that it would set friend against friend and drive brothers apart. He felt a tear run down his cheek as he rode westward. *This is going to tear this country from one end to the other*, he thought, *and all of it is over the question of slavery.*

He stopped at Andres' farm and told him what he had witnessed.

"What were you expecting, with the Federal Government presiding as the 'Satanic Majesty' and issuing rulings and demands?" said Andres. "They be butting their noses into everything where they've got no right. It's time that folks stood up to them."

"But this whole matter of secession is over the question of slavery," replied Abraham, again covering familiar ground with his friend. "Mary and I traveled thousands of miles to be rid of that system and now the whole country be torn apart by it. You don't approve of slavery, do you Andres?"

"No, Abraham, I don't. But it be up to the states to say whether it be permitted or not, not some political hacks back in Washington."

"Those people in Washington work for us," replied Abraham. "And if'n we say slavery is wrong, then they have to enforce our will. Surely, the ties that bind us are stronger than the winds that pull us apart. And right or wrong, America is our country, yours and mine."

Andres looked at him for a long moment. "Look, old friend, you see the situation through the window of slavery and I'm sympathetic to your view. But I see it through another window—states rights against the Washington power-grabbing politicians who, given the chance, want to tell everyone how to live their lives. Power begets money, and both produce officials who think they know better than we folks do. There be a deep-seated division in this old union of ours, and separation may be the only way—two countries instead of one."

"I worked hard to find an alternative to slavery," Abraham heatedly replied. "You know that. There be no crop important enough to warrant a slave system. Thank God, Missouri be almost free of it."

Andres let out a sigh. "Well, is it?" he asked, fingering a strand of his beard.

"Yes, there be some slaves in the county, but nothing like we had back in North Carolina."

Studying his friend for a moment, Andres continued, "Look at the farm help we use right here in Lost Creek Valley. I have fourteen children and you have nine. Have all of them worked on our farms? Do they really have a say on what they want to do? Do you or I pay them a wage beyond their keep? You and me, we expect and demand that they work for us."

"Surely, you ain't saying that slavery and our children working on our farms be the same?" Abraham answered angrily.

"Not exactly, but it be worth thinking about, isn't it?"

Abraham was stunned. Linking the two had never occurred to him. He had worked on his father's plantation just as his father had before him. It'd been like that forever as farms passed down within a family, so it wasn't like working for someone else. "I'm sorry you see the situation as you do, Andres. I couldn't disagree with you more."

Andres shrugged. "Alright Abraham, let's agree to disagree, yet I think there be other important matters to think on. Dangerous times already be here with deserters from both sides joining up with the bushwhackers. Those animals are terrorizing people and destroying farms carved out of the frontier. I also believe this here land we love is likely to become a battlefield."

Abraham looked at him quizzically.

"Armies need supplies and guns and musket balls. This area has lead deposits running from Amos' land clear up to Joplin. Unless both sides back down, they're going to be fighting over those mines right here in Six Bulls country and it'll make no difference what you and I think about this war. I'm wondering if our prairies will soon be covered with blankets of blood."

Abraham stared at his friend. *Could he be right? Would there be battles right here in Lost Creek Valley?* He was at a loss for words. Instead, he sharply replied, "I hope you're as wrong about that as you are on the question of slavery. Good day to you."

With that, Abraham slowly rode home. *It's already started right here in Six Bulls,* he thought, *with neighbor turning against neighbor. If'n Andres is right, maybe even battles will be fought on our farms. Why, Lord, have thee allowed this?*

He stopped beside Mary's grave, painfully dismounted, and sat on a stump. Speaking to her aloud as he often did, he said, "We had so many happy times in this valley, Mary." Pulling a few weeds, he rearranged the flowers on her grave.

"There be terrible pain coming. I fear for our younguns and our friends." Laying his hat on the ground, he looked at the horizon. "And Mary, it be hard to understand, but the question of slavery be at the center of the quarrel. Can you believe that? We've come all this way and after all these years . . . that issue is now dividing our country."

Chapter Twenty-three

K neeling at Mary's resting place, Abraham quickly wiped his eyes and nose with a handkerchief at the sound of an approaching wagon. Looking up, he rose as saw John Leach stop his team.

"How goes it today?" asked the younger man.

"Oh, about the same," replied Abraham, managing to control his emotions.

"Good. I'm going to Joplin in the morning to buy supplies for my trading post. Come along with me, why don't you?"

Abraham shook his head. "Thanks John, but I got my chores to do. You go ahead."

Stepping down, John stood by the grave. A wooden cross was at one end, already starting to weather. "It'll do you worlds of good to ride the prairie and visit the big town. It'll give you a chance to talk with folks. As for your chore of tending Mary's grave, the weeds will wait. What do you say old friend?"

"No need bothering for me," replied Abraham with a small smile.

"Hey, I'm looking out for myself. I've made that trip so many times that I get bored. I'd like the company and besides, given the times, it's best not to travel alone."

Almost reluctantly, Abraham nodded. "Alright, maybe it'll do me some good."

🐾 🐾

The next day the weather was mild and the trail was good for wagon traffic. Abraham figured the trip would likely take all day if the weather held. They traveled north most of the morning over the prairie, watching for game trails and waving to the few travelers going south toward Seneca—most folks avoided being alone out on the prairie these days.

"God, this country be pretty," said Abraham. "I never cease to be amazed at the length and breadth of the horizon when you see it from a hilltop. Mary

-167-

loved Lost Creek Valley. I think back to the places we lived and this was her favorite. It's mine, too."

John nodded and looked at the older man.

He wants to comfort me, thought Abraham, *but he's unsure what to say.* "It's alright, John. Losing Mary has hit my soul some hard licks, but I talk about her all the time . . . and, when the weather permits, I talk to her daily at her resting place."

Trying to sound positive, John carried on. "This land be different now than when we first arrived, but I like the feeling I get when I'm out like this with the big sky before me. Ohio was alright, but I really like Six Bulls country. I often think kindly about the trip Sarah and I made with the other families traveling on the big rivers and the adventures even though we lost . . ."

Abraham guessed that John had stopped in mid-sentence to avoid talking about death. He knew the stories about the baby the Leaches had lost on their trip to Six Bulls. To change the direction of their discussion, he said, "Out here on the prairie, a man feels as big as the horizon and there's nothing he can't do. That's why I hate this war and I'm damn mad at the way the bushwhackers can roam over the land. "

"You got that right, Abraham. When I think about Six Bulls country, there is also a special feeling that folks get when they come together to build something like all of us have done here on the frontier. A special relationship develops and I feel it with you and Andres. Can you understand what I be saying?"

"I do. And I completely agree."

They rested the horses briefly on a rise while surveying the valley before them. The trail was apparent, and in the distance, there was a line of trees indicating a stream passing through.

John's two-horse team started out again and Abraham could tell the love this man had for his animals.

"Giddy-up, Flora, move over, Queenie. That's a good girl."

Beyond the next ridge, they passed close to the trees that Abraham had noticed from the hill. Crossing the stream, suddenly three, then perhaps half a dozen, horsemen brandishing guns were upon them, bandanas covering their lower faces, their horses snorting as they excitedly pranced.

Abraham shouted, "John, look out!"

"Stop yar wagon and drop your guns," one bandit commanded loudly.

In the same instant, John slapped the reins on the backs of his horses and they bolted ahead, tossing the rattling wagon from side to side.

The Seneca men were too far from the safety of Joplin, and Abraham knew they couldn't outrun the outlaws. He shouted, "John, head for the next hill up yonder. Maybe we can find some cover and make a stand there."

John nodded. "Aha!" he shouted, urging his horses up the hill. "C'mon Flora—faster Queenie!"

Abraham glanced back at the bushwhackers. Their intent was clear despite the lack of gunfire. He figured they were after their horses and money.

Minister Hood had railed from the pulpit about the bushwhackers riding freely in the territory. They took strength in riding in gangs, easily overcoming settlers on remote farms, plying their trade of thieving and killing. Seneca had hired a sheriff some years earlier, but he had quit and moved on. With the war, men were in short supply and the lawman position remained open.

"There's no accounting for the likes of these kinds of men," Abraham shouted.

Lashing the horses up the hill, John spun the team and wagon around and pulled up. Abraham climbed down with his rifle and he and John took cover behind a fallen tree.

The thieves reined in at the bottom of the hill, and took cover. Still, there were no shots fired.

Abraham surveyed their position and found that it was poor. The bandits could take several routes to outflank them.

"What do we do now?" John wondered aloud.

"It looks like a Carolina stew," observed Abraham. "I guess we'll wait and see what the day has in store for us. I think I'll go to the other side of the hill and see how the land lays out."

"Alright, but you be careful. I don't want to be carrying you back in my wagon with you bleeding all over it." John meant it as a joke, but it came out well short of humor.

"Be back soon." Abraham ran for the opposite side, keeping low. There were other places to hide, but he also noted this was equally true for anyone coming up the hill behind them. Scurrying back to John, he reported, "We could make a run for it down the back side of this hill, but there aren't any good places for us here."

John looked at him. "The men below haven't changed position much. Wonder what they'll do next?"

His answer was not long in coming. A shot rang out, clipping a branch over their heads. "Throw out your guns where we can see them," the leader shouted. "Then step out from behind that tree. You've fine horses and money we be wanting. Do as I say and you can stay alive."

Two bandits disappeared, riding westward around the base of the hill. "Those two will likely come up behind us," Abraham noted.

After a few minutes, the bandit shouted once more. "All we wants be your horses and money. Take your kit and leave. We'll give you two minutes to think it over."

"Them two fellas will be rounding on the other side of the hill in the next couple of minutes," Abraham whispered.

"I know. There be no sense in giving in to such men. They're as likely to kill us as let us go, depending on their whim."

"Reckon so," replied Abraham. Their situation was perilous.

"Let's make a run for it," suggested John. "You drive the wagon and we'll go down the other side of the hill. I'll lie in the bed with our two rifles and see if I can wing one or two to discourage them."

"I think it's the only thing we can do," agreed Abraham. "I'm ready when you are."

At John's signal, Abraham quickly climbed to the seat and John rolled into the wagon bed.

"AHA!" shouted Abraham, reining the horses hard to his right. "Oooeeee, get up you little darlings, let's fly!" he shouted as he brought the whip down sharply on their haunches. The wagon hurtled down the hill, spewing dirt back over their trail.

Suddenly, one of the bandits coming up the backside of the hill rode out of the trees in front of them.

"If'n that man thinks I'm stopping, he's got a surprise coming," Abraham shouted in the wind. Never flinching, Abraham veered the horses and wagon right at the man. Abraham could see the surprise on the outlaw's face, then his mount bucked and bolted, throwing the bandit under the team's pounding hoofs.

"One down," yelled John over his shoulder as he desperately held on to the sides of the bouncing wagon.

Abraham quickly glanced over his shoulder and saw the second bushwhacker riding hard on their trail. A shot rang out and Abraham heard a cry from John. Looking back, there was blood on the side of John's head and he was no longer holding onto the sides of the jarring wagon. Behind, the bandit was riding low in his saddle and kicking his horse to overtake the slower wagon.

There was little time for thinking as Abraham slapped the reins calling out to the horses, "Aha, aha! Run your legs off, my beauties!"

Looking back once more, he noticed that the rider was much closer now and was preparing to jump to the wagon. Just as he was poised, John rolled over, leveled his gun, and fired, the bullet knocking the man off his horse.

"Halleluiah," yelled Abraham. He looked back once more and, in the distance, the other bushwhackers had now come around the hill and had reined in.

After a long run, Abraham eased the horses up so he could tend to John. The younger man was lying on his back with his eyes closed as blood streamed from the head wound. There was no sign of the bushwhackers as Abraham headed for a stand of trees, before sliding the team to a halt.

Jumping out, he bent over John.

The younger man was dead.

Uncontrollably, Abraham found himself weeping as he held and rocked the younger man in his arms. "Here be a fine enterprising man with a wife and six younguns," he cried out, his voice filling the prairie. "He be off to a better place now, but lost to his family. Why is all this happening, Lord?"

Chapter Twenty-four

Wailing sounds came from within the Leach home as Abraham stood by the fence. With him were Andres and his sons, the Vogel boys, Frederick, Tommy, and many from town.

Suddenly, the back door burst open and John's oldest daughter, Emaline, ran out clutching her father's blood-soaked shirt. Sobbing, she headed toward their barn. Behind her, Sarah came out of the door. She stopped and watched her daughter disappear before she turned and strode toward them with purpose. Her eyes were red, but her features were set.

"You fellows owe it to this family to track down them no-good bushwhackers that did this terrible deed to my John," she said. Getting no instant reply, she went on in a strong voice, "Are you listening to me?"

Abraham nodded. "We'll try and get them, Sarah."

"No, you didn't hear me, Abraham," she quickly responded. "I didn't say 'try.' I said you go out and find them low-lifes! Then, you hang them vermin from the closest tree until they be properly dead. And don't you rest until you've got it done. Now, be that clear enough for you?" Her pale and drawn face belied her deep inner rage.

Turning to Captain Vogel's oldest son, she said, "George, you got the best hunting dogs in these parts. Them can find these scallywags, can't they?"

"Most likely, ma'am."

"And you, Curtis, you be tracking game all your life. Think you can follow those animals that killed my John?"

"You know I'll do my best."

"Abraham, you've been in the army. You'll take the lead?"

Abraham nodded.

Sarah, her tight-lipped mouth set and her bearing straight, continued, "Good. I'll wait until you bring them back—dead or alive—before I do my crying."

Abraham thought, *this be a woman had a lot of sand.*

🐿 🐿

His aching bones warmed by the sun, Abraham sat his horse on a high ridge overlooking the river. George's dogs had had difficulty holding the trail, but Curtis was savvy about tracking and the posse had come quite a distance following the bushwhackers. An old chap in neighboring Cassville had told them about Roaring River and the narrow canyon, including the loud magnified sounds made by the water rushing out of the heavily rocked cave.

They sure named this river right, Abraham thought. As the twelve Lost Creek men stared down from the ridge, he knew that they had a fight on their hands. Rising smoke near the mouth of the cave indicated a campfire, although there were no signs of the bandits.

"Probably preparing to fix their midday meal," Andres observed.

Abraham studied the lay of the land, then turned to his men. "Curtis, do you think you can find a way to get down to the river without being seen?" When the young man nodded, he continued. "I'd like to know where their horses are and if'n there be another opening to the cave. Think you can do that?"

"Yes, sir."

"But for heaven's sake, be careful."

With a determined set to his mouth, the young man left.

Abraham looked at the others and said, "We'll stay over the hill and out of sight. George, you get them hounds out of here fast. I don't want any sounds to give us away."

After dismounting, Andres asked, "What do you have in mind, Abraham?"

Abraham shrugged as he recalled having asked Big Jen a similar question many years earlier. Big Jen's answer had been, "Something will come to me." *Looks like we'll have to wait for something to come to our minds, too,* he thought.

"Don't rightly know yet," he answered Andres. "Not being familiar with the caves in this neck of the woods, I don't know whether there be another entrance. I reckon we'll have to wait for Curtis."

Half an hour later, the young man returned. "Mr. Rallemore," he reported, "it's hard to tell, but it appears that there only be one way in and out of that cave. There be three or four men around the cooking fire and I didn't see any shelters or bedrolls so they must be sleeping in the cave."

"Did they see you?" asked Andres.

"Nope."

Abraham was thoughtful for a moment. "My biggest concern is them slipping away in the dark this evening if'n they know we're here. How about their horses? Did you see them?"

"Yep," replied Curtis. "On the right side and beyond the mouth of the cave, there is a small meadow. They are hobbled there."

"Think you can get behind those men and get to their horses without giving yourself away?"

"Yep."

"Good," said Abraham. "Now all you fellas gather around. I've got a plan."

With difficulty, Abraham got down on one knee, and began drawing a rough semblance of the situation in the dirt with a stick. "I be thinking that getting their horses be the key. Men on foot can flee, but they can't get far. Curtis and Frederick, I want you to circle around and get to their horses. Think you can slip their hobbles quietly?"

"Yep," replied Curtis and there was a hardness to him that bespoke rage and determination. "John was my good friend and taught me everything I know about horses. We'll get it done."

Frederick simply nodded.

"Tommy," continued Abraham pointing with his stick, "I want you and four others to take cover across the river here. Get yourself positions that give you protection and a good firing angle into the mouth of the cave. You men will also have to be careful so you don't alert the outlaws. Got that?"

"Yes, sir," Tommy said.

Andres asked, "You fixing to hole them in the cave, Abraham?"

"Something like that. Curtis, you and Frederick free the horses and spook them toward the campfire. Then you take firing positions where you can see into the cave and be careful. I don't want to lose anyone in this party."

Andres asked, "They'll surely make for cover in the cave. How're we going to get them out?"

"I figure the same as you," replied Abraham. "We've got a couple of things going for us. One be surprise. Second, we may hit a couple before they make it to the cave. Given the roar of the river, I'll wager that there are many rocks inside that cave. Our gunfire may not hit the bushwhackers directly, but those balls are going to be ricocheting around and giving them fits."

Abraham saw the men nod. "So, men, first we got to relieve them of their horses. That will alert them to our being here. Curtis, do you think you can give an Injun war cry when the horses are free?"

"Yep."

"Good. That'll be the signal for us to start shooting. Then you boys get those horses really moving into that camp area." Stiffly, Abraham stood and looked at the group of men. "Any questions?"

Abraham thought it was about as good a plan as they could devise. There was still the possibility that another opening existed which would allow the bushwhackers to escape. It was a risk they would have to take.

"The bushwhackers can figure out what we have in mind, Abraham," Andres stated.

"Probably—question is what they'll do. Will they surrender or do we have to starve them out?"

Andres nodded.

Abraham and the posse finally heard Curtis' loud, "Yeooowaaawee!" as the horses ran through camp. Immediately, everyone in the posse opened fire. Ducking and dodging, the outlaws made for the cave, firing blindly at their attackers.

Abraham heard the whining of ricocheting lead, confirming that there were many rocks inside the cave.

After a few minutes, a white cloth on the end of a limb began waving from the cave's entrance.

"Hold your fire," Abraham's voice boomed out over the roar of the water.

From the cave came a loud shout. "Who are ya fellows and why are ya shooting at us?"

"You attacked a wagon several days ago and murdered our friend," answered Abraham, his loud voice trembling with emotion. "We are a large posse of armed riders and you've got two choices. You can die here and let the turkey buzzards pick over your bones. Or you can give yourself up and we'll take you in for trial."

"That'll be the day," was the reply, as the bushwhackers opened fire again.

Once more, the posse rained bullets into the cave and kept the barrage going during the next hour.

Finally, a white cloth came out again and someone yelled from the cave, "Hold yar fire. All of us be wounded and one be real bad. We'll surrender if'n ya stop shooting."

"Alright," shouted Abraham. "Throw out your guns first. Then come out."

Grimacing, Andres noted, "If we take them back to Seneca, we'll have to keep them away from Sarah."

Shadows were beginning to lengthen in the canyon as Abraham watched the posse prepare to leave for Neosho. They had decided to take the outlaws to the county seat, as the circuit judge would eventually show up making his rounds. In any event, that town had a jail and Seneca didn't. One bushwhacker died before they could tend to him. Now bandaged, the other two sat bound on their horses.

Curtis double-checked the outlaws to make sure that their hand and foot ties were secure. Finishing, he came over to Abraham and whispered, "I overheard them two talking. As I make it, there still be one more bushwhacker in the cave, a fella they called Hooker."

Astounded, Abraham's face paled. "You're sure the name was Hooker?"

"That's what it sounded like to me. Why, does that name mean something to you?"

"Yep, it sure does," replied Abraham stoically. "We need to make sure. How about you take that tall fella off in the woods and have a 'Come to Jesus' talk with him? I'd also like to know what the man in the cave looks like." Curtis eyed him curiously but nodded and left.

Abraham motioned Frederick over to him and spoke in a low voice. "Son, Curtis overheard them two bushwhackers talking and he thinks there still may be one more left in the cave. One of the outlaws called the man 'Hooker.'"

A disbelieving scowl appeared on his son's face. "Hooker?" Frederick responded. "Here? Good Lord."

"Curtis is talking to the tall one right now to find out more."

Soon, Curtis returned with the bandit's horse. "That tall fella tried to escape and he'll not be returning with us. Before he departed this world, he told me that this fella, Hooker, is in the cave and unhurt. Said he was a cagy-type that keeps mostly to himself. He also told me that he be bald and strange looking with no ears."

Pale and anxious, Frederick stared at Curtis.

Straightening himself and with a grim look on his face, Abraham said, "Well, that's one man who ain't getting away." Turning to his men, he called out, "Hey, you fellas listen up. We got another bushwhacker holed up in the cave."

As the posse gathered around, Abraham briefly told them about Hooker and finished by saying, "He is part of the gang that killed John, and he nearly killed my son years ago. You fellas know I've never been a violent man or one who preaches it. But I've known Hooker for over thirty years and he be evil and mean. I'm telling you straight out—I'm not leaving until we capture him or he be dead. Are you with me?"

Andres replied, "Count me in."

All of the men agreed.

"You got a plan on how we smoke this varmint out of his cave?" Curtis asked.

"Not right yet," replied Abraham.

"Well, why not do just as I said—smoke him out?" asked the younger man. "We can throw brush from the sides and the top of the cave into the opening and light it. By keeping it going, the smoke will eventually flush him out."

Abraham looked at the young man and then at Andres, seeing him nod.

"Sounds like a good plan to me. Let's get ourselves down there. George, tie that last wounded bandit to a tree so he don't slip off."

🐾 🐾

With the posse safely positioned outside the cave, Abraham hollered, "Hooker, this is Abraham Rallemore. The rest of your gang be dead or tied up. We aim to catch you and we're not leaving until we do." Hearing no response, he shouted again, "Hooker, are you hearing me?"

"Ya possum-brain, I hear ya," came an echoing voice from deep within the cave. "How are ya keeping yarself these days? Ya must be surprised to come across yar old pardn'r again. Hell, if'n I'd recognized ya on that wagon the other day, I'd have blown ya to yar maker."

"Come on out, and I give you my word, you'll get a fair hearing before the judge in Neosho," answered Abraham.

"Be that some more of yar justice, Rallemore? Not this time as I've got me a big deep cave here. Anyone coming in will be outlined against the light.

Next thing ya know, that fella is going to be dead with my shot in his head. So, stay out there and holler all ya like, ya soft-headed jackass."

"Alright, boys," Abraham told his men. "You heard the idiot. Start building the burn pile."

In short order, an enormous mountain of brush and limbs was stacked high at the cave's opening.

Once more, Abraham shouted into the cave. "Hooker, this be your last warning. Throw out your guns and then come out with your hands up. If'n we don't see them weapons coming out, we aim to light this pile and smoke you out. What's it to be?"

"Go to hell, Rallemore" came the echoing voice. "I regret that I missed killing yar brat some years back. At least he has spunk in him. He must have taken after Mary and not his slave-loving pa."

"To hell with him," Abraham commanded, "light it up."

They kept the fire blazing for a good long time, throwing everything they could find into the inferno. The flames roared and curled against the cave ceiling as black and brown smoke boiled out and rolled back into the cave. Soon, the smoke mixed with the rushing water giving it the appearance of rising steam.

As he watched the blaze, Abraham recalled the many times that he and Hooker had crossed paths going all the way back to the runaway Indian slave. Frederick was standing near him and Abraham knew his son was also reliving his terrible encounters with this evil man.

The canyon was nearly in shadows as the posse kept feeding the flames.

Suddenly, a loud shout came from within. "Alright Rallemore, ya goddamn dimwit, I'm coming out. And I'm going to be aiming for yar heart as ya're the first one I'm gunning for," Hooker yelled, coughing heavily.

Abraham and Frederick tensed, guns at the ready.

"ABRAHAM RALLEMORE, YA'RE GOING TO MEET YAR MAKER THIS DAY, YA SON OF A BITCH!" Like an evil apparition, the earless Hooker came running full tilt out of a swirl of heavy smoke, his face and baldhead blackened. He held a rifle in one hand with a pistol in the other. Strapped to his back was another gun and there was a knife his belt. With the words still eerily echoing, Hooker fired his rifle. The shot went wide as he tossed the gun aside and raised his pistol.

Abraham and Frederick fired simultaneously.

An instant later, ten other guns let loose.

The bald earless man stopped in mid-stride, violently jerking as shot after shot struck him, forcefully turning him in a pirouette of death until he collapsed and tumbled into the raging inferno, sending up a huge shower of fiery embers.

"Good God almighty," Frederick exclaimed.

For long moments, Abraham stared at the funeral pyre and then, in a voice filled with emotion, he hoarsely whispered, "Nothing erases a man's black cloud like a firestorm. For a slaver, theif, murderer, and bushwhacker— this *is* proper justice."

Sarah listened and remained somber until Abraham had finished. As it turned out, the last outlaw had died while the posse was at the cave dealing with Hooker.

"Them scallywags got what they deserve," she said. "I hope you left their bodies hanging in the trees for the turkey buzzards." She looked at them quizzically and then shrugged. "It's time now for me to do my crying."

Abraham tipped his hat to her and turned for home with Andres. He had never seen a woman with so much grit. He said to his friend, "Well, we showed those outlaws that they can't take us Lost Creek folks for granted."

Andres fixed him with a long look. "You know, I be saying those very same words years ago. I'm not sure that the bushwhacking days are over, but I hope I'm wrong."

Chapter Twenty-five

The September 12, 1862 edition of the newspaper reported that the South had won a major fight in Virginia at the Second Battle of Bull Run and featured the exploits of General Thomas J. "Stonewall" Jackson.

With the Union Army now occupying Springfield, a second article noted that it gave the North complete control of the valuable lead mines from nearby Granby to Joplin. Still another told of local citizens seeing Confederate cavalry scouts and speculated on the possible return of southern troops to the county.

Abraham and Frederick watched as fifteen hundred Union soldiers came through Lost Creek Valley from Fort Scott on their way to the small town of Newtonia, which was twenty-five miles east of Seneca.

On the morning of September 30, the Battle of Newtonia took place. As Abraham later heard the news, the fight was a seesaw event with both armies making gains at different times. The Union army finally fled the field of combat in the late afternoon leaving the Confederates as the winner. Strangely, thought Abraham, the southerners pulled back and some said they had returned to Arkansas.

Between the armies and bushwhackers, the once game-filled plains and horse-eye-high grass that Big Jen had marveled about were gone. With many of the Lost Creek men and older boys fighting in the war, pickings for the bushwhackers were even easier.

In Abraham's view, men who preyed on helpless women and youngsters were the lowest form of human existence—the scum of God's creations—and their practice of burning cabins and farms was a madness of mindless violence.

Folks did their best to survive or flee the armies and bandits. Some made their way east to Springfield while others went west to Fort Scott. Arkansas was the destination for those with Confederate sympathies.

Abraham knew that he and his sons could no longer protect the homes and farms of each family. They decided that they'd enlarge and reinforce

Frederick's stoutly built farmhouse and all were residing together. When Abraham later returned to his cabin, he found it burned to the ground.

🐾 🐾

He was sifting through the cabin ashes when he saw Sarah walking his way. Studying the woman, she looked thinner and haggard, wearing an old quilt pulled around her shoulders. Her graying tightly braided hair hung down her back.

"How do, Abraham," she said.

"It's been a while since we last saw each other, Sarah. How're you and the family doing?"

With a forced smile, she answered, "As well as can be expected. Life has become hard and a challenge for survival."

She pulled the quilt closer around her and he glimpsed the frayed blue dress beneath.

"The bushwhackers have near cleaned me out. A gang of maybe twenty showed up last month and ran off all my livestock."

"I'm very sorry to hear that."

Abruptly, she asked, "Do you remember that John and I were at your birthday party years ago?"

"Of course I remember," he answered, surprised at the question.

"You gave a little talk about the evils of slavery. Do you still feel the same way?"

Her red-rimmed eyes were deep-set and haunting. He was unsure where this was going, but answered truthfully. "Yes, and I feel even stronger now."

"Good. I feel the same," she said, almost relieved. She paused, looking over his shoulder at the hills bordering the valley and then back to him. "You were a friend to my John and I'm going to ask you to help me. My two eldest sons joined up with the armies—David for the North and James for the South. They were both in Newtonia during the fight."

Abraham could see the pain on her face as she controlled herself with great effort.

"I had my three girls and my youngest son with me and we were on our way to Springfield, trying to flee all the madness. On the road, the bush-whackers caught us and stole our remaining horse and everything else they could carry. I begged them to leave us some bedding and this quilt. We made it as far as Newtonia."

"You didn't get caught in that battle, did you?"

She nodded. "Yes, a farmer and his wife gave us some food and told us we could take shelter in their stone barn. We had no inkling what was coming."

Stopping, tears clouded her eyes and ran down her face. "Oh, Abraham, it was horrible. My younguns and me lay as flat as we could while the minie and cannon balls flew. Thank the Lord for that stoutly built barn. In the middle of the battle, who should come through the door but my David, seeking shelter from the gunfire with his arm broken."

A thin smile creased her face. "And after the battle, I was twice-blessed as we found James alive on the battlefield, but he was hurt bad. Can you just imagine my happiness, Abraham? The good Lord was finally smiling down on us. We came back to Seneca, as I had no way of knowing where the armies had gone. Now, I have my boys back from the war, but they need time to mend. We're going to Fort Scott and we're going to stay there until this insane war ends."

Abraham was silent for a moment. Her story touched him deeply as he wiped away a tear. *First John and now this,* he thought. "My God, Sarah, that's the most moving story I've ever heard. I'm happy you found your boys and sad for all your troubles. It's a long way to Fort Scott. How you aim to get there?"

Again, she fixed Abraham with a long look. "There be two things I came to ask you. God gave me and my younguns two legs and we'll walk, if necessary. My concern be for James, as he has lost considerable blood. Those scalawag bushwhackers done stole everything including John's prized horses. I have one wagon left and no animal to pull it. Abraham, would you please sell me a mule?"

Abraham was thinking as she spoke. "My whole family is staying at Frederick's cabin and we sure ain't doing much farming these days other than our vegetable garden. We have a mule you can use, but I'll not take any of your money. Keep it for your needs."

Sarah looked at him and, for the first time, her face seemed to soften. "You're such a kind man. I accept and praise you to the Lord in heaven."

"We can let you have some food, too," he said, watching her face brighten.

"Ahh, Abraham, you're an angel to share in such bad times. Your hair be white, but your heart be overflowing."

"Why don't I bring over the mule and some food to your cabin?"

"There's nothing there. Those evil low-lifes burned down my place just like they did yours. We're staying in the chicken shed. Thank you, Abraham. You and John were close at one time and I feel as though I've nowhere else to turn."

Her statement surprised Abraham knowing how close the former Ohio families had been.

She must have seen the look on his face, as she went on, "Yes, I know what you're thinking. My family was very close to Andres', but I can't hold with his views on this war. It's just not in me anymore." Another tear slid down her face. "I'd be obliged if you'd do me one more favor."

"Of course—what is it?"

"John and me saved some money and I converted it to gold after he died being fearful of the times that were coming. Would you please hide it on your farm for me? I fear being robbed again as we travel west."

Abraham was surprised. "Are you sure you want to do that?"

"Yes. Will you do me this last favor? Please?"

"Yes, if you're sure. I'll locate a burrow that no one else can find. If'n you don't mind, I'll tell Frederick seeing as . . ." he paused, searching for the right words, ". . . as I'm getting a bit long in the tooth, Sarah. Is that alright with you?"

"Yes, I understand. Thank you, Abraham. Now, would you mind turning your back to me?"

Mystified, Abraham complied and thought he heard a rustling.

In a few moments, she said, "Alright, you can turn back." She was now holding a leather pouch.

"Where in the world did that come from?" he asked in surprise.

A thin smile crossed her face. "When those bushwhackers waylaid us, they searched to find my valuables, but they didn't find this bag because I've had it hidden on me. Please take it and keep it safe for us. And may the good Lord keep you and yours safe through this insanity."

"Thank you, Sarah. I'll ride over this afternoon. I pray that God protects you and your younguns on your journey."

Chapter Twenty-six

In his advancing years, Abraham found it difficult to mount his horse or to sit a saddle, yet his visits to Mary never stopped. He found peace knowing that she was near.

On this particular afternoon, there were angry clouds in the sky, threatening rain. He was tending her gravesite when he heard gunshots coming from the direction of Andres' farm. Concerned for his friend's family, Abraham rode there, stopping his horse just short of the clearing around the house. Amazed, he saw horsemen milling about. The dozen or so were armed and two carried lit torches.

"Andres Sommer," a voice called out. "Come out, you damn rebel sympathizer,"

Abraham noticed that some of his neighbors were among the riders, including Tommy Burked and George Vogel.

"Get yarself out here or we'll burn the place down with ya and yar family in it," the leader shouted again. "And we ain't going to be waiting more than a moment longer so ya best get out here right now."

The cabin door opened and his friend walked outside. His hair was mussed and his clothes looked rumpled. He carried a musket, but it was in the crook of his arm, pointed down.

"What you fellows be wanting?" Andres asked. "I ain't done anything to you."

"We aim to string up rebel sympathizers starting with ya."

"You know I got a son fighting with the Union Army up in . . ."

"And we know ya got sons in Arkansas with the rebels, so don't try justifying yarself by them means."

Several men dismounted and grabbed Andres' gun, tying his hands behind his back. With a shove, they walked him towards Lost Creek.

"I don't understand why you're doing this," Andres said, reluctantly walking with a man on each side.

"Yar slave-loving kind is bringing this country to its knees. For years, we worked hard as free men to build our lives on the frontier, only to have it all kicked away by the war and ya rebel-lovers. Ya and the others think ya can get away with it, but yar wrong. We're going to hang ya from that big tree near Lost Creek as a warning that we're just not going to take it anymore."

As they marched him to the tree, Abraham overheard his friend say, "You boys aren't thinking clearly. You ought to see yourselves for what you are, nothing but a bunch of wild ruffians who ain't any better than them bush-whackers. I hope you've made peace with the Lord as you're surely going to rot in hell."

Abraham followed, sticking close to the cover provided by the greenery as the vigilante group made for the hanging tree. He pulled his rifle out of the scabbard and wondered what to do next. He knew there were too many of them, but he wasn't going to let these men hang his friend without a fight.

Someone threw a rope over a limb and fashioned a noose. *Andres looks scared and who can blame him*, thought Abraham. *If he had struggled back at the cabin, he might have put his family in danger.*

One of the men put the noose over Andres' head and they forced him to climb up a woodpile stacked beneath the tree. The noose tightened as he tried to balance on the uneven footing.

"You got any last words, you damn slave-lover?" asked the leader.

Digging his spurs into his horse, Abraham came out of the trees, startling the angry mob. "Stop this nonsense right now!" he shouted. "Have you fellas gone plumb crazy? Take that rope off of my friend."

As he rode forward, a shot rang out and Andres tumble down the wood-pile as the lead ball cut through the hanging rope. Abraham looked around, and there, confronting the men was Ella Mae, pregnant again and looking determined. Her hair had fallen down and her mouth was set.

She had apparently followed the mob carrying two rifles. One was now lying on the ground, smoke curling from the end of the barrel, while she aimed the second at the armed men. "You free my husband right now, you hear me, or the next shot is going right through your heart," she said to the leader.

Abraham reined in beside her, his gun pointed toward the mob as his hand trembled. "Untie his hands," he commanded with a hard edge in his voice as his friend struggled to his feet. "And do it now!"

"Abraham, ya old fool," said one of his neighbors, "Ya got sons and grandsons fighting for the North. Why are ya siding with this southern sympathizer?"

"Tired and old I am, but I've not lost my senses. I don't believe in seeing a friend die at the hands of an angry senseless mob and I don't believe in killing innocent people as a warning to others."

All of the men were staring at him.

"Tommy, what're you doing here?" Abraham asked, staring at the younger man. "How're you going to explain this hanging day to Samantha and your younguns? What'll your mother say? I know that your papa is looking down at us this very moment, and I can tell you, he surely is angry—angry that his son be caught up with a vigilante mob." The young man looked away.

"And you too, George? Think about the shame you're about to heap on your family. You've known Andres Sommer all your life and you know him to be a good man. Don't that count?"

Some of the men looked uneasy, but no one made a move to untie his friend.

"And look at the rest of you," Abraham continued. "You be a dozen men and there be one of him. Ain't that just what them evil bushwhackers would do—cowardly gangs of many against the few."

As his pulse raced and his hands trembled, the Carolinian realized that his words weren't swaying the men and that he and Ella Mae were in a poor position. His only hope was that a break in the mob's momentum would get them thinking straight. He looked again at George and Tommy, but they refused to meet his gaze.

None of the men spoke.

Talking passionately, Abraham continued, "Many of you have known Andres most of your lives. You know him as a man of his word, an honest man. You've seen him at church where we pray together every Sunday. He was with us when we chased after them bushwhackers that killed John Leach. Some of you grew up with his younguns. Everyone knows how hard his family has worked to turn virgin prairie into fine working lands. That's the real mettle of this man."

In a softer tone, he went on, "Whether he has the same beliefs as you or not, are you really ready to become murderers by killing this innocent man?"

The leader's face was red with anger. "Did ya know that this here upstanding citizen of Seneca used to own slaves? Eh, do ya know that."

Taken aback, Abraham looked at Andres.

"It be true," said Andres, in a subdued voice. "A long time ago, a neighbor in Ohio owed me some money and couldn't pay. Instead, he gave me a young Injun boy. Before we left Ohio, we gave him his freedom."

"Well, what about that," demanded the leader as Abraham stared at his friend.

Turning to look at the blustering gang leader, Abraham thought, *in one way, he reminds me of Hooker. The difference is that the times have made him and his men afraid for the lives of their families.*

"That doesn't prove anything?" continued Abraham. "You heard him say that he set the boy free. Ain't that enough for you?" Pausing, he looked at each man before he continued. "I, too, had some slaves back in North Carolina at one time. I didn't cotton to the practice because I believed it was wrong, but most of my kin and friends practiced it in their tobacco fields. Does that make me an evil man? You boys need to think for yourselves and not be so gall-darned fired up by the words of politicians . . . and rabble-rousers."

The gang leader demanded, "Give way, ya damn old fool."

Without hesitation, Abraham spurred his horse forward a few strides, leaving Ella Mae behind. Straightening in his saddle the best he could, he replied, "I can't give way and I won't let this happen without trying to stop it. What you're doing is wrong. Before you can murder my friend, you'll have to kill me." The silence was thick as the mob stared at him. In a stronger voice, Abraham went on, "Are you boys prepared to slaughter two innocent men on this day of our Lord?

The men shifted uneasily in their saddles and some exchanged whispers with the man next to him.

Lowering his voice, Abraham continued. "There be more than one kind of slavery. Even free men can be slaves." Most had curious looks on their faces. Adjusting himself again in the saddle, he continued, "Free men can easily become slaves if'n they let others do their thinking and talking instead of using their own heads. Do you want to be remembering this day for the rest of your lives—the day you murdered two innocent men? I guarantee you, it'll haunt all of you forever and there won't be any eighth day after the Sabbath in your lives." As he spoke, his own experiences with bandits and Hooker flashed through his mind.

The two men holding Andres loosened their grip and stepped aside. Ella Mae ran to her husband and took off the noose.

"Now, please untie his hands," Abraham continued, lowering his rifle.

The leader signaled the men to untie Andres' hands. "Alright, old man, ya win this time, but hear me good and clear. If'n Andres so much as provides one more chicken to the Rebs, I swear, we'll be back and nothing will stop us from stringing him up. We're going to do everything we can to take back our country," he stormed, turning his horse away. The others followed. Tommy gave him a slight nod as he left.

Ella Mae was sobbing, holding her husband.

Andres stood her aside and went over to Abraham. "Thank you, dear friend. You surely saved my life this day."

Abraham slowly dismounted. "What has this country come to?" Shaking his mane of white hair, he stared up at the branches of the hanging tree. "Most folks do know right from wrong and there are two armies in the area. Yet nobody will enforce the law or the decency of man." Looking at his friend, he said, "What're you going to do now, Andres? I'm afraid for you and your family"

Rubbing his bruised wrists, Andres looked at him and then at his sobbing wife. "I expect we best be packing up and going south, perhaps to Fort Smith where we are known. We'll stay there until this terrible war be over."

"That makes sense," said Abraham. "How can I help you?"

"You already have. We'll pack up this afternoon and leave at first light. The bushwhackers have already run off most of the stock."

Andres held out his hand. "Abraham, you've been a good friend and I'm glad that we're neighbors. I knew it would be that way the first time I met your boys coming over that hill up on the prairie. You take care of yourself and your family and may God bless you."

With tears in his eyes, Abraham shook Andres' hand and the two men clasped each other. Stepping back, the Carolinian said, his voice cracking with emotion, "And may God bless you and your family, Andres. I fear we'll not be seeing each other again in Six Bulls country."

"Perhaps you're wrong," Andres said as Ella Mae continued to sob at his side. "But after the good Lord takes us both, we'll meet up again someday in a better place."

With considerable effort, Abraham mounted his horse and tipped his hat to Ella Mae. His hands still trembled as he slowly rode away.

His mind was a muddle of thoughts as he sat his horse next to the old wooden cross. *You and me, Mary, we done some good in this life—like our younguns and breaking new ground with the tenant plan and our stand against slavery. From Flat Swamp Creek to Lost Creek, we've come a long way, haven't we?*

Hesitating, he looked to the rainclouds on the new horizon. "Why, God? You made man in your own image. Why then do so many lack good sense? And why is it that we are so easily drawn to hate and kill each other? Why, God?"

His only answer was the silence of Six Bulls.

Author's Notes

Cumberland Gap

The Appalachian Mountains were a barrier to westward expansion for two centuries. Containing a baffling string of ridges and valleys running from the Canadian border southwestward for nearly two thousand miles, they vary from one hundred to three hundred miles wide, with peaks averaging three thousand feet.

Tectonic plates collided eons ago, uplifting and converting the ancient seabed into strings of mountain ranges. Erosion nearly flattened them into high plateaus before further uplifting took place.

Thousands of years ago, the Yellow River carved a valley through these mountains. As the land rose again, the direction of the river reversed, leaving a notch in the ridgeline. Bison used the pass for centuries, traveling to the rich bluegrass in the area that became Kentucky. Indians traveled the same track and referred to it as a "warriors' trail."

The mountain barrier was finally breached in 1775 when Daniel Boone and his axmen marked a trail through the notch called the Cumberland Gap. Pioneers streamed through and, by 1792, the territory known as Kentucky grew to a population of over one hundred thousand. Admitted to the union, it was the first state west of the Appalachians. Improvements in the trail occurred in 1805 to accommodate Conestoga wagons.

Some estimate that over three hundred thousand settlers crossed through the pass in the first thirty-five years following the trailblazing done by Boone and his men.

It is said that one of the axmen in Boone's party was a young lad by the name of Edmund Jennings.

North Carolina Gold

Johannes Reith, later known as John Reed, was a mercenary Hessian soldier who fought for the British in the Revolutionary War. Afterwards, he stayed in

America and settled in an area east of Charlotte, North Carolina, acquiring a farm on the banks of Little Meadow Creek.

In 1799, John's son found a large rock in the creek and marveled at its color. It weighed seventeen pounds and served the family as a doorstop for the next several years. A local jeweler bought it for three dollars and fifty cents, identifying it as a gold nugget.

With that discovery, North Carolina became America's only significant gold-producing state in the first half of the nineteenth century. Over the years, the Rowan County settlement of Gold Hill became the richest gold mining town in America until the California discoveries.

Most of the gold came from hard rock mining areas along the slate belt running through the state. Over the centuries, gold nuggets and flakes washed down creeks and rivers, lodging in potholes.

The War of 1812

On December 24, 1814, diplomats from England and America met at Ghent, United Kingdom of the Netherlands (present-day Belgium) to sign a peace treaty. With the slowness of travel, battles continued in America, the most significant being the battle for New Orleans.

The English wanted to lay claim to America's western territory by landing a force of ten thousand troops near New Orleans. Several skirmishes occurred and, before the main battle, the British seized or sank five American blockade barges.

A thick fog covered the land on the Sunday morning of January 8, 1815, as the crucial British attack began. General Andrew Jackson's army numbered some four thousand, all located behind a mile-long, hastily constructed fortification.

As the English advanced, the fog quickly lifted, exposing them to heavy fire. A series of blunders, confusion among the ranks, and inexplicable "non-orders" from the British generals resulted in a bloodbath. The Americans suffered twenty-one casualties, while the British sustained over two thousand. After the battle, British reinforcements and a siege train arrived. Despite this, the British viewed continued fighting as too costly and, within a week, they departed in their ships.

The battle resulted in a surge of patriotism and, years later, boosted the reputation of Andrew Jackson as he sought the presidency.

Indian Removal Act of 1830

This law continued efforts to relocate Native Americans begun in the administration of President Thomas Jefferson. Under the plan supported by President Andrew Jackson, Native Americans were relocated to the frontier west of the Mississippi River. To this end, the army constructed a string of forts in a north-south line that ran from Fort Snelling in present-day Minnesota to Fort Jesup in Louisiana.

By treaty and force, thousands of people journeyed to Indian Territory, then the homeland and hunting grounds of still other Native Americans. Before reaching the new lands, thousands died from the lack of food, shelter, difficult travel, disease, and demoralization.

The term, "Trail of Tears," describes the forced marches of the Cherokee Indians, in particular, and, in my view, aptly applies to all Native Americans that endured these journeys.

The Black Hawk War

The Black Hawk War of 1832 was the culmination of disputes and acrimony between the Fox and Saux tribes and the US Government. A series of treaties beginning in 1804 ceded tribal homelands in Illinois for lands west of the Mississippi River. Chief Sparrow Hawk, know as Black Hawk, later maintained that the Indians were cheated.

Repeated incursions into Indian lands by white settlers finally prompted Black Hawk to return to his former homelands in 1830 and 1831 with small groups of men. Each time, his stay was short. In April 1832, he crossed the river once more, this time with over a thousand people, including women and children, seeking to retrieve his homelands.

Illinois settlers panicked and the governor called out the militia and urged the nation to come to their aid. The Federal Government and local militias from neighboring states responded with a force that grew to nearly four thousand.

The Indians proved to be elusive despite a number of encounters and battles. Three times, Black Hawk tried to withdraw or surrender—these failed. Black Hawk finally divided his band, sending half across the river where they were slaughter by the Sioux Indians. Of his remaining band that fought at Bad Ax River on August 2, only one hundred and fifty survived.

Basilica of St. Louis, King of France

Consecrated in 1834, it was the first cathedral west of the Mississippi River and named after Louie IX, the King of France, later canonized as St. Louis. The cathedral has beautiful neo-classical marble altars and a magnificent painting of Christ's crucifixion presented as a gift by King Louie XVIII.

In 1961, Pope John XXIII signed a decree naming the original Cathedral of St. Louis a Basilica and bestowing its present name.

Battle of Newtonia

Southwest Missouri was a battleground for the control of lead mines. Located within this region, the small village of Newtonia had little strategic value during the Civil War other than its grain mill, which provided flour for Union army troops.

The area was the scene of battles in 1862 and 1864. The first involved the most men. The second battle occurred when the Confederates paused in their retreat to Arkansas. A rear guard provided cover for the retreating troops, which overpowered the advancing Union cavalry force.

The stone-built Ritchey barn and mill drew the fire of both sides during the battles, yet it managed to survive.

The SIX BULLS novels

The Six Bulls series of novels draws on life stories set in the 1800s. My sincerest thanks for all your support. The next book is *"Missouri Vengeance."* It's an adventure story about Andres Sommer's boys and events that set them on golden paths of adventure.

Here are excerpts from it and the first novel, *SIX BULLS-The Ohioans.*

Missouri Vengeance

1856
LOST CREEK VALLEY

. . . Ella Mae's voice now had a sharp edge, as she said, "My situation be hard enough without you shouting at me and flogging me with your wounded pride. I've been beaten and wronged. Can't you understand that? I've got people telling me that I'm bad—telling me what to do and what to think and what to say. It's been hard for me to keep my wits about me and your shouting is no help at all, Marion Franklin."

The young man stood there, speechless.

Standing and straightening herself, Ella Mae went on, "I've got to think about my life and the future and I've got to do it right now, not next year or when it's more convenient or when it suits you. I've got to think about a life for my baby."

"Why didn't you come to me and tell me about this. You know I love you."

"And do what?" she replied, her angry voice now cutting like a knife-edge. "You got no land and you got no money and you got no means to support yourself, much less a family. Why in many ways, you're still a boy."

Marion sagged under the weight of her words. "Ella Mae, how can you say such things? I love you and I know . . . you love me. Why if'n I was in your place, I think I'd rather . . ."

"DIE?" she finished his thought. "Be that what you're about to say. Kill myself? KILL my baby?" Now she was standing ramrod straight, he mouth strangely curled with anger. "Grow up boy so you can face the world as it is."

Hurt, he shouted, "You're just as bad as your pa . . . and my pa. You're nothing but a money-grubbing used-woman . . ."

AUGUST 1832
Beanblossom Creek, Wisconsin Territory

Very quietly, the Captain leveled his flintlock musket. The hammer was half-cocked and the pan primed. He used his thumb to bring the hammer all the way back. There was the unmistakable soft click as the cocking device caught. He looked out of the corner of his eye and saw some of his company of fifteen men. Like his, their guns were raised and pointed toward the creek.

In the dawn light, a low ground fog softened the outlines of trees, rocks, bushes, and the Indians. Seventeen or eighteen were astride their horses, making their way along Beanblossom Creek to join Chief Black Hawk's large war party several miles downstream. These Indians, too, were stealthy and wary. They knew the white man's militia was somewhere in the area trying to track Black Hawk's elusive trail.

Captain Renke Vogel's shot broke the stillness as the gun butt recoiled into his shoulder. The ball sailed through the trees, clipping leaves, and downed one Indian. Immediately, the rest of his men fired, as the air filled with black powder smoke. Four Indians went down in the opening volley with another five thrown as musket balls struck their mounts.

An instant later, Captain Renke was charging the Indians, mouth open, emitting a gut-curdling roar, rifle balanced in his left hand. Dodging tree limbs, brush, and stone outcroppings, he continued his charge as all two-hundred-ninety pounds of him hurled toward his opponents. His right hand now held the tomahawk he had drawn from his waist belt . . .

See the richardpuz.com website for more family books.

www.ingramcontent.com/pod-product-compliance
Lightning Source LLC
Chambersburg PA
CBHW071310200626
46813CB00015B/1440